3.42

B P Walter was born and raised in Essex. After spending his childhood and teenage y he worked in bookshops th of Southampton to study Film A in Film & Cultural Manag e Faber Academy and form in social media coordination for Waterstones in London.

twitter.com/barnabywalter
facebook.com/BPWalterAuthor
instagram.com/bpwalterauthor

Also by B P Walter

A Version of the Truth

Hold Your Breath

The Dinner Guest

THE WOMAN ON THE PIER

B P WALTER

One More Chapter
a division of HarperCollins*Publishers*
1 London Bridge Street
London SE1 9GF
www.harpercollins.co.uk
HarperCollins*Publishers*
1st Floor, Watermarque Building, Ringsend Road
Dublin 4, Ireland

This paperback edition 2021
First published in Great Britain by HarperCollins*Publishers* 2021
Copyright © B P Walter 2021
B P Walter asserts the moral right to
be identified as the author of this work

A catalogue record of this book is available from the British Library

Epigraph reprinted by permission of HarperCollins Publishers Ltd
© Agatha Christie 2014

ISBN: 978-0-00-844610-9

Printed and bound in the UK using 100% Renewable Electricity
by CPI Group (UK) Ltd

MIX
Paper from
responsible sources
FSC™ C007454

This book is produced from independently certified FSC™ paper
to ensure responsible forest management.

For more information visit: www.harpercollins.co.uk/green

For Emma, Meg, George, Corinne, Pippa, Sam, Virginie, Chris, Andy and all the other amazing people I met whilst studying at university

A mother's love for her child is like nothing else in the world. It knows no law, no pity. It dares all things and crushes down remorselessly all that stands in its path.

— *The Last Séance*, Agatha Christie

You cannot know what it is to fear until you have a child.

— Mr Woodhouse in *Emma* (2009), screenplay by Sandy Welch, adapted from the novel by Jane Austen

Prologue

December. Two months to go.

MICHAEL KELLEY: Hey, you there?

JESSICA MACLEOD: I'm here. I can't talk long tonight, though.

MICHAEL KELLEY: That's OK. I'm tired too.

JESSICA MACLEOD: I'm not tired. It's my mum. She's pissed me off again.

MICHAEL KELLEY: How come?

JESSICA MACLEOD: Oh, just stuff. But she wants to have a chat about my work. She thinks I'm failing at school.

MICHAEL KELLEY: You're not though. Are you?

JESSICA MACLEOD: Would it matter if I was?

MICHAEL KELLEY: Not to me.

JESSICA MACLEOD: It does to her apparently. As if she can talk. She dropped out of uni. Likes to tell everyone she went to Oxford but she couldn't hack it past the second year. Used the excuse of getting a job in TV.

MICHAEL KELLEY: You're stronger than her.

JESSICA MACLEOD: I know. She's weak. I used to think she was this strong person who always knew best.

MICHAEL KELLEY: Me too. About my mum. But she's not strong at all.

JESSICA MACLEOD: I'm just so tired of getting angry. I just want to talk to you all the time at the moment. I feel like I have so much of this stuff – people's secrets, things I just would prefer not to know. All of it's like weighing down on top of me.

MICHAEL KELLEY: I think I know what you mean.

JESSICA MACLEOD: Well I'm glad someone does at least.

MICHAEL KELLEY: I want to talk to you. I wish I could see you.

JESSICA MACLEOD: You can see me. My photo's in my profile. Isn't that enough ;)

MICHAEL KELLEY: No, I mean I want to see you in person.

JESSICA MACLEOD: I want to see you in person too. It's just difficult right now.

MICHAEL KELLEY: OK. Can we talk on the phone again?

JESSICA MACLEOD: Just wait until we meet. We can do more than talk ;)

MICHAEL KELLEY: Wow. OK. That wink definitely got me a bit excited.

JESSICA MACLEOD: You just wait.

Chapter One

THE MOTHER

May. Three months after the attack.

L aini makes that face while she waits for me to answer. That *I'm not convinced this is healthy* face. She's made it a lot lately. I think she's unaware of it. I've found that, in the past. People who know a lot about human behaviour tend to know very little about themselves. I glance around the room whilst trying to think of something to say. There's a strange stain on the floor by the door. It upsets me. Ever since I've been coming to see Laini, there's been that odd-looking patch. Coffee, perhaps. I consider about asking her about it, but she's sucking her teeth now – never a good sign – and I sense she's about to pass judgement.

'Well, if you're not sure about what led you to write a piece of work so violent, can you tell me the emotions it caused within you? How did you feel after you tried to write the murder scene you mentioned?' She moves her glasses slightly up the bridge of her nose. *She's a bit of a shrink cliché*, I think to myself. The sofa, the calm, slightly superior voice, the glasses that she peers over. If this were one of my screenplays, I'd get a red mark in the margins from editorial about 'tired archetypes'.

'I felt upset,' I say flatly. I then reach for one of the tissues on the table in front of us and, although I'm neither crying nor close to sneezing, I dab it to my nose. I'm playing for time, and she knows it. I avoid her gaze as I push the tissue deep into my pocket. She takes a slow breath in and waits. We wait. The seconds tick by. Eventually I give in and say, 'I thought I could just dive straight in. I know it was foolish, not writing for months and then trying to pick up where I left off. You see, the show I was in the middle of developing for ITV was something I was very keen to be part of. It's based on a terrific series of crime novels; it has a really interesting cop as the main character. Not one of those we've-seen-it-all-before types with an alcohol problem, poor diet, and marital issues. He was athletic, kind, did outdoor rock climbing in his spare time. He was a really interesting character for the screen – or would have been. But the first episode, it starts with the torture of someone in a basement, which is strong stuff, of course... then the plot starts to hinge on the disappearance of a teenage girl...'

I let the silence return and, after a few moments, Laini steps in this time.

'And you felt the subject matter wasn't helpful.' She says the sentence matter-of-factly. It isn't a question, but she's hoping I'll want to react.

'It all just... it reminded me of some of the lower moments. The fifth scene in the episode is where the girl's mum is trying to call her daughter on the phone, then reporting her missing...' I trail off. She nods understandingly.

'Caroline, I can understand how the idea of returning to your work might seem therapeutic to you. In fact, I don't think it was a bad decision. You should trust your instincts and it's good to see you're making steps in a positive, progressive direction.'

There's a but coming. I can sense it.

'But, I would caution you about the intensity of such content. Go easy on yourself. Be kind to yourself. Take it slowly, one step at a time, and be mindful of the impact graphic or highly emotive material might have on you after your experience earlier this year. An experience you are still living through.'

I want to leave now. I can feel myself getting prickly, feeling defensive. This is the part of therapy I really don't enjoy: knowing that they're right and having no option but to accept it.

'Honestly, it really wasn't that strong. I've done a lot harder stuff than that before. Did you see that three-part drama last year about the child finger murders? Based on the real case of the man who sent mothers the fingers of their dead children through the post? I wrote that. I handled it without even blinking. I mean, I understood it was upsetting stuff, of course, but I just got on with it and did the job.'

'I'm sure you did,' Laini says, staring calmly at me. 'But I think you need to be more aware of your own emotional bandwidth.'

Emotional bandwidth. The phrase irritates me, but I don't interrupt her.

'I'm not sure it's the most helpful way to work through your grief, dealing with the darker aspects of human behaviour.'

I nod. 'I just feel frustrated. It's been four months now.'

Laini offers a sad smile. 'I'm not trying to hold you back, Caroline. I'm just advising you against pouring salt on your wounds.'

I sigh. 'OK.' I look away from her, then, when she doesn't say anything immediately, switch my gaze back to her. She's still smiling.

'Good,' she says, laying her palms flat on her knees.

I like Laini, I do, but there's only so much of her I can take. I keep paying her. Paying her a fortune. I could have got therapy on the NHS – only a limited number of sessions, and I did go along to the first, but I didn't like the woman they gave me. She reminded me of Barbara Hershey – not nice, *Beaches*-style Barbara Hershey, more *Black Swan* Barbara Hershey. Any moment I thought she might flip and start clipping my fingernails in a violent rage. Laini isn't like that, though. I don't think she's ever done anything violent in her life. She probably doesn't even swat flies; she'd just brush them gently away with a glide of her ringed hands.

'I took your advice, from last time,' I say now, trying to avoid another lengthy silence. 'I've avoided disturbing content on TV. Alec still watches stuff, though. I caught him watching a rerun of *Spooks* in the lounge the other night.'

She raises her eyebrows a little.

'Have you seen *Spooks*?'

She indicates with a tilt of her head that she has.

'The Matthew McFadyen years or the Rupert Penry-Jones years? Or the later series after that when they chop and change the main character?'

Her smile is tinged with slight impatience now. She'd deny it, but I know it's there. 'I don't recall, I'm afraid.' Unspoken meaning: *We're not here to talk about TV shows.*

'I preferred Matthew McFadyen,' I say, and the image of him that swims into my mind pleases me.

'And did you speak to Alec about how some of the themes in *the programme* may upset you?' Laini is obviously keen to bring me back on track.

'Yes. We had a row.'

Laini glances at her notes. 'Do you feel your relationship with your husband is still, using your words from last week, "tense and taut"?'

I nod, keeping my eyes to the floor.

'You mentioned before that you've been able to talk to a couple of other people. A friend...'

'Yes, a friend I made at the support group. *Friend* is probably a bit too strong a word. But she lost... She was a mother too. And at least that means I'm able to speak to someone who knows what it's like. To lose that status, you know?'

'Status?' Laini asks, gently.

'Yes. The status as a mum. It's like this thing that you are. And then suddenly you're not. Suddenly you're just... just you again. It's like going back in time. Although you don't feel like you. You just feel empty. I'm not saying I was some amazing example of motherhood. But growing up, let's just say my own mother didn't exactly shine in that department, so I was determined to do better… determined to shine in a way she never did. And then, suddenly, all that just… disappears.'

Laini waits for a bit, as if allowing the room as a whole to digest what I've just said. Then she says, 'Your husband's brother…' She pauses to look down, her eyes scanning her notepad once again, apparently for a name, 'Robert, was it? Have you found talking to him helpful? You said how he'd helped you, especially in the first weeks.'

'Rob,' I said, 'Yes. Well, I was able. To talk to him, I mean. Like I said a few weeks ago, he was great just after Jessica died. I would phone and he would just listen. It helped that he was someone outside of the house. Of course, he knew and loved Jessica – he was a great uncle. But of course it's not the same as it is for Alec. And if I talk to Alec, I have to take into account his grief and everything that goes with it.'

A look up to see a slightly more engaged expression on Laini's face, as if she's more than a little impressed. 'I think it would be helpful to focus on this next time – how Alec's grief and the way he shows it can make it hard for you to talk to him.'

I don't reply, but I don't really need to. She'll get me to talk. It's part of her strange witchcraft and to be honest, it's the only reason I keep coming back. In spite of everything, I usually do end up talking.

I leave her room feeling that now familiar sensation of tired vulnerability. It wears you out, talking about your innermost fears and hopes and regrets and dreams. I'm fairly sure Laini sometimes lets her opinion shine through more than is professional. Alec would suggest reporting her to whatever monitoring body one reports bad therapists to, but at this point I'm not sure I could deal with another change to my weekly routine.

On the stairs to her rather gorgeous office block I bump into a young man. He has a pale, haunted face, as if he's being eaten up by some dark secret. There's a dentist in this building, an osteopath, an acupuncturist and then Laini. I bet he's going to see Laini. He looks like he needs to confess something. *Don't we all*, I think to myself as I cross the road to my car.

The Range Rover is filled with thick, warm air when I get into the driver's seat. It's only May and already the weather is baking hot. I check my phone and see I've got a voicemail from Alec asking me to pick up some milk if it's not too much bother. The choice of words makes me tut. *Too much bother.* I know what it is – it's a deliberate attempt to rile me. He does that – has always done it, if truth be told – but especially now. It's as if he wants me to flip out, wants to watch me crumple, watch me overreact so he can be the bigger person. Just because I forgot to get his Earl Grey teabags last week I am now being treated to a succession of tiny digs.

I drive defiantly past the Tesco Express on the way back to the house. Fuck his organic, semi-skimmed milk, I think to myself as the car sails by, the wind rushing through the windows. After ten minutes, I slow down as I steer along the road until I reach the turning onto Oak Tree Close. The neighbourhood's tidy line of trees, the large houses, most of them new-ish and unremarkable, a small handful either tastefully mock-Tudor or weird and modern. I used to love it here. Used to enjoy the sense of calm – clean, neat suburban calm. Now I just want to stand outside each and every home, one by one, and scream until I have no strength or working vocal chords left in me.

In the house, Alec is there by the kitchen counter, staring into the distance. The staring drives me up the wall. I clatter about loudly as I get in, pulling out the blender and going to the fridge to get strawberries, raspberries, and then, from the fruit bowl, a banana. I throw them all in the blender – I don't even bother to take the green bits off the strawberries – and enjoy the satisfying grind of the propeller blades as they turn the jar's contents into a dripping red mush.

'Did you get the milk?' Alec asks as the blender growls on and I pretend I can't hear him. He's white noise to me. He looks at me, then, just to make sure, comes right round, so he's almost facing me. 'Caroline? The milk?'

He bellows this over the top of the blender's roar. When I think about it now, I really am astonished I ever found his voice attractive. I would have once described it as deep but lyrical, earthy but sophisticated, his Scottish accent lending it a boyish charm. Now, it grates like broken glass in my ears.

'Just go away,' I mutter at him under my breath.

'You what?' he says. The blender ends and I make sure I'm especially attentive to the way the liquid enters my large glass tumbler in folds, as if it were made of silk. He watches me as if he's part disgusted, part baffled.

'I'm going for a nap,' I say, walking past him.

'You what?' he says again. He lays a hand on my arm, trying to stop me leaving, but I shrug him off.

'Nap time,' I say, heading for the stairs.

'With a big glass of sugar?' He follows me, hands on his hips now. He thinks he looks impressive, like a dominant, manly man. He doesn't. It just makes me sigh sadly.

'Why didn't you get the milk?' He shouts this up the stairs as I disappear.

'Good night!' I call back, as if responding to goodnight wishes from him, even though it's only 4pm.

In the bedroom I fire up the TV and navigate to the Netflix app. I stick on some awful-as-hell comedy – a dire pastiche of old cowboy movies – and sweeten my tongue with the berry pulp. Then I reach for my phone.

He answers on the fourth ring. 'Caroline,' he says, and there's something in his voice that's impossible to ignore. A tinge of impatience.

'Rob, I'm sorry… I just had a row with Alec. I just need to talk for a bit.'

I hear him sigh. I've been trying to ignore this side to our calls for a while now, but it's impossible to disregard. I'm becoming a burden on him. He's getting bored with my grief. He's starting to withdraw his support, slowly but surely, like a liferaft steadily losing air. 'What was the row about?' he asks eventually.

'What it's always about. Us. This shit life we're now leading. How we're broken. Smashed up and fucking broken.' I pulled myself up a little on the bed, feeling myself get into my stride, ready to open my soul in a way I've

13

never done to Laini. 'Do you know what my mother once said to me, back when I phoned her to tell her I was getting married? I hadn't seen her in years and I told her I was engaged, and do you know what she said?'

A few beats of silence, then Rob says, 'What did she say?'

I take a deep breath, feeling tears start to sting the backs of my eyes. 'She said, "It won't last." And do you know what I hate the most? The fact she was right. Couples are supposed to support each other through the very worst. So how can it last if we can't even do this?'

There's some more silence. Then at last Rob says, 'I've got to go, Caroline. I'm out shopping and I need to go and pay and...'

It's exactly the wrong thing to say – something so crass and insensitive, so different to how he used to be. 'Oh, well, I'm sorry to interrupt your fucking grocery shopping,' I snap at him. I hear him say my name, once more with that tired-sounding tone, before I cut the call. Then I fling the phone across the bed. It falls to the floor with a thud. I don't bother to pick it up.

As the film starts to play with a burst of orange and red colour filling the TV screen, I glance around my perfectly organised bedroom. The crisp white duvet cover, the pale-blue curtains, the neatly ordered bookshelves. All of it is just so heartbreakingly mundane. This is my life now. I just have to live it.

Chapter Two

THE MOTHER

January. One week to go.

'You'll probably just say no, but I said I'd ask. Can I go and visit Hannah in Somerset next weekend?'

I looked up from the script I was perusing on my iPad. It was something I wrote two years ago. The project was originally with the BBC but they decided they had too many crime dramas in the pipeline. Now it looked like another broadcaster might give the green light, but the production company had asked me to rewrite it so it was set in Birmingham rather than Central London. Cheaper on the budget, apparently.

'Hello? Mum?'

I realised I'd been sitting there with a rather glazed expression on my face, my mind still picturing Midlands architecture. 'Sorry, darling? What did you say?'

Jessica sighed; one of her more frequent demonstrations of impatience towards me. 'I said, I know you'll probably say no, but I promised I'd ask if I can go to Somerset to see Hannah next weekend.'

This threw me a bit. 'Hannah? But I thought she lived in Sevenoaks?'

She rolled her eyes. Her second most used demonstration of impatience.

'She does. With her mum. But her dad has moved to Somerset to open some seafood café or something and has married this awful new woman and Hannah's asked if I can go and stay with her there for a few days. To distract her from the wicked step-mother.' There was a silence while I digested this before she prompted: 'Well, can I?'

I laid the iPad down on the empty side of the sofa next to me and focused properly on her. 'Somerset? For how long?'

'I'll go on Saturday morning and come back late Sunday night.'

I felt my brow tense. I wouldn't have considered myself overly protective, but the West Country was a long way and the thought of Jessica doing that journey late in the evening, with school the next day, didn't have me jumping for joy.

'Can't you wait until the holidays? How about February half-term? And you've got all those modular exams to be preparing for too. I really don't think you should lose a whole weekend of revision when you could—'

She cut me off. 'I can do all that on the train. If you think about it, I'll be kept prisoner for hours there and back, so I'll definitely be able to concentrate.'

'Hmmm,' I said, because I wasn't convinced the revision would last any more than ten minutes before it was replaced by Instagram and a Cassandra Clare novel. 'Well, I'll talk to your father.'

Jessica made a huffing sound and rolled her eyes again, then wandered away and upstairs, clearly deciding to save her energy for convincing her father. He'd let her go. Almost straight away, I predicted, but not to please her. To make him look like the calm, cool, relaxed parent. The one that said, 'You know what, let's have extra ice cream today!' whilst pestering me to watch what Jessica eats and how diabetes and obesity are real things to be concerned about. I told him his concerns weren't necessary – Jessica was very healthy, ate a perfectly normal diet, and didn't show the slightest chance of developing an excessive addiction to sugar. But if she ever did, I was pretty sure the blame would be laid at my door.

Sure enough, when Alec arrived home from work at 7.45pm, Jessica immediately started the campaign before he'd even properly got through the door. 'Hold on, hold on,' he said jovially, trying to get his bag strap off around his neck and hanging up his brown blazer. 'When is this trip planned?'

'Next weekend,' Jessica said enthusiastically. 'Mum said we need to hear what you say before she says I can go. Something about revision – but I know I can do it. I'll work on the train there and back, and…'

'Let me go and talk to Mum while you go and carry on with said revision now, OK?'

I couldn't see her, but I was sure she would have offered him one of her I-love-you-Dad grins, before running back up the stairs.

It took a few seconds before he came into the kitchen, but as soon as he'd walked in, I could tell he was annoyed.

'Good day?' I asked, not looking up from the lasagne I was lifting out of the oven.

'No,' he said bluntly. 'The soft drinks company has asked us to go back to the drawing board with our campaign. They're worried about the amount of soft-drinks-are-bad-for-you stuff circulating and now want a campaign that tells people to ignore the advice and just drink it anyway. Not exactly an easy tagline, but we've just got to find a way to say it.'

I nodded, offered him a weak smile, then waited a few moments to see if he asked how I was or how my day had been. But he didn't. It wasn't on his radar.

He sat down at the kitchen table and let out a long, exasperated breath. I could tell what was coming. 'I do wish you wouldn't get Jessica all hyped up about going on a minibreak with her friend so close to her module exams.'

I gripped the large spoon in my hand, trying not to get angry.

'I know you had an easy-come-easy-go approach to your teenage years, running away from your home, shacking up with a bunch of hippies once you'd got to London, but I think Jessica needs rules and stability. Giving her hope about things like this only makes her get her priorities mixed up. It confuses the message we want to send her.'

The message we want to send her. He even talked about parenting like it was a marketing campaign for a new sportswear brand.

'I didn't say she could go. And it isn't a "minibreak". It's a two-day trip to the West Country to see her friend. The one she was close to before she changed schools.'

I could hear him breathing as I set the lasagne in the centre of the table. I was bracing myself for more jibes, more criticism, but before he could speak, Jessica rushed into the room.

'Ah great, I'm *starving*.'

She sat down at the table, iPhone in hand. One glance told me she was editing the caption on an Instagram photo.

Alec took the seat opposite her. 'Less of this at the table,' he said, waving a finger at the phone, but his tone was kind and jovial. Jessica finished her tapping after a few seconds and put the phone down. 'So, I hear you're keen to go on a little trip to visit your friend... Karen, was it?'

'Hannah,' Jessica said, grinning. 'Karen's the one with the three mums who now lives in London. Somewhere shocking, like Southwark or something.'

'Is Southwark shocking?' I asked, placing the lasagne in the centre of the table. 'I always thought it was quite a nice area of London. You've got so much near you, like Borough Market and London Bridge and along near the Southbank you've got—'

'Some kind of table mat would be nice,' Alec cut in, 'just so as not to ruin the surface.'

My eyes automatically shifted to Jessica, to see if she'd noticed the edge to her father's tone. Apparently not. She'd turned her attention back to her phone. Silently I reached for one of the spare table mats on the side and, using the oven gloves, slipped it under the Le Crueset oven dish. I noticed how it was starting to look a little old, with a mark on the side I haven't been able to get rid of. Alec would have noticed it too. I'd have to do something about it soon, before he mentioned it.

'Anyway, back to your little trip,' he said to Jessica, tapping the table in front of her. 'Your mother thinks you should be staying here to revise, but I've made your case – that you'll do extra revision in the evenings leading up to the weekend, with no movie nights or lengthy swim sessions – and have managed to persuade her that you should be able to go.'

I saw Jessica's joy light up her beautiful, soft, pale skin. 'Really? I can go!' She turned to look at me, and I force a smile. I knew he'd do this. I just knew it. I was now the pantomime villain, once again. The joy-killer. The one trying to hold her back. And lovely Daddy was the parent of the year. The one who gave her everything she wants.

'Yes, you can go,' I said, gripping the stack of plates in my hand so tightly I could hear them grinding into each other. I then distributed them round and took a seat. 'You'd better tell Hannah so she can let her dad know.'

Jessica was already typing away on her phone. 'Already done. Cannot wait!'

Alec smiled at her. I started to ladle out the lasagne in silence.

Chapter Three

THE MOTHER

May. Three months after the attack.

'What's the point?' I ask.

Alec stands before me, in front of the TV, blocking my view of what is now my second Netflix film – a raucous comedy drama about a group of girls who go to Ibiza. He seems shocked at my words.

'What do you mean, what's the point? Surely that's obvious. It helps. Talking helps.'

'What will it solve?' I ask. I know I'm sounding cruel, but I can't help it. I know he's looking for comfort. But I just can't stand the sight of him. Everything about him reminds me of how I've wasted most of my adult life trying to please him. Trying not to piss him off. Trying not to let so many things bother him: that I bring in more money than he does; that I have a social life with friends I actually like; that it was impossible for me to have another child after Jessica. These subjects were his 'trigger' issues. Ones for which, if he were exposed to them too much and too often, he would punish me. Not physically. Alec has never laid a finger on me. He probably likes to think of himself as more sophisticated than that. But now Jessica has gone – now our lives are without her laughter, her sadness, her joy and teenage tantrums – he's lost one of his main weapons against me. And he's very much feeling the loss, wrapped up within normal parental grief and guilt.

I look him up and down as he stands over my bed. Slim frame, smart, sensible shirt, black trousers. All of it just smacks of dull, dull, dull. I once overheard one of the secretaries at his work Christmas party describe him as 'privileged, middle-class Britain at its very worst'. Couldn't have put it better myself.

'Charlotte phoned,' he says, sitting down on the side of the bed.

I pull myself up, my back pressing uncomfortably into the headboard. 'Detective Inspector Close. Calling her Charlotte is… weird.'

'She told me to call her Charlotte,' he says, defensively.

'Of course she did,' I mutter.

'What?'

I shake my head. I haven't got the energy for an explosive row. 'Nothing. What did she say?'

Alec sighs. 'He says you've been bothering her about that man Jessica was seen talking to. The one in the shop at Stratford station.'

I fix Alec with a hard stare. '*Bothering*. She really said that, did she? Detective Inspector Close said I had been *bothering* her?'

Alec rolls his eyes. 'No, not quite, but it was implied. She says there really isn't any need to look into it further. She mistook him for a member of staff at the shop. She asked him if they had a book she was looking for. He just told her he didn't work there, she said sorry and went off to browse the shelves alone. And he went and caught his train to Braintree. Nothing strange or suspicious about him at all.'

I look at my hands. I wish DI Close had spoken to me personally and not explained everything to Alec. I couldn't shake off a suspicion about the man she'd mentioned. She said it was innocuous at the time – said it didn't bear any relevance to what happened later. But I still hoped it would offer something... some kind of explanation...

'I think you should stop. Stop *looking* for things, just... wait for news. If there is any news. And try to be OK with the fact that there may never be.'

'Be OK with it?! How can you even...? I don't understand why you're not doing the same thing. Why you're not interrogating people yourself, not camped outside the police station, ringing up all of Jessica's friends.'

'Because you've already done all that,' he said quietly. 'And all you do is get people's backs up, make them feel awkward, afraid – or, like Jessica's friends and their parents, block your number and threaten to report you for stalking them.'

I'm angry at how often he likes to remind me of this. 'Well, if you wanted proof of how many seemingly ordinary people are actually insensitive, selfish, cruel...'

'They're nothing of the kind – you know that. You need to let it go, Caroline,' he says, looking at me sadly. I can see the tears starting to fill the corners of his eyes. They stay there for a few moments, then he catches them roughly with the back of his hand as they start to fall, as his expression grows cross, as if I should have warned him that he'd started to cry. Like he'd been caught unawares.

I shake my head. 'No. The police aren't doing enough. Nobody's doing enough. I wonder sometimes if I'm the only one who cares.'

Alec's rubbing his face now with both hands, then, after one more heavy sigh, he gets up, letting the bed spring back to its normal shape with a twang. 'I think they've got more than enough on their plate. And I hope you know that's not true. That you aren't the only one who cares.' He stares at me for a few seconds, then looks down at the floor. 'Why don't you come down and have some dinner?'

I shake my head and turn back to the TV to start the film up again. He stares at the remote in my hand as if it's an abomination. 'You'd rather watch television than…'

'Right now, yes.'

He shakes his head, as if I'm some unfathomable creature that a sane person couldn't even begin to understand. I hope he's about leave, but he lingers near the door, his eyes now on the TV screen.

After nearly a full minute, I decide I can't bear it any longer. 'I'm going to get some more smoothie.' I get up and pad out the room, my bare feet silent on the carpet, ruined by the heavy stomp of his hard shoes as he follows me. He used to care so much about taking his shoes off at the door when we had the new carpet laid. It's amazing what rules can be abandoned when you suffer like we have suffered.

It's like there's no laws any more. I even saw him leave a teabag on the side of the kitchen counter the other day, brown stain left there – forever, potentially – tainted water making its dripping marks down the cupboard doors and onto the floor. My mind immediately began imagining what Alec would have said if I had done such a thing in the days before everything changed.

We do end up having tea together. Nothing fancy or adventurous. Just cheese on toast. When dinner was a family affair, with the three of us sitting down to a cooked meal at least three or four times a week, depending on our work and Jessica's social engagements, Alec used to 'entertain' us with endless trivia, as if he were the fount of all knowledge. He'd tell us snippets about psychology and history and even creative writing tips, aimed at me – the woman who has written for two major TV soaps, created four reasonably successful series of her own, one of which won multiple awards, penned six stand-alone TV films and miniseries, and contributed to many other established dramas. But Alec knows better about everything, it seems. Once, during a shop at the local Sainsbury's, he started advising me of the best way to structure a narrative. I laughed straight at him. I couldn't have hidden my contempt even if I'd wanted to. 'Why are you being like that?' he said, looking shocked.

'Because you're lecturing a BAFTA-winning screenwriter on how to write a good story.'

'What? Oh come on, nobody does that – refer to themselves as "a BAFTA winner" or "Oscar winner". It's...'

'It's what?' I asked back, allowing a woman with a pushchair and full basket under her arm to get some Ready Brek off the shelves.

'Arrogant,' he said, then did his disturbed, puzzled face, as if he'd just discovered something deeply troubling about the woman he'd married. 'Honestly, Caroline. You really need to think about how you come across to others sometimes. Not everyone's as... well, as forgiving as I am.' He wandered off at that point, leaving me standing with my trolley and not knowing if he'd left the store or just gone to another aisle to sulk.

Many months on, with our lives turned upside down, he no longer does this. No longer offers me regurgitated I-bet-you-never-knew-this facts he's remembered from the previous night's episode of *QI*. He now just spends the mealtimes we do happen to share together either sitting in silence or trying to get me to talk about Jessica. Help him unburden himself by telling him what a great father he was.

Night-times are even more difficult. Before it happened – before my daughter was murdered and my world changed so irrevocably – I'd presumed couples who underwent trauma never had sex again and that somehow their libido and sense of intimacy would be swallowed up by the hole now left in their lives. I was wrong. Our sex life carries on. But I think it's because it was never that 'normal' to start with. It was never about closeness and comfort. It was about him getting what he wanted. The release he wants. A release he still wants now. The only difference is, he now goes to the bathroom to cry once we're done.

After the cheese on toast, Alec goes out for a walk while I lounge on the sofa, feeling my hands brush against the soft, expensive materials. Out of the corner of my eye, I see my iPhone's screen light up in my pocket with an incoming text. It's from my friend Kirsten. She's one of the few friends I still speak to now. The others think they speak to me, or rather think I speak to them. But I don't. Not really. I just tell them that everything is terrible but 'we're working things through and taking each day as it comes, one step at a time'. They love that kind of thing. They lap it up. *Good*, they think. *She's still sad (she has to be, otherwise she wouldn't be human), but she's not loopy-sad. She's doing it in a respectable, normal way.* But of course, what they don't know is that there isn't any normal way to cope with what we're going through. No textbook guide, even though there have been many self-help volumes written on dealing with the struggles of grief.

But Kirsten, on the other hand, always stares at me blankly and I'm never entirely sure if she's heard me until she finally speaks and gives me disconcerting advice. 'Start doing laundry,' she says, 'and I mean *really* do it. Focus on folding each item before you put it into the washing machine, then again once you've dried them.' I told her it was a bit pointless folding things when you're putting them *into* a washing machine and I didn't think it would be the best way of ensuring they were cleaned, but she shook her head: 'It's the process; the perfect symmetry of doing it before and then after – honestly, it's soothing.' I said it sounded like she actually *wanted* me to go nuts, but she just smiled her strange, sweet smile and stirred her tea. And, oddly enough, it turned out she was right. It was therapeutic. More therapeutic, to some extent, than my sessions with Laini.

'Did this help *you*?' I asked her, when I went to see her a few weeks later. We were wandering around an open garden; one of the few times I'd agreed to go somewhere that wasn't my house or hers. 'Did this help when everything that happened with your husband became so unbearable?' I thought she was going to cry then, the memories of her sudden divorce and his very public arrest. He'd killed a dad and his two children due to dangerous driving. Ploughed into them on a zebra crossing at a huge speed. He was on his way home, drunk, after visiting a woman he'd been having an affair with. He fled the scene, arrived home in tears, and had to be dragged away from his own driveway by the police. Probably reflecting back on all this, Kirsten nodded. 'Yes, of course. Although what happened with me and my family was nowhere near as bad as what happened to those two little girls and their dad. Nowhere near as bad as what their mum must have gone through. And nowhere near as bad as yours,' she said. I nodded. She was right. It couldn't even compare.

I stare at the phone, trying to focus on the text.

Are you going to Denise's fiftieth? We can talk about it if you want?

I read Kirsten's message a couple of times, its meaning sinking in. I knew Denise's fiftieth was approaching. She'd dropped a card by, probably comfortable in the knowledge there's no way I would attend. I hadn't really thought seriously about going, but had put it in the little pouch in the calendar in the kitchen. I'd meant to talk to Kirsten about it but it had gone out of my mind as soon as the card had dropped out of sight, hidden among phone bills and council tax forms. Once upon a time there would have been things in that calendar about Jessica's school. Trips to London to galleries, museums, university fairs. Not anymore. It had been another of those weird milestones, going past the months where there was nothing written in or added into the calendar about her at all. No dental appointments or school things. It was as if she had faded from our lives; steadily sponged out as the days went by.

I text back to Kirsten:

I haven't decided.

And click send. Then type out an extra message as an afterthought:

Alec wouldn't agree to going. No hope in hell.

I wouldn't want him to, either, I think as I lie back into the cushions. Not because he would be embarrassing, though there's a chance he would be, but because I'd sense him watching my reactions, judging me, waiting for me to fall.

Regardless, since Kirsten's text the prospect of the party

plays on my mind. I lie on my bed, turning it around in my head, allowing my mind to fantasise about what it would be like, trying to be nice to people, attempting to smile and make it look natural. It would be an effort. An extraordinary effort. But something within me wants to do it just to see the looks on their faces. It sounds cruel, but I've always rather liked doing that. Disconcerting people. Challenging their sense of the norm and throwing their presumptions back in their smug faces. It's what makes me a good writer, I think. A writer has to be brave enough to 'go there', I've always thought. Tackle the problems you don't want to talk about. Make people feel uncomfortable. Because that's where they find out the most about themselves. And usually – not always, but usually – they don't like what they find out.

Chapter Four

THE MOTHER

February. The day of the attack.

'Have you seen the News?'

I in was the foyer of the BBC's Broadcasting House on Regent Street. I wouldn't normally be there on a Saturday, but the drama producer I needed to meet was about to go to America for three weeks to oversee a show being produced with HBO and I was keen to go through a few things before his trip. We were going up in the lift to the floors full of brightly coloured chairs and photos of famous TV stars on the walls, when I noticed something odd. There weren't many people in the offices, but the ones who were there were grouped around the large TVs on the walls to the sides, watching the BBC News that was being broadcast in the very building we were standing in.

'What's going on?' the producer, Mike, said to a young woman waiting for the lift.

'There's been another terrorist attack.'

I saw Mike's eyes widen. 'Where? In London?'

The girl nodded, 'Yes, in Stratford. I think at the train station.' She looked worried. Maybe she knew someone in Stratford. Maybe she was supposed to be getting home that way. She got into the lift and pushed one of the buttons, and the doors closed.

'God, another one,' Mike said, leading the way towards an empty meeting room. He swiped it with his pass and we went inside. A large photograph of Nadiya Hussain was on the wall. 'Take a seat. I'll grab you a drink. Tea or coffee?'

'Tea, please,' I said, settling down and taking out my iPad. Mike left the room, and as he walked off I saw him glance at the TV screen on the wall. I couldn't see it properly, and part of me wished we'd stopped to watch on our way through. Unlocking my iPad, I navigated immediately to the main BBC News homepage. And there it was. The main headline read:

STRATFORD ATTACKS:
MULTIPLE VIOLENT INCIDENTS IN EAST LONDON

The photograph was of the outside of Stratford station showing police vans and ambulances, their lights glowing in the late-afternoon winter gloom. The page had one of those useful bullet-point timelines summarising the confirmed information, but I didn't have time to click onto it before Mike came in carrying the tea. He noticed the page on the screen.

'Do you need to call anyone?' he asked as he set the tea down.

'No, no,' I said. 'My husband's at home and my daughter's in Somerset visiting a friend. I might have some trouble getting home, though.'

The thought had only just occurred to me. Should I be leaving London? Will there be a rush on the trains?

'Oh goodness. Do you go through Stratford? Will you be able to find an alternative route? I suppose it depends on whether they close the train line. I imagine they probably will.'

'You're right,' I said, trying not to look too worried. 'Although I don't go through Stratford. London Bridge, so hopefully that's still open and running. Well, let's go through everything as planned and I'll see how things are when it's time to leave.'

I switched my iPad over to the notes on the TV series we'd planned to talk about. Mike opened a laptop in front of him and we got to work.

———————————

'Do you want me to call you a car?' Mike offered as we went down in the lift just over an hour later.

'I'm sure I'll be fine,' I said, gripping my phone in my pocket. I was getting a bit worried now, eager to work out how I'd be travelling.

'I now feel a bit bad you've come all the way up here on a Saturday.'

I smiled and shook my head, 'It's nothing. I had planned to do some shopping on Oxford Street, but I think it's best if I just work out my way home.'

He nodded and we got out of the lift.

On my way out of the BBC I walked in a bit of a daze down towards Oxford Circus. I took out my phone, but at my first glance I ended up careering into someone who tutted loudly and rushed past me. 'Watch it!' someone else said.

I needed to stop and think. I was walking past a Caffè Nero and quickly nipped inside. I didn't bother going up to the counter to order, just headed over to an empty table and sat down. There were already two messages from Alec and a missed call.

Something's happened at Stratford. You OK getting home?

Said the first one. Then the second, sent half hour later:

Message me to say you're all OK getting home.

I tapped out a message straight away:

Yes, all fine, just looking into journey details. Will call if I have problems.

I then navigated to the BBC News site, clicked on the main item and began to read:

At least 17 people have been killed in a series of major incidents in Stratford, East London. The Metropolitan Police have confirmed they are

34

**treating this as a terrorist attack. Below is a
timeline, based on information from the police, on
how the events unfolded.**

- At 4.35pm six men carrying knives and firearms
  alighted from an incoming train and attacked
  members of the public and two police officers on
  platforms 9 and 10 at Stratford station as they
  waited for trains to London Liverpool Street,
  Southend Victoria, and Norwich.
- At approximately 4.40pm the attackers then entered
  the main concourse of Stratford station and
  continued to shoot civilians as they tried to flee to
  safety. The BBC understands two further police
  offers were shot.
- At 4.44pm the attackers then walked the short
  distance to the exit of Stratford station and opened
  fire on police and crowds of people near the
  entrance to Westfield Stratford City shopping centre
  and the lower ground-floor food department of
  Marks & Spencer.
- At around the same time, reports of multiple knife
  attacks came in from two restaurants on the dining
  level of Westfield. It has been confirmed nine
  people were stabbed by two masked attackers in
  Pizza Express and TGI Fridays and at the entrance
  to the Vue multiplex cinema. Police consider the
  incident to be connected to the attack on Stratford
  train station.
- At 4.50pm, during the mass evacuation of the

shopping centre, a suicide bomber, believed to be one of the Stratford station attackers, detonated a bomb in the main entrance hall of Westfield Stratford, causing further fatalities.

- The Prime Minister has been informed and is journeying to 10 Downing Street, cutting short a visit to Brussels, and will chair an emergency COBRA meeting in the morning.

I found the details, laid out in a cold, simple list, both shocking and strangely numbing. Shocking because such callous, horrific violence against innocent members of the public naturally repulsed me, but numbing because – and I felt guilty as I thought it – it had got to the point where this kind of thing wasn't only a part of life, it was to be expected.

Everyone knew the tempo had changed over the past year when there were a series of attacks in quick succession throughout the summer and autumn. After the lull in atrocities since the multiple attacks of a few years back, it felt as if people had just forgotten there was much of a threat. Other things started to become main news, and the attacks grew less frequent. Whilst there were still terrible attacks a short distance away in Europe, and our national terror threat level went up and down, people's minds weren't really on extremists and people who may wish us harm. And then, just as things were starting to edge back to normal and people were celebrating the end of a very dark era, a man walked into a crowded Sainsbury's in Battersea with a load of Semtex strapped to his chest. I don't think many people had thought of supermarkets as being a target. Not until they saw the carnage on their TV screens. Thirteen people dead. Then a week later another bomb, left on a luggage rack, detonated on a train just as it was pulling into Walthamstow Central. Nine people dead. Just over two months later, a man left a rucksack in a packed bar on the King's Road in Chelsea on a Friday night. Twenty people dead. And, finally, just before Christmas, a bomb which failed to fully detonate went off in the Eurostar terminal in Ebbsfleet. Multiple people with major injuries, and one person dead; a teenage girl, close to Jessica's age.

With all this in my mind, I switched to Facebook Messenger and sent a quick message to her:

> You may have seen that there's been another attack in London. Hopefully it won't affect your train journey home tomorrow, but let us know if so.

I tapped send, then, worrying it sounded too calm and distant, added a touch of caution as an afterthought:

> If anything looks wrong or unusual or if you're unsure of what to do, please phone me or your dad immediately or speak to a police officer. Don't want to worry you, but I'd prefer it if you message me when you're on the train and then when you're passing through London Bridge. Just so I know you're safe. No detours!

I felt uneasy as I went to my home screen and opened the National Rail app. *Maybe I should offer to drive down to*

Somerset to get Jessica tomorrow, I thought. *It would take hours and hours, though. And she already has her return ticket, too.* The National Rail departures list to Sevenoaks made it very clear: major disruption until end of service. After some more research (via *The Guardian* and the *Daily Mail*), I discovered that most major train stations in London had been evacuated pretty soon after it became clear there was a coordinated attack on Stratford station. Many of them were still closed. London Bridge had reopened but services were far from normal and people were being advised to seek alternative transport. And, to be entirely honest, I wasn't sure a train station platform was a place I wanted to be lingering at that moment.

I messaged Alec, telling him I was going to get a car home – I couldn't face the train commotion. I then ordered a car using the dedicated app on my phone, bought a panini from the smiley young woman at the counter, and walked while eating towards Langham Place, near the BBC, where the car was collecting me. It took longer than advertised, and I spent the time looking at Twitter, seeing the hysteria unfold. Both #PrayForLondon and #PrayForStratford were trending. I thought we'd abandoned the 'Pray For' hashtags, but they seemed to have started up again. I rarely used social media myself; just occasionally, to retweet trailers of TV series I'd worked on and keep an eye on viewers' reactions to them when they aired. The idea of using it – actually updating one's status or posting photos – in the midst of an emergency situation rather baffled me. I couldn't imagine taking out my phone to tweet, as one woman had:

> OMG I just saw a woman got stabbed in front of me
> when coming out of the cinema in Westfield – never
> seen something like that in real life before. So horrible.
> I'm so shaken. #Stratford #StratfordAttacks
> #PrayForLondon.

Another person had tweeted an image of what appeared to be bodies, photographed from afar, lying on one of the station platforms. The user, named @OddJobJimmy1991, had included the words:

> So fucking sick. Slaughtered like animals. This needs to
> be SORTED.

He'd tagged in a few notable politicians, including the prime minister and home secretary, along with two far-right journalists and social commentators, perhaps hoping for a retweet from them.

The car eventually arrived, and it was only once I was inside its warm interior that I realised how frozen I was. I felt my icy fingers start to regain feeling as I continued to swipe my phone, typing out another message to Jessica:

> Hi, did you see my message?

It was a bit pointless, as I could see she hadn't seen it. She was probably busy Instagramming some big hill she'd just trekked up with her friend, or the meal they'd just had in a gastro-pub. I checked her account to see, but there was nothing – the last thing she'd posted had been the cover of a large fantasy novel by Sarah J. Maas, along with the caption:

It's official: I'm addicted and in LOVE with this.

But that was yesterday, before she'd left for the West Country.

Suddenly, I was filled with an overwhelming need to speak to her. Hear her voice. *Everything will be fine*, I tried to tell myself. She'd been out of Kent and London for hours and hours. Long before the whole commotion happened. And besides, she wouldn't have needed to go anywhere near the East End. I tapped the 'call' button on her contact details and her face filled the screen. The dialling tone went on for what felt like an age, and then a woman's voice said, 'Welcome to the O2 messaging service,' and I cut the call.

'It's going to take quite a while getting back,' my driver said in a bored-sounding voice. 'Everywhere's seized up. The main task is going to be getting out of London. Normally it should take just over an hour, but today – well, I think you're in for a bit of a long ride. And there's trouble on the A13.'

'Great,' I murmured, trying Jessica again. This time, at the sound of the voicemail, I didn't hang up: 'Hi love, it's me. I don't know if you've seen my messages, or the news, but there's been another attack in London and I just wanted to speak to you – hopefully it won't affect your trip home tomorrow, but… well, can you just give me a call? I love you.'

A few seconds after I'd cut the call, the driver said, 'You got family in the area?'

I shook my head. 'No, my daughter – she's in Somerset but will be travelling back tomorrow. Shouldn't be a problem, but you know what it's like – neurotic parent and all that!'

I saw the young man shrug. 'Don't have kids. Never found a girl I've liked longer than six weeks.'

'Right,' I said, unsure what to do with this information.

'But my mum was the same. Always calling me, checking if I'm dead.' He seemed to have got onto a subject he liked and started waving his hands, imitating someone I presumed to be his mum, saying, 'Text me when you get there! Call me to say you're safe!'

I made a small half-laugh sound, hoping to put an end to the conversation, but he carried on:

'I mean, I'm thirty in July and she's still like that. Never stops. Is your mum the same?'

My stomach gave a small lurch. 'No,' I said, looking down at the dark screen of my phone in my hands. 'No, she was... something else.'

He seemed to take this as an end to the chat, and I was relieved when we started to inch our way down Haymarket in silence.

The young man was right: what should have been an eighty-minute journey became two and a half hours. By the time I stepped through the front door and into the lounge, I'd already worked myself up into something of a state.

'Caroline,' Alec called from the lounge, 'you've been ages. I had to eat without you.'

How can he be thinking about his stomach at a time like this? I thought to myself as I walked through into the lounge. He was lying back on the sofa in his jeans and a casual light-pink shirt. My eyes flicked over him and even in my distracted state I noticed three things: his slightly flushed appearance, the lack of socks on his feet, and, from where his shirt had ridden up at the side, the fact that the waistband of his underwear was a different colour to the pair he had been wearing when making breakfast that morning. To many people, these details would hardly be perceived, but to me – to the experienced eye – they shouted out, loud and clear. He had the TV on, playing BBC News, with a reporter speaking from somewhere outside, with flickering blue lights in the background.

'When there wasn't an attack over Christmas, apart from that Eurostar thing, I thought maybe that was it,' he said, his eyes on the screen. 'But I suppose it was only a matter of time before it happened again.' He pointed the control at the screen, lowering the volume. 'Was the journey dreadful?' he asked, turning his eyes to me.

'Yes,' I said. 'And I can't get hold of Jessica.' I tried to make the words sound as light as possible, but sensing the rise of tears behind my eyes, I walked away from him and into the kitchen. I reached for a large glass and filled it with water, my eyes flicking to the drying rack, loaded with plates and a saucepan. And two wine glasses. Two of them.

Just sitting there, upside down. I turned my back on them, wishing I hadn't seen them, and took a long, deep glug of the cool water.

Alec must have wandered in behind me, because when I turned back towards the doorway, he was standing in front of it, looking confused and concerned. 'Jessica? But she's in Somerset.'

I nodded, 'I know. But I'd like to speak to her. She might be... upset.'

He looked even more confused. 'Yes, but, well, this isn't the first thing like this that's happened. She'll be getting used to it now. Like the rest of us.'

I felt my eyes flare. 'Are you implying I shouldn't be upset with the idea of a bunch of sociopaths gunning down innocent people? That our nearest major city is fast becoming a warzone?' I was talking quickly, my bottled-up worry about Jessica flowing freely into my diction, making me garble my words.

Alec watched me, his eyebrows raised. 'Christ, you're sounding hysterical. London isn't a warzone.'

I didn't have the drive to fight him. I took out my phone and went back to the lounge. Once inside the room, I stood in front of the now muted TV and phoned Jessica again. Voicemail. 'Hi, it's Mum. Getting a little worried now – just phone me so I know you haven't fallen down a ditch or something!'

I knew the closing few words probably sounded manically bright and happy, but it was too late. Jessica would hear the message, roll her eyes and tell me she was fine, and then she'd return home as normal tomorrow and all my concerns would be for nothing.

Welcome to the O2 messaging service…

I turned back to the TV. The news announcer was issuing us with an update: the newly calculated death toll stood at seventeen.

It was the middle of the night when we heard the doorbell. Some parents speak of denial when they're told the worst. Their brains refuse to believe it. Mine didn't. I knew, as soon as I heard the doorbell at two in the morning, that I wouldn't be seeing my little girl ever again. I knew it throughout every fibre, every muscle, every bone.

Part of me expected them to tell me Jessica had been hit by a car on some road in Minehead. Or perhaps fallen over and fatally injured herself on some long country walk. But it became clear very quickly, from the first words the two kind police officers said to me as they sat down in the living room, that this wasn't an accident. My daughter had been murdered in the terrorist attack on Stratford station. They had checked her debit cards, and her 16–25 Student Rail Card, which included photo ID. They were sure they hadn't got it wrong, but they would need either me or Alec to formally identify her.

'This… this must be… this can't be…' Alec said in consternation, running his hand through his bed-ruffled hair. 'There must… But she's in Somerset…'

I couldn't speak. The young police detective was saying

44

something, but it had all started to blur and slow down, and I couldn't make the room stay still. I just sat in silence. Eventually I became aware that Alec was trying to talk to me – something about if Jessica had told me she was going back to London. I shook my head. 'She wasn't supposed to be there... She wasn't supposed...' I couldn't finish the sentence. I walked over the soft carpet to the large windows that faced onto the garden. I looked out into the darkness, and for a second I thought I could see the outline of a slide and a swing, which we had bought when Jessica was a child. But as I took a step closer to the glass, I could see the lawn was empty. As it has been for years.

'Caroline?' Alec said, as if he'd just asked me a question and he was prompting me for an answer.

After a moment or two, I stepped away from the window, and walked back to be with my husband so we could listen to the two police officers describe how our daughter died.

Chapter Five

THE BOY

When I was six, maybe seven years old, my dad pulled me from the back seat of his van from under an old blanket. I was in pain and had been crying, and he told me to 'grow up' and 'get in the house'. Inside he ran a bath for me and lifted me in as I was still too short to climb in myself. I told him then that it was the worst day – the worst day of my life. And I didn't want to go in the van. Ever again. He told me to shut up. To have my bath and be quiet. Then he said that I would know lots of bad days. Many worse than this one. And one day, when I was older, they would all blur into one.

There was one bad day though, years later, that would never blur into all the others. It would stand out as if written in fire on my mind.

I saw it on the BBC News website. That red globe with the rings round it that alerts you to a breaking news story was at the top of the page. Reports said shots fired at Stratford Station, East London. I watched as the facts became clearer. The Met were at the scene, along with special armed first responders who floated around London waiting for things like this to happen. I had to go and be sick for a bit. I knelt on the bathroom floor and let my dinner from earlier pour out of me. I've always hated being sick – I mean, no one likes it, but I especially don't. But this time, I didn't really think about it. I just thought of her.

I kept the 'Live Updates' feed open on my desktop for the rest of the evening and into the night, watching the news roll in. Sometimes, when the BBC updates were slow, I switched over to Twitter where rumours spread like STIs, but disturbing details had a habit of floating to the surface quicker than on the official news sites. It was all a mass of opinions, retweets, videos and photos that may or may not have been taken from the scene. They started to fill my newsfeed. Some showed police and dancing blue lights outside the entrance of Stratford station. Others had images of people being evacuated from the Westfield shopping centre next to the station, their hands held above their heads. Some photos even showed bodies and people running over them, desperate to get to the exits.

At around half past midnight, nearly three hours after the news alert popped up on my screen, the BBC website updated the headline to say the police had confirmed 'multiple fatalities'. The Metropolitan Police hadn't yet released an official death count, but the word 'multiple' hit me between the eyes and then sank in, slowly and horribly, like a slow-burning headache, spreading across my temple, making my whole face vibrate. *She's going to be OK*, I told myself. *She will be OK. I'll text her,* I decided. I reached for my phone and hit the Facebook Messenger app icon.

> I'm worried. I've just seen the news. I'm so sorry I
> wasn't with you. Please tell me you're safe.

More hours passed and the message went unseen and unanswered. The *Daily Mail* was leading its homepage with the heading 'TERROR STRIKES THE EAST END'. The text underneath said a group of masked men with machine guns opened fire on people waiting for a train at Stratford station, East London and that explosions had been heard coming from the Westfield shopping centre. *The Guardian's* report was similar, though didn't mention the rumour of explosions.

My message remained unanswered. I typed:

> Please. I get that you're probably mad. I'm really sorry. I
> can explain why I didn't meet you. Please can you just
> tell me you got home safe. Please?

And clicked send.

Three hours later I returned to the bathroom and was sick again, even though I had very little left to throw up. A small knock at the door made me start.

'What's going on?' It was my mum's voice.

I told her I was OK and she should go back to sleep.

'Were you being sick?' she asked.

'Yes, but I'm fine now. Just go back to sleep. It must be flu or something.'

A few moments' pause, then I heard her say, 'Or those dodgy fish fingers,' and then the sound of her moving back to her bedroom. I went to the sink and turned the cold tap on and threw handfuls of water onto my face, soaking my clothes, the cold temperature making my face tingle. It felt good. As if it was giving me strength. Brought me back to my senses.

I tried to tell myself everything was going to be OK. I was just being silly. The attack happened an hour after we were supposed to meet. I couldn't imagine anyone would linger an hour, waiting for a date to show up. *It wasn't just a date, though, was it?* I ignored the little voice in my head and left the bathroom. On the landing I paused to remove the sodden T-shirt and boxers and threw them into the washing basket we keep near the airing cupboard, then grabbed some old pyjamas that had been in there for ages and pulled them on. They felt soft and smelt clean and comforting. Reminded me of when I was a kid. I walked quickly back to my room and almost yelled with shock when I saw my brother sitting at my desk.

'What the fuck are you doing?' I hissed at him, trying to keep my voice low.

'I saw your light was on. Have you heard about Stratford?'

'Yes. Can you go? I'm not feeling well.'

'It was on your laptop screen. It says seventeen dead.'

I thought I was going to be sick again.

'I need to sleep.' I tried not to shout. I just needed him to leave.

'Why are you wearing those?' he said, looking at the pyjamas.

'I was sick on my clothes,' I lied. I couldn't be bothered to explain about the water. 'I want to sleep.'

'OK, OK.' He took his hands away from the keyboard and walked out, closing the door behind him.

Back on my computer, I saw the BBC's site had been updated with the new death toll, as he'd said. They also had one of those bullet-point timelines summarising the confirmed information. I clicked on the link and read through it – every single one. Each paragraph of the article felt like a physical pain. I stumbled away from the computer and realised I was shaking. From the floor I found a hoodie and pulled it on and then collapsed onto my bed. Instead of going properly under the sheets, I backed myself into a corner and pulled the duvet around me so I was cocooned in.

I don't know how long it took me to fall asleep. It could have been hours, it could have been minutes. No dreams came to me that night, surprisingly. They would arrive another day.

When I woke, I had that strange, dazed feeling you get when you've been in a very deep sleep. A feeling that took me back to the days when I would wake up as a kid and not know how I'd got back to my own bed after being out late with my dad. How my memories of the night were blurred, as if scrubbed away by sleep.

My back hurt from my odd position and I ached as I stood up to face a bright, hot but horrible morning. The laptop was still open but had gone into hibernation and when I clicked it, part of me hoped it would never come back to life. But it did, of course. The screen glowed instantly at my touch and the BBC website refreshed itself to show a new headline:

STRATFORD ATTACKS: DEATH TOLL RISES TO 37

I knew what I needed to do. It had been a while, but the scab was still there. I opened the little drawer of my desk and reached right to the back and pulled out the cold metal compass. It still had blood on the point, dried to an almost-brown colour. I stared at the sharp tip for a few seconds, then, my eyes filling with tears, I brought it down and pressed. Hard.

Chapter Six

THE MOTHER

May. Three months after the attack.

We're going to Denise's fiftieth birthday party. I had fully intended to ignore the invite, but now, for reasons best known to the inner workings of my brain, I've decided we're going. That is, if I can convince Alec to come too. Initially, I text Rob – not to ask him to come, but to just get some emotional support in the decision. A hope that someone would acknowledge how hard it is for me to even contemplate going to something like that, but encourage me all the same. All I wanted was a nudge in the right direction. But my message went unreplied to for a good hour (unusual in itself), then came back with a response that made me feel furious with exasperation:

You should do what you feel comfortable with.

It was such a useless piece of vague, wishy-washy

advice, I almost flung the phone across the room again. And now I'm sitting on the edge of the bed, trying to find the right words to broach the subject with Alec.

Much as I'd love to leave him behind, I think I know deep down I would need him if it all went to pot, even if he was just on chauffeur duty. As I expected, he isn't best pleased when I tell him. He has just come from one of his 'evening walks'. His face once again has that flushed look and the collar of his shirt is bunched and crumpled at the back. I realise I should have picked a better time (he usually doesn't want to talk when he's got back) but the words spring from me before I have a chance to stop them.

'Denise's fiftieth birthday party is tomorrow. We're going.'

He looks at me as if I'd just told him we were going to Raqqa. 'What the fuck?' he says, and follows me into the lounge as I start to walk away from him. I settle onto the sofa so that I'm comfortable while he rants. I don't say anything; just watch him go from sheet white to ruby red in the space of ten seconds.

'We're *not* going.' He is pacing around the room now, gathering momentum. 'I can't… I just can't.'

'You'll be fine,' I say, sounding far more confident than I feel.

'It's not happening. I'm not going to spend three hours standing in a room with those smug, posh twats while they all point at me – at us – and say how awful they feel to our faces, and then go away to thank God that it didn't happen to them. That it didn't happen to *their* daughter.'

This is predictable. I could have written this beforehand

on a piece of paper and practically every single word would be verbatim as he was saying it right now. He pauses the pacing and stands awkwardly, leaning up against the mantelpiece, avoiding looking at the photos of Jessica that are just a head-tilt away from his line of vision.

'You don't even like Denise. You said she was a two-faced, old cow who still thinks she's twenty-five. Christ, you even invented a character in a television show that was bloody based on her. I mean… what friend *does that*?'

I fix him with a stony stare. 'I believe at the time you said it was a "genius move" and laughed for days about it. I thought I did it quite well.'

'You did,' he says, rubbing his forehead. 'And you're so bloody lucky she never watches crime dramas otherwise she'd have spotted it for herself. You even had her living at a place called Four Hedges House.'

'It's a little different.'

'Not by much,' he snaps.

Denise lives at Three Trees House, christened thus, one presumes, on account of the three large oak trees that surround her beautiful property.

'Don't pretend you care what I write about Denise. It doesn't make the slightest bit of difference.'

'So why do you want to go?' He is down on his knees now, almost begging, holding onto my legs. I can smell him – the Ralph Lauren scent he uses, along with something else, something sweeter. Something feminine.

'Caroline, are you listening to me?'

I take my time to answer, then eventually say, 'I just need a change. We can't go on as we are. Surely you know that? We don't *do* anything. You go along to your... walks,' I see him look away at this word, as if something on the carpet has caught his attention. 'I go to therapy and the gym and that's it. I'm not writing anymore. I've tried and I can't. I just can't, ever since...'

I can't bring myself to say it. We still haven't got there yet. We haven't found a way to articulate what happened to our daughter – unless it's within the heat of a blazing row – without stumbling and backing away. How do you condense something so terrible as that into a short, accessible phrase? You can't. And so we just flounder and grasp at words in the air.

He looks at me and I think he's going to cry, then he looks at the floor and says quietly, 'I think... I might go on another walk.'

I can't cope with that. I just scoff. 'Oh come off it. Walk? Who's next on your list? That receptionist at the dentist I saw you making eyes at last time you picked me up? Or that "old work friend" you refer to carefully so as not to give away their gender – or the fact she's only twenty-eight!'

I shout these last words, recoiling away from him. It was about three weeks after the Stratford attacks, when we'd had time to digest, at least to a small extent, what had happened and who was responsible, when his 'walks' started back up again. It was the day they'd properly identified all the terrorists that had taken part. We'd even heard their names on the radio and seen their faces splashed across the front page of every newspaper in Britain: 'FACES OF EVIL'; 'BUTCHERERS OF THE

INNOCENT'. The headlines seemed to revel in it all – the horror, the fear, the outrage. Alec, to my surprise, seemed to swallow all this tabloid hysteria with an enthusiasm that rather dismayed me, and started to regularly trot out bizarre rumours about 'immigrants' and 'extremists', as if the two things were inextricably linked. I greeted his preposterous, untrue statements with all the respect they deserved – a look of disgust and a refusal to talk. The only time I did properly respond was when he made a comment about most of London and the south being now 'overrun with immigrants'. I snapped back at him that it must be 'awful to be married to one'. This did make him pause a bit, then he said, 'Well, that's different; you're Australian.' I couldn't help but laugh, 'Oh I see, so some countries are OK, are they? You do know I spent most of my childhood in Saudi Arabia, don't you? I'm surprised you haven't tried to have me deported just for that.' He didn't respond. We settled into a tense silence on the subject after this discussion, but it didn't last long, and finally, when it all got too much, we had another explosive row about it. He accused me of being a weak-willed liberal with my head in the sand and how I, of all people, should want all the 'vile monsters' removed off this earth. Then he slammed out of the house, shouting inevitably that he was 'going for a walk'.

Now, confronted with the image of him in front of me, looking both angry and sad, I fall back on my main coping mechanism when I no longer have the strength to continue fighting with him: I get up and walk away. He then has to make the choice to follow me, which he often does, but it speeds up the process. It means he can get hysterical and, as a result, reach his apex quicker than he would normally.

'So, that's settled, right?' he says, following me into the library as I walk towards the end-most bookshelves. I survey the titles before me, an array of hardbacks and paperbacks, all jumbled together, no rhyme or reason. 'We're not going, OK? I can't begin to imagine why you ever thought it would be a good idea.'

'I think I'm going to start reading again. There are so many here I haven't read. And I'll rearrange them, too. Alphabetically. And who knows, with the reading might come the writing. Maybe I could find something nice to adapt – something less violent.'

He raises his hand to his hair and runs it through it, messing it up, making him look like a teenager who has just returned back home after a wild night out.

'I am *trying* to have a conversation with you about a single important issue, so can you please not try to distract me and change the subject?'

'It was you who wanted to stop talking and go out and roam the streets! You'd like me to start writing again, wouldn't you?'

'Er… I… well… yes, of course…'

'Well then, just leave me to get on with it,' I say, pulling the little step stool to my right so I can climb up and reach the top shelf. 'I've always meant to try my hand at adapting a classic novel. Like a Brontë, or maybe an Austen. But I got distracted by brooding crime thrillers.' The book I've reached for is *Little Women*. I'm not even sure why I have it here amidst a bunch of Edinburgh-based murder mysteries, but that's the case with most of the books in our library. I have an expensive habit of ordering up mountains of books. Even if I don't read them, it still makes me feel like I'm keeping my finger on the pulse of the literary world.

Alec sinks down into one of the tasteful cream armchairs that are dotted about the room. 'Caroline, please, *please*. Denise's party. Can we talk about it?'

'We have,' I say, climbing back off the stool and then sitting down in a chair at the other end of the room. 'We're going. Or at least I am. Do as you wish.'

He does his teeth-clenching thing when I say this, which usually means he would really like to say something back that's both hurtful and intelligent but, as always, fails under the time pressure. And then he comes out with something that does actually make me gasp. 'Do you know,' he says slowly, in a low, dangerous-sounding voice, 'you're really starting to remind me of your mother right now.'

I stare at him, stunned into silence for a second. Then, when I regain my voice, I splutter back: 'What? How can I? You've never even met her.'

He surveys me, folding his arms in a belligerent way. He knows he's got to me now, and I'm kicking myself for letting it show. 'I have a pretty good idea, from what you've said in the past. You know what I mean.'

I feel defiance inside me and I become determined to hold his gaze, to not back down. 'No, actually, I don't.'

He pulls a weird face, like a half-grimace, half-smirk. It makes him look uncharacteristically ugly. 'Well… unhinged. I just wonder if I need to watch my back when I'm around you. I don't know what you might do next.'

The blood surges into my face and I feel myself going red – red with rage, with hatred, with pure, hot fury. 'Get out!' I shriek at him.

At first he doesn't move, then after a few seconds he gets up and marches out of the library, slamming the door behind him.

I take some deep breaths, calming myself down. It's strange – before the disaster, I wouldn't have dared speak to him like that. Even when he occasionally went to nasty, bellow-the-belt places. Even when he tried to make out I was stupid or conniving or crazy. But now the worst has happened, I find a spirit within me I never knew existed. The spirit to fight.

Trying to stop myself trembling, I turn the book I'm clutching over in my hands. It's a Penguin English Library edition – one I think I bought a few years ago when I thought I'd start collecting the series. I remember reading *Little Women* when I was at school, but my memory of it has been mixed with various adaptations I've seen – one with Winona Ryder I think, and another with Emily Watson, and a more recent one at the cinema.

Christmas won't be Christmas without any presents.

The first line brings with it a wave of warmth and familiarity, tinged with the same sweet sadness one feels at the end of the summer holidays, when the golden days are over and the funfair is packing up its wares.

Remarkably, I make it through the whole novel without crying once about Jessica, even during the moments of death from scarlet fever. It might be because the time and setting, with the American Civil War backdrop, are far removed from our lives here. It's because I've got my writer's eyes in. I do this sometimes. Alec accuses me of doing it when I'm watching TV. If we're in the middle of a drama or film and he sees me crouched forward, my eyes squinting slightly, he says, 'You're doing it, aren't you? You're writing the rest of the plot for them. Figuring out the mechanics of it.' I'll nod vaguely in response, slightly embarrassed to admit it, but it's true. And now here I am, doing it to *Little Women*. And I've become serious about the thought of an adaptation. I think it will help. It will give me a motivation, or purpose, something to wake up for. In some way, I might be able to give myself some sense of peace. I'm not delusional enough to think I'll ever get real peace or total mercy from this terrible world we live in. But at least it will offer me something new – relief from the fear that Alec and I might carry on forever as we are now, floating our way towards a new normal, carrying on like automated androids, sniping at each other, testing each other's tempers and then falling into a stony silence when we can't think of anything else to say.

Jessica used to read. She was an outspoken critic, but she regularly found a series she liked and threw herself headfirst into it, devouring book after book. As soon as she was old enough, she read *The Chronicles of Narnia*, *Harry Potter*, and a little later, *The Lord of the Rings*, cover to cover and memorised all the characters and place names. 'Maybe you could be an author when you grow up,' I once told her. 'If you like fantastical characters and magical lands, you should make up some of your own.' She used to nod and giggle at this when she was very young, but if I hinted much about any future careers once she had hit her mid-teens, she smiled but her mouth twisted in that way that told me I'd best not pursue the subject. She never liked to think about adulthood, her future, life beyond being sixteen and carefree.

My legs have become stiff and I feel a bone click as I get up off the sofa. It has become dark as I've sat there, immersed in *Little Women* for the past few hours, the only light coming from the small reading lamp I turned on halfway through. I have no idea what the time is, but Alec is still awake. I can hear the TV in the lounge playing some documentary about sharks. I decide to leave him to it.

Upstairs, I instinctively move towards Jessica's bedroom. I used to come in here every day, each time like climbing a big, emotional mountain, only to find a cold, cruel abyss on the other side into which I'd fall. I keep myself together tonight, as I wander round, taking in the books, the neatly folded clothes, the movie posters on the walls – dystopian science-fiction films like *The Hunger Games* and *Divergent*. She put these up when she was twelve or thirteen and I'd been happy she'd kept them up. I thought it was sad so many teenagers would strip away their childhood passions and interests when they hit their late teens, as if embarrassed they ever cared so much about something. I move over towards the books, all of them neatly stacked in alphabetical order; a smaller model of my grand plans for the large library of titles we have downstairs. She kept all her books from her early teen years, as well as others that go back further to when she was in primary school. Enid Blyton jostles for space up against the likes of Suzanne Collins and Stephenie Meyer, along with the C.S. Lewis and J.K. Rowling favourites.

I turn away to her desk, where her laptop and iPad have lain untouched for months. She had her phone on her during the attack and the screen shattered at some point, probably when she hit the floor. I haven't even tried to get it working; I don't know if it still would. Curious, I feel along the side of the desk for the charger and connect it to the bottom of the iPhone. Nothing happens at first, then the screen lights up with a battery symbol, telling me the phone is chronically starved of power. But it seems to be charging. Eventually, after a glimpse of the Apple logo, the home screen appears and Jessica's face greets me. She is in a bikini and smiling, standing next to me and Alec. We were in Florida on a beach and she had the phone extended on one of those plastic arm things so she could take a photo of all of us. I'd thought at the time how ridiculous it was that young people couldn't do as we used to when we were young and wanted a group shot: we just asked someone else to take the photo. Jessica just rolled her eyes when I said this.

I don't know her password, but it doesn't matter. There isn't any need to go any further. This photo is enough for now. I take the phone with me and in my room plug it into my charger so it can be with me throughout the night. A little piece of my beautiful daughter, sitting quietly on my bedside table as I drift off to sleep. She's there, in cyber form; a little hard drive of memories. Waiting to be unlocked.

Chapter Seven

THE MOTHER

May. Three months after the attack.

On the morning of Denise's party, I wake early and attempt to do some yoga. I consider going to the gym, but decide doing it in the conservatory will take up less time. I want to leave the house by 8am.

The yoga never really takes off, so I abandon it after less than ten minutes, shower quietly so as not to wake Alec and start to get dressed. I'm just doing up the zip of my jeans when I hear him stir. He thuds out of his bedroom on the way to the bathroom. Sometimes I wonder if the stomping to the loo each morning is him making a point about no longer having an en suite, now he's in the guest bedroom and I'm in the main one. I think about making a run for it down the stairs while he's peeing, but before I can move he's there, standing on the landing. His hair's ruffled, the T-shirt he's slept in all creased. I used to like the sight of him in the morning; he had a sense of dishevelled attractiveness about him that I could never quite resist. But this has gone. It's not so much that he's changed, it's just the way I see him. It's like getting a glimpse of a car on the road that you used to drive – identical to your old one, but now a thing of the past, still existing somewhere but no longer part of your life. I find it strange to think the sight of him used to inspire excitement and lust. Now the most I feel is a sad sense of detachment.

'What are you looking at?' he asks, noticing me staring. Then, when I don't answer straight away, he adds: 'Do you want to have sex?'

This makes me look into his eyes properly and shake my head in disbelief.

'What?' he says, as if surprised I haven't said yes. 'I thought you did, by the way you were checking me out.'

'*Checking you out?*' I say in consternation. 'Christ.'

'Well, if you're going to be like that…'

'I'm going to the group meeting today. I missed the last one.'

'You're… what? Why?'

I start gathering some things from the drawer in the bedside table – a new packet of tissues, pre-empting my likely tears, and a box of antihistamines. I put them into my bag and walk past Alec and go downstairs.

'Caroline, please don't ignore me.'

I sigh as I get my shoes on near the front door. 'I'm going because I missed it last time. And it helps. It really does. You…' I pause, about to say *You should come too*. But I stop myself. Because I don't want him to come. And if he does and doesn't like it – which is more than likely – he'll probably refuse to go to Denise's party later.

'Don't you think you're doing enough today without adding this to your stresses?' he says, almost gently.

I shake my head, 'It will do me good. Really, it will.' I walk through into the kitchen and take my keys off the end of the island countertop.

'Where is it?' Alec calls from the hallway.

'Whitechapel. In a community town hall or something.'

'Why the hell is it there?'

I open the front door. 'Because it's close to Stratford without it being actually *in* Stratford. The organisers thought that might be a bit...' I pause, swallow, then carry on, 'A bit much. For the parents.' I see a flicker of something in his eyes. His grief stirring. And then he nods.

'I'll be back in the afternoon,' I say, then close the door, leaving him standing there, sad and alone.

———

I arrive at the community centre early.

The previous meeting was held in a conference room in Canary Wharf, which felt strangely corporate; another was just a few streets away in Limehouse, and another near Barking, which I missed. Alec accompanied me to the first one, but walked out after ten minutes. We had been speaking to a couple whose two daughters had been killed in the bomb attack in the Westfield shopping centre. One had been thirteen. The other ten. They had been there with the mum of a family friend. She had survived the explosion, and so had her own daughter. But the two girls in her care never came home. The mother of the two girls who had died was almost unable to talk when we met them over coffee and biscuits before the group session properly began, but the dad seemed able to talk. He told us the facts almost as if he were narrating a documentary about another family, a cool sort of detachment neither Alec nor I had been able to experience since the atrocity. But then, of course, everyone copes in different ways. We all just try to carry on existing. It was this conversation that finished off Alec, though. I could see him trying to control his expression while the man in front of us was describing his terrible ordeal, then, when we were starting to gravitate towards the chairs in the centre of the room, he went all rigid and refused to move. 'Alec,' I said, trying to get him to shift, but he just stood there, staring into the distance. Then the tears started to fall. He shook his head and said, 'I can't do this,' then just walked out of the room. I went to go after him, but felt a touch on my arm. A short woman, about the same age as me, with a kind face and a sad, sweet smile, had laid her hand on me. 'Let him go,' she said. 'Honestly, it will be better if you don't try and force him. Come and sit down next to me.' And so I did. And that's how I met Fareeda.

Today, the meeting follows a similar pattern to the first, although this time the theme is about 'how our grief has progressed' since the events earlier in the year, and whether our feelings of anger have 'increased or tempered'. I don't speak; I'm not sure I'd have been up to it today, but Fareeda does. She stands as she talks, and something about her calm, soft voice and quiet confidence makes her presence almost mesmeric.

'I still have feelings of anger. Sometimes I feel angry at God for giving me a life with such loss. Such sorrow. As a few of you know, my boy died outside the cinema in Westfield. He was stabbed to death. And he was sixteen years old. But he was not the first child I've had die. My daughter died when she was five of bone cancer. So I thought I had experienced enough suffering in my life. But it seems that wasn't a limit. There isn't a quota of suffering that gets assigned to everyone. And for that, I feel angry. Fiercely, fiercely angry. So the biggest hurdle of all for me, right now, is managing that anger and attempting to turn it into a love and celebration of the time I had with my beautiful babies. Because it was the sweetest, warmest, most wonderful time. And I'm grateful I had it, even if it was brief. I am...' He voice quivers a little, and after a little choke, she finishes: 'I am grateful for the time I had with them.' Then she sits back down. I can't help it. Like many of the other people sitting, listening to these saddest of stories, I start to cry too.

After the meeting, some people linger to chat, but I find myself gravitating towards Fareeda. Although I haven't seen her for over a month, I feel we have a connection after she took me under her wing at the first meeting. 'It was very moving, what you said,' I tell her, and she nods.

'It was hard, but things are often hard before they get easy.'

Some of the things she says would sound rather limp and fortunate-cookie-like in some people's mouths, but she manages to sound both sad and profoundly wise at the same time. I nod. 'I was wondering if you fancied getting a coffee? Not here,' I say, worried she'll think I mean the watery rubbish that's been laid out for us on the tables at the side. 'Somewhere in the high street, maybe? We must be close to a Costa or something.'

She smiles at me, 'That would be really lovely. Thank you.'

The heat wraps itself around me as I walk out of the air-conditioned building. 'God, it's hot,' I remark as we walk towards what looks like a pedestrianised area near the start of a shopping centre I saw from my car on my way in. 'I can't believe it's practically summer already.'

'We'll be saying that about autumn in a few months,' she says.

'Very true.'

I feel embarrassed that we're talking about the weather, but I don't really want to tackle anything too emotive until we're settled somewhere. We soon find a Costa inside a Waterstones bookshop and a smiley young woman brings us two black coffees. The first ten minutes of our chat see us tiptoe around the main thing that connects us – the fact we've both lost our children – but eventually I can't hold off any longer. I have to come right out and say it.

'I don't think I'll ever be able to let go. Like they said in the meeting, about letting go of anger. Because I think to let

70

go… I think you need a sense of closure. And I don't have that.'

I see Fareeda examining me silently over the top of her mug. She takes a slow sip, then lowers it and speaks in her gentlest, quietest voice. 'Is that because you don't feel the young men who committed the terrible crime have received a fair punishment?'

I shake my head, frowning slightly, 'No, no. That's not what I mean at all. I mean, they died, didn't they? That hasn't really crossed my mind.'

More slow nodding and sipping, then she replies, 'Yes, but for many it hasn't been enough. It all went exactly as they planned. They knew what would happen if they brought guns and knives and explosives into such a public place. They knew what would happen if they used them on innocent people. They knew they would very likely be killed during their attack. So I think many feel like they escaped punishment. And the grieving can't achieve true closure because of it.'

It takes me a few moments to digest this. 'Do you feel that way?'

She gives a little shrug, 'I try not to dwell on it.'

This talk of retribution and punishment has stalled me a little, and I try to steer the conversation back onto the course I originally intended. 'I meant that, well, for me, closure seems impossible because the whole thing is still a mystery to me. A mystery as to why… why Jessica… was there in the first place.'

I see the realisation dawn on Fareeda's face. 'You mean, you didn't know she was in Stratford?'

I shake my head, 'No. We thought she was in Somerset visiting a friend. But I knew there was something wrong when she didn't respond to my calls and messages, on the day the attack happened. For a bit, I worried that she'd had an accident or something. But then the police arrived and...'

I have to stop myself before I get upset, and Fareeda lays a hand on my arm to show she understands.

'Have you checked her Facebook and Instagram and things like that?' she asks.

I reach in my bag for a tissue and nod, 'Yes, it's one of the first things we did. The police advised it too, but you could tell they weren't really that interested. I mean, they were really supportive with everything in the aftermath of the attack, but they didn't really see Jessica's presence there as anything to worry about. Probably just thought she was a typical teenager, lying to her parents, going a bit rogue. But this wasn't like Jessica. She wasn't deceptive. She didn't ever wilfully try to mislead us or anything.'

Fareeda looks concerned, 'If it was so out of character, surely the police would understand your worries?'

'They did, I think,' I say, dabbing at my nose, 'But I suspect they saw it as... well... too late to do anything about it. After all... she'd already been murdered. What could be more sinister than that?'

A dark shadow seems to pass over Fareeda's eyes. 'Some things are,' she says quietly. After a second or two, she jerks a little and waves her hand, 'Ignore me, please. That wasn't a helpful thing to say. I think it's just that there is so much cruelty in the world... it's hard to know what the very worst thing is.'

I know what she means, but it isn't a subject I especially want to get into. 'I just mean, I don't think they saw my worries as that credible or important just after the attack. And… I think I may have come on too strong. I was told to stop bothering one of the detectives.'

Fareeda doesn't say anything, but raises an eyebrow, waiting for me to continue.

'The young police officer who came to tell us what had happened – he was very nice to us. So I sort of… clung onto him a bit. I found out where he lived. And I started going there, trying to speak to him. Asking him to let me see CCTV and stuff like that. It all got… a bit awkward.'

Again, Fareeda stays silent, letting me take the time to choose my words.

'I ran into him, in a supermarket near where he lived. It's true that I had driven into East London to try to talk to him, but he was out and the house was dark, so I decided to drive home. On the way, I decided to get some food in the big Sainsbury's nearby. Well, just out of sheer coincidence, he was in there – shopping with his family. I think they thought I'd followed them, and I'd clearly been a topic of conversation in their household, because I heard the guy with him say 'Is this her?' when I tried to speak to them and got upset. Then I made the mistake of trying to push him away, and I must have underestimated my strength, as I knocked him down. It all got a bit out of control after that. Alec had to come and get me and I was given some "friendly advice" by the police. I think they just see me as this grief-addled mother who has taken leave of her senses.'

A small, understanding smile lingers of Fareeda's lips.

'We all have our little episodes – moments where the world seems to be working against us. Rubbing salt in our wounds. I wish I had an easy piece of wisdom to pass on, but I really don't. I know it doesn't seem helpful to say to someone, "Just keep going", but when it all comes down to it, I think that's the only true piece of advice anyone can offer. Just keep going.'

I nod slowly, dabbing at my eyes with the back of my hand.

'I know... I know that's all I can do. I just wish Alec was easier to talk to about all of this. He's either desperate to talk but doesn't like what I have to say, or he's just spiteful and surly and impossible to get any sense out of. I did... I have...' I take a breath, trying to stop myself descending into full, proper tears, 'I have been able to talk to Alec's brother, Rob, a little, especially after it all happened. We've always got on- he's more laid-back than Alec. And it helped, being able to talk to someone who was grieving but not in the same way as Alec and me. But lately he's become... more distant. I wonder if I'm just... I don't know... boring him now.'

Fareeda shook her head. 'You shouldn't think like that. It can be hard for people to know what to say to those who have gone through what we have. Do you have your parents still?'

I shake my head, 'No... that's a whole other saga.' I try to laugh a little, as if it's funny how my family life is just one big drama, but it comes out like a strange, strangled cough. 'My mother's alive – she lives in Australia, where I grew up. We don't really speak. And my dad's... no longer with us.' I feel a familiar prickle of something down my spine, a weird sensation that often occurs if I get too close to the subject of my father. 'The problem is…' I pause and swallow, trying to gather together my thoughts. 'The problem is less about not having people to talk to, and more about just not really moving forward… not moving on. And I can't really start to move on until I know the truth. So much of the whole situation feels wrong. I know something like this could never feel… right. That's not what I mean. It's just that… Jessica lied. She lied *to me*. About something so important – saying she was going to stay with a friend when she was intending to go somewhere else.'

Fareeda shakes her head, 'Teenagers – they don't think of it as lying. They live in their own little worlds.'

I know what she means, but that's not it. This is something else. It must be.

'Jessica… in her teen years… she started to become different. More – I don't know how to describe it really – more reactionary. She'd get upset about little things. I thought it was just changes – natural teenager changes, the strains of puberty. That sort of thing. But it wasn't that. It was like she was trying to distance herself from us. She even started to make comments towards me – the kind of things her father's said. That I'm too wrapped up in my work. Care more about fictional worlds than I do the one in front of me.'

I can feel myself falling into the dark heart of the past, its strange magnetic pull dragging me in, and I can't stop it. 'When I was a teenager, I ran away from home. My home life was… difficult. To put it mildly. My mother wasn't like other mothers, and her relationship with my father was... odd. Sinister, some may say.'

Fareeda raises an eyebrow, but doesn't interrupt me. 'I know most people probably look back and see things in their parents that they didn't see before. But I've tried to spend my life not looking back. Especially at why I left. It's too much. And I think Jessica knew that. I never properly told her about the whole ordeal, but she picked up on things Alec said to me. Fragments of conversations. And one day, out of the blue, when I was pestering her about homework or something, she said, *Maybe one day I'll run away from home, like you did – and see how you like it.*'

I have to stop for a bit. The tears are flowing too freely now.

'She probably didn't mean it,' Fareeda says softly.

'I know, I know. But it felt... I don't know... personal. Like she was attacking me, pouring salt on my wounds. She wasn't to know how painful those memories were, but I could tell she meant it to unsettle me. To use it as a weapon of some kind. And then... before she died, there was a big row with her dad. I only caught the tail end of it, but... she said some things. Things that have stayed with me... and I can't get them out of my mind. They're always there. Never letting me go.'

Fareeda focuses her kind, deep eyes on me. 'What did she say?'

My tears are properly running now. I take another sip of the now lukewarm liquid, then start to tell her.

Chapter Eight

THE MOTHER

February. One day to go.

I was just getting out of the shower when I heard the shouts. A strong, unbridled shriek that ripped through the house. It was Jessica. It must be. I stepped into the bedroom, the carpet soft and warm under my bare feet, and ditched my towel in favour of a dressing gown.

'Just fuck off!'

This shocked me. Although Jessica wasn't exactly a stranger to four-letter expletives, it was unheard of for her to hurl one at either me or her father. For a second, I wondered if she was having boyfriend trouble – maybe she was on the phone, dumping someone, telling some two-timing Year 11 boy to clear off. But then I heard a distinctly male-sounding 'What?!', making it clear she was arguing with her father.

I took the stairs quickly, my wet hair sending channels of water coursing down my neck and into the sides of the dressing gown. As I got near the lounge, I made out more words in what seemed to be a diatribe from Jessica.

'You think you're so cool? So fucking important? I've seen the way you act around the mums at school. And so have my friends. And I try to be all fine with it and make myself think it's cool to have a dad that both my friends' mums and my actual friends want to fuck, but I never thought you'd actually... actually...'

I stopped dead still in the middle of the lounge, but my presence had been noticed. Alec was facing my direction and I saw his eyes widen. Jessica noticed and turned around. I must have looked a bit strange standing there, my dressing gown wrapped around me, but I couldn't move. I could barely utter a word.

'What?' Jessica yelled at me. 'Are you here to tell me to calm down? That it's all in my head?'

I managed to raise a hand, trying to get her to stop. 'Darling, I'm not sure what you've heard or what... what this is about, but I think you should—'

'Should what?' she cut me off. 'Should just shrug and move on? Get on with my schoolwork and stop worrying what my parents are up to?'

I saw her cheeks were becoming flushed, her lashes glistening with tears as she looked at me, and I struggled to keep eye contact with her. 'I think you should stop shouting.'

She looked like she was going to do the opposite – start properly shrieking at me like she had been at her father mere seconds ago, but she took me by surprise. She raised both hands to her face and rubbed her eyes, as if she were exhausted and just wanted to go to bed. 'God… I'm just so tired of…'

She didn't finish the sentence, just dropped her arms and went to push past me. I took her arm and held on, trying to stop her, but she shook me off. She snapped at me to let her go, but I had to know: 'What do you mean? Tired of what?'

'Everyone,' she said and then, almost imperceptibly as she left the room, 'and their secrets.' Her words jolted me. I followed her, calling up the stairs, asking her what she meant. What secrets? But she didn't reply. Just slammed her door.

The next day, she left for Somerset. She was civil in the morning, offering me some coffee from the machine as I came into the kitchen, but she clearly had something on her mind. I helped her with her bag, kissed her goodbye as I dropped her at the station, telling her to text me once she was there. She rolled her eyes as she normally did and gave me a smile. But it wasn't one of her bright, cheery smiles that told me she was off to conquer the world. It was slightly distant. Slightly sad. A complicated shadow of a smile from someone wise beyond her years. I almost asked her again then, asked her about what she meant by 'secrets'. How much she knew about what her father was up to. How she found out. What triggered last night's blow-up. But I didn't. I just hugged her and waved her on her way. Then she was gone through the station doors, her bag on her arm, phone in her hand. And I never saw her again.

Chapter Nine

THE MOTHER

May. Three months after the attack.

I drive home in a daze, my thoughts still reverberating around Jessica's last day at home. The things she said. The look on Alec's face as she shouted at him. I stop at a McDonalds on my way through Kent and sit in the corner with a box of chicken nuggets. A family sit nearby at one of the table booths, laughing and chatting. The children look about eleven or twelve. One girl and one boy. The mum is showing the girl something on her phone, to which the girl responds, 'That's an awful photo!' The boy laughs at it, which seems to enrage the girl at first, but she ends up laughing too.

Maybe things would have been easier if Alec and I had managed to have another child. We haven't mentioned it, since the disaster happened, but it's there between us – an awareness of our loss, and the lack of focus that makes us feel as if we're now drifting through time rather than actually doing anything to aid our grief.

I find myself fantasising about how different life could have been all the way home. If we'd had a younger sibling for Jessica. Another little girl, perhaps, or a boy. Would things be better or worse with another child in the house? Or is that selfish of me to wish such a thing, knowing full well the brutal murder of their sister would quite possibly scar them in a deep, visceral way for the rest of their life?

Alec's on the sofa when I walk in, stretched out in his skinny jeans and a Nike T-shirt, a can of Coke Zero lying empty near his feet. *It's probably good I don't have another teenager – I have one right here,* I think to myself.

'I fell asleep,' he says, by way of a greeting.

'So I see.' I don't hang around for a chat, but instead grab some water with ice and leave to go upstairs. 'We're still going to the party,' I call back to him.

A couple of hours later, we're in the car, on our way to Denise's. Alec's not pleased about it. He's got a few choice phrases he's been trotting out throughout our time getting changed, locking the house, getting into the car. 'Too soon' is his favourite. And 'madness' has also been said at least twice. If he doesn't speak, he just shakes his head, as if marvelling privately to himself at someone's – my – great folly.

As the car glides, almost silently, along the country lanes and back into the edges of suburbia, I become gradually aware of a mounting sense of panic inside me. Maybe he's right. He's pissing me off, but maybe there's some truth in what he's saying. Maybe it is too early. I spoke to Laini about my plan to come to the party in my recent session and she was fairly positive about the idea. 'If you feel able to try it, do it. Listen to your mind, Caroline. You don't need to go for long. Try it and see how you feel.'

So here I am, trying it. Seeing how I feel. Denise answers the door with a smile that very quickly disappears into a look of shock. If I were in a less anxious mood I'd find it comical. She clearly didn't expect me to come. I sent her an email to say we were and she responded, claiming she and Craig were so glad we'd be there, but it's obvious now she never really thought Alec and I would follow through and actually come. But here we are, clutching a bottle of wine and a box of chocolates, waiting to enter her home.

She recovers quickly. 'Caroline, Alec! How lovely it is to see you.' Quick kisses and hugs. I can almost feel her brain whirring. She doesn't know whether to repeat how sorry she is. It was the first thing she said to me the last time I met her. I tried to go for a coffee with her and another friend a few weeks after Jessica's death. It was a mistake. I cried in the loos for most of it, then left without properly saying goodbye. And because of that abrupt ending, she's not quite sure if she's expressed enough sorrow and understanding. She settles for a squeeze of my arm and proceeds to lead us into the house.

Denise's home is almost offensively gorgeous. She's never been poor, but ten years ago she divorced her second husband and ended up £2 million richer. Throw into that a surprisingly well-paid column for the *Daily Mail*, an agony-aunt position in a woman's magazine, and the jolt of a new, younger, and extremely attractive husband, and the results are plain to see. She and her home seem to glow in unison.

'It looks like a luxurious orphanage,' Alec murmurs to me. 'You know, like the one you'd get in *The BFG* or *Annie*, but done up for a millionaire.'

I smile in spite of myself and put my finger to my lips, hoping Denise hasn't heard. She's touchy about the subject of children, ever since her two kids decided it was more fun living at their father's townhouse house in Islington rather than out in the suburbs of Kent. Howie, her son, comes back most weekends to play rugby, but I think Annabelle, still only about twelve, has barely visited. And Denise is quietly cut-up about it.

After the meet and greet, it's obvious she's a bit unsure what to do with us, so we come to rest by a table of drinks and food. She has professional caterers in, as I presumed she would, and she thanks us for the wine and chocolate – 'So kind of you, you shouldn't have' – and then there's a terrible awkward silence. Alec shows no signs of coming to my, nor Denise's, rescue and eventually I say, pathetically, 'You've been blessed with good weather.' My weird phrasing makes me sound like someone out of *The Handmaid's Tale*. Automatically the three of us glance out to the far end of the living room, where a large lawn filled with huddles of people chatting and drinking can be seen. The evening light casts a warm golden glow over the whole thing and under any other circumstances my spirits would have been high. I love summer evenings. Especially early summer, when the heat is still new and people encourage it rather than moan about it, cherishing each ray, each baking-hot day as if it might be the last.

'Yes, it's such a nice evening,' she replies, then turns back. The awkward smile is there again. 'Kirsten is in the kitchen, if you want to speak to her,' she says.

I know she means well, but I can't help feeling a little offended. Is she really so desperate to group together all the 'difficult' guests so early on in the evening? Put them in a corner so they don't frighten the others away?

'So awful, isn't it, what happened with her husband,' Denise says in a hushed tone, then adds quickly, 'Of course, not as awful as… I'm sorry, I just meant…'

'I know what you meant, don't worry,' I nod and attempt a smile. I can feel Alec draw in a pointed breath and transfer his weight onto another leg. He's right. This is painful.

'I mean, nobody had a clue. To be honest, looking back, it doesn't surprise me he was having an affair. Never trusted him, not really. He had shifty eyes, and I once witnessed him listening to a Hear'Say song in his car as he was parking outside Waitrose. Very odd behaviour.'

She finishes saying all this, then slips a little stick laden with cheese and olives into her mouth. I'm aware Alec has some strong opinions on the matter of Kirsten's cheating violent husband, so I try to steer the conversation away and remark how lovely all the food looks, but Denise presses on. She's clearly been a bit starved of gossip while I've been out of action. 'I watched a news report about it only the other night. Well, it was actually about how that awful show's viewing figures have tripled since one of their cast members – can you call them cast, if they're not acting? – anyway, since one of their number was caught shagging a guy in a club and then tried to kill her boyfriend. I know she's dropped out, but apparently their ratings are through the roof!'

I shake my head, 'I don't watch much TV. At least, not on the normal channels. Just Netflix, really.'

'Oh really?' Denise raises her eyebrows and looks both impressed and disconcerted, as if I've just revealed I can speak Japanese. 'Well, I suppose that's the way things are going, isn't it? All on-demand these days. Apart from things like sport and the news.'

'I don't watch the news,' I say, a little too quickly.

She looks instantly appalled. 'Oh gosh, of course not. What a stupid thing to say.'

'Don't worry,' I say for the second time. 'Sorry, Denise, can I use your loo?'

The relief is immediately evident. 'Of course you can, come this way.' She marches off and I turn to Alec and pull a face. 'Just get a drink or something. We won't be staying long.'

I follow Denise's departing figure, saying 'Excuse me' to the guests as I slide past, trying not to catch anyone's eye in case I meet someone who recognises me. 'Here we go,' she says when I've caught up. I thank her and duck into the predictably beautiful bathroom. I don't actually need the toilet, but I lock the door and settle down on the seat regardless, and pull out my phone. A familiar sense of unease is tugging at me inside. *I shouldn't have come. I shouldn't have come. Alec was right. How could this have been anything other than utterly awful?* I tap the home button of the iPhone to wake the screen up and then almost drop it in shock when my daughter's face comes into view. She's smiling at me. The beach in Florida. Me and Alec next to her, our faces slightly obscured by the clock dial at the top. It takes me a few seconds to work out what's happened, the numbers distorted through the slightly cracked screen. This is Jessica's phone. I must have picked it up instead of mine from the bedside table. The models are identical – both iPhone 8s – the large, plus-size version with a glossy back. It's fully charged and even has a 4G signal. Neither Alec nor I have cancelled her phone contract. It's tied up with ours as one big O2 package and all comes out of our joint account each month.

I go to the lock screen and tap in her birthday as a password, feeling a wave of triumph when it works first go. Faced with the array of apps, I'm now at a loss what to do. Eventually I tap on her photo album and a colourful collection of stills and videos unfurls. I scroll through a few, my heart beating hard each time her face appears. Then something hits me. The WhatsApp icon. Its green speechmark shape, glowing in front of me. I trawl the app, looking for clues from her friends as to why she might have been in Stratford on the day of the attack. And there's the iMessenger app – the way Jessica and I usually communicated. But there's one I haven't thought of. Hurriedly, I swipe through the app screens until I get to the penultimate page. And there it is. The Facebook Messenger icon. I tap it immediately and her chats come up – a menu of faces. A lot of them are unread, their words still in bold next to their faces:

> I know you can't read this now, Jessica, but I just
> wanted to message and say how much you meant
> to me

A girl named Suzanne Randall had written. I never heard Jessica mention her. The same could be said for the endless people who've written publicly on her Facebook wall. I had to stop looking at it in the days after her death. It made me so angry to see people I was sure didn't even know my daughter – who probably just sat in the same classroom with her or brushed past her in the corridor – write long essays explaining how devastated they were she was no longer part of their lives. Devastated? They didn't even know the meaning of the word. They didn't have a clue.

I'm about to close the app and put the phone away when one of the messages catches my eye.

> I'll always love you. I'll never forgive myself. I'm sorry.

It's from a boy. His face isn't very clear in his profile picture, but I can tell he's quite good looking. Olive-tanned skin, short hair. Michael Kelley is his name. I click on the message so I can see the full conversation, reading it in reverse order:

I'll always love you. Always.

Jessica, please. This is honestly killing me.

Tell me you're not hurt.

Please. I get that you're probably mad. I'm really sorry. I can explain why I didn't meet you. Please can you just tell me you got home safe. Please?

They're dated the day of the Stratford terrorist attacks. The day she died. And then I get to the sent messages from her. Loads of them, with no reply from him between them.

I can't believe you'd just leave me here and not tell me. I lied to my parents about coming here. Couldn't you just tell me that you're running late? Where are you?

OK… It's nearly an hour since we were supposed to meet… Have I got the right place? At the chairs near the sandwich shop? Getting a bit worried now.

Is everything OK? Have you been held up?

Hi, I've been here for twenty mins now and haven't heard from you. I presume you're stuck on a train or something.

I'm here – have you arrived or you still travelling?

Just getting into Stratford now. Can't wait to see you.
We've been talking about this for so long. SO excited
we're finally doing it.

I think I'm going to be sick. I am going to be sick. I slide
off the toilet seat and spin round just in time to throw up
into the bowl. Someone knocks on the door. 'Caroline? Are
you OK?' It's Alec. He's probably pissed off I've left him for
so long. I try to answer but another load of nausea hits me.
Then the tears start. They're running down my face and my
breathing becomes tight.

That boy stood her up. She didn't go to Somerset. She
went to Stratford to meet a boy. And he abandoned her. He
was the reason she was there. It's his fault.

I have to tell someone. I have to tell the world. I have to
find him. Make him see what he's done. I have to tell Alec. I
scrabble to the door and unlock it and he bursts in. 'Christ,
Caroline, what's wrong?' He shuts it quickly behind him
when he sees the state I'm in.

'He left her!' I shriek, not caring about the noise. I don't
give a fuck about Denise or her party guests. I just want to
scream, to hurt, to break something. I'm scrabbling around
on the floor, my face a mixture of tears and vomit. 'He
arranged to meet her there and he fucking left her. He's the
reason she's dead!'

'What? Who?' Alec says, trying to pull me to my feet.

'A boy,' I say emphatically, as if this is enough. 'She went
there on a date to meet a boy. She was only there because he
said he would meet her there, and he stood her up.' I crouch
back down on the floor, my hand feeling along the cold tiles

for the phone. I grasp it tightly, smearing the screen with a fleck of vomit, but I don't care. I unlock it and click on the profile picture of Michael Kelley so his tanned, grinning, oh-so-fucking-happy face fills the screen. 'Him!' I spit. 'This is the boy who killed our daughter.'

Chapter Ten

THE MOTHER

May. Three months after the attack.

Alec doesn't talk much on the way home. He just lets me talk. And God, do I talk. I'd left the house, helped out by Alec and Denise, borderline screaming. Screaming all manner of words I wouldn't normally scream, especially not at a tasteful dinner party, but I couldn't stop myself. No amount of words, no amount of promises of violence and revenge would match the anger that soared inside me when I read those messages on Jessica's phone.

'He is a fucking *murderer*,' I spit at Alec as he drives through the winding suburban streets towards the motorway. 'I want him dead, do you hear me? I want him to know exactly what he did, exactly what he's done, exactly how much he's hurt me.'

'Hurt *us*,' he says quietly. I ignore him.

Back at home, Alec makes me a mug of hot chocolate as I sit and sob on the sofa. It's the first properly kind and generous thing he's done for me in months and I'm not really sure how to cope with it when it arrives. 'Do you want to talk about it?' He takes a seat next to me as he says it; another change. Usually he's standing over me or pacing somewhere out of reach.

'Yes. No. I don't know. I want to scream.'

He takes a slight breath in, as if he's about to say something, then stops. Eventually he says, 'I can understand your anger, Caroline. I mean, believe me, I'm angry too. But I don't think this is really going to help anything. I don't think… well, I don't think it matters.'

I almost spit out the tentative sip of cocoa I've taken. 'Doesn't matter?' I can't believe he's just said it, so simply, as if it's obvious. 'Of course it matters. This is… this is a breakthrough.'

'In what sense?' he says calmly. 'In what way is this a breakthrough? It's not as if Jessica's death was part of a big mystery…'

'It *was* a big mystery, one that I have now solved!'

He carries on, speaking over my shouts: 'She wasn't the victim of an elusive serial killer the police have been hunting down for months. We know who killed her. Jessica was killed by a member of ISIS. A twenty-year-old lad from Birmingham, who was part of a group of Islamist extremists. She wasn't killed because a boy decided to blow off a date. That boy didn't open fire on all those people. That boy didn't purchase an illegal weapon to slaughter innocent people or detonate a bomb in a shopping centre. *They* did that. The terrorists.'

I gape at him. Surely Alec, a man who has for months been clawing around, looking for someone to blame, would be cheering at the thought of finding an actual candidate. Not the masked sociopaths who were killed at the scene. Someone who is actually alive, living a presumably normal life free from punishment. 'Maybe you don't want the boy to be blamed because it takes the attention away from blaming Muslims.'

I see his eyes flare at this. 'I'm not getting into all that,' he says quietly. There's a tight edge to his voice now. 'I'm just saying that if we're going to blame everyone who merely caused someone to be in the place of an atrocity, where does it end? What about that nine-year-old victim? Melanie Robbins or Robberts or something – is it her mother's fault for taking her to the Westfield shopping centre, where she worked, because she couldn't afford to take time off when the kid had a cold? She'll blame herself for the rest of her life, but is she really actually to blame? Or that young couple from America on their honeymoon who had gone to see the Olympic Park. They were supposed to be travelling back the day before, apparently, but due to a confusion with their booking at the airline, they ended up having to stay an extra day. Would it be the fault of a member of staff at British Airways that they died? If he or she hadn't made a mix-up with their flights, they would probably be alive right now. But of course it isn't the fault of the airline, or the fault of Melanie's mum, or the fault of this random boy our daughter was off to meet. It was the deliberate action of a group of sociopaths.'

I wait for him to finish his little monologue then muster the strength to fight back. 'And ours. It isn't just the boy I'm blaming. It's our fault too. We always told her she could tell us everything, and said how important it was to know where she was if she was dating. And she kept secrets. That's what she said to me, the day before… she said… she said she was tired of keeping so many secrets, and I can't stop that spinning and spinning around in my head. She lied to us. She lied about where she would be. Why couldn't she tell us that she was going to meet a boy?'

Alec holds his hands up, shaking his head. 'She's a teenager… *was* a teenager. They do things like that. I'm sure I did.'

'That's what Fareeda said,' I mutter, partly to myself. I feel myself starting to cry again and lie back onto the cushions of the sofa, wishing I could just sink into them.

'I think she's probably right,' he says softly.

I let a few beats of silence pass, then say slowly, 'You're trying to exonerate yourself. You feel guilty, too. And so do I. But the main bulk of guilt – it's with *him*. It rests with *him*.'

He sighs again, then moves away from the sofa, giving up. 'Drink your hot chocolate,' he says, as if he's the responsible adult in the room and I'm a moping, weeping child. Regardless, I do as he says for half an hour, watching the late-evening sun turn to darkness as the clock ticks its way towards 9pm. Eventually, after I've drained the last thick drops of chocolate from the bottom of the mug, I stand

and walk slowly towards my office. I've got pins and needles from how I've been lying on the sofa and my back clicks as I straighten up. The ordered calm of my workspace is comforting to me, reminding me of my day-to-day routine before everything ended. Before I became 'grieving mother' rather than 'successful screenwriter'. I would come in here as early as 6am some days and answer emails from my agent or the producers I was working with, getting the admin out of the way first, before doing a bit of light social media. I'd then see off Jessica as she left for school, reminding her to take her packed lunch with her and checking what extracurricular activities she had that night – piano, violin, Latin club, netball, book group, swimming. Then I'd return to my office to start the real work, the writing, before stopping for lunch at around 1.30. I'd either pop into town to lunch with friends or find something in the fridge and take it into the garden, or watch a bit of TV if the weather was bad. The afternoons I usually reserved for going over what I'd written and making phone calls and other admin.

I've only been back in my office a couple of times since the disaster, and that's only been to get blank envelopes or stamps. I haven't worked. The deadline for my next project passed weeks ago. I haven't tweeted or bothered to respond to emails, other than essential ones from my agent, Jane, and those I did from my phone. Now, opening my laptop for the first time in months, it feels strange to see my desktop there as normal – all my apps and minimised windows glinting at me as if nothing has happened and barely a second has gone by since I closed it. Right now, though, I'm not here for working. I navigate to Facebook and type 'Michael Kelley' into the search box. It takes a little while to find him, but since he's a mutual friend of Jessica's it isn't too hard. His handsome face stares back at me, almost tauntingly, as I save the image to the computer and then follow the options to print. The A4 sheet comes out of the machine to my right a few seconds later, his face filling it, slightly pixellated, the resolution of the Facebook profile picture not coping well with the enlargement. I then scroll down his page, looking at the type of things he likes. Nothing very remarkable. A couple of superhero films, a few bands I've never heard of. He doesn't post much, either. Nothing at all this year, in fact. I hoped to see a stop in all activity from February onwards, after the terror attack, but he didn't seem to use Facebook much even before that point. The most recent post is from a few summers ago – of him and a girl on a beach, him playfully licking her cheek and her caught mid-shriek. It didn't look like an exotic location – too British – and the geotag proved me right. The photo had been taken in Southend, Essex. That explained the lack of sea and expanse of mud.

After a few more minutes of fruitless stalking I close the laptop and journey to the kitchen with my print-out. There, on the door of the fridge, above the ice button so I know Alec will definitely see it, I stick the photo of Michael Kelley, keeping it in place with two magnets at either end.

'Fuck you,' I say, staring at the photo, surprising myself slightly by the strong language. But it feels right. Fuck him.

Chapter Eleven

THE MOTHER

May. Three months after the attack.

I immediately think of the boy the moment I wake up. I stare at his face as I silently crunch through a bowl of cereal, sitting at the breakfast bar in the kitchen. I then spend the rest of the morning cleaning the kitchen to clinical levels of cleanliness, even though our cleaner Kate only came three days ago. And after every swipe of the surface wipes, every tug on the hoover handle, every close of the dishwasher, I look up at his smiling face, and hate him that little bit more each time.

The afternoon changes everything. I pick up my phone to order some groceries and my hand accidently nudges the screen over to the Apple News stream.

I almost scream. I can feel the panic rising. The world turning, knocking me into the cool glass of the oven doors.

'Alec!' I call out and he runs into the kitchen.

'I've just heard,' he says, breathlessly. 'Piccadilly Circus. It's on the TV.'

'I don't think I can watch.' I glance through into the lounge, taking in the TV that's playing, muted, a special BBC News report.

'I'm going to. Let's sit on the sofa. We'll watch together.'

I shake my head. 'I can't,' I say, stepping away from him and running up the stairs.

Alec follows me. For almost a minute, we sit on the bed in silence. Then I move to the left side of the bed, leaving a spare side for him to get on properly. He takes up the invitation, pulling his shoes off and lying down. Then I reach for the television control. It's strange, us lying on a bed fully clothed in the middle of the day, watching a terrorist attack unfold in front of our eyes. My hand is trembling and Alec takes it. It surprises me. Comforts me, slightly.

The BBC reporter is in full flow. 'The bus to Hackney Wick was passing through the busy tourist hot-spot of Piccadilly Circus when the bomb detonated. As you can see from the images on the screen right now, the top level of the bus was blown off almost completely, in images chillingly reminiscent of those of the 7/7 attacks in 2005.'

I watch the screen, showing footage captured from what must be a helicopter, and see the lumpy long bundles with material over them on the floor. I try to think of them as bodies – as people, someone's daughter, son, girlfriend, boyfriend, wife, husband, sister, brother, mother, father – but my mind protests and they go back to being bundles. I didn't think news reports showed such things. I thought they'd wait for them to be cleared away before their cameras swooped in from helicopters to capture the scene. But apparently not. It's almost like war photography. Only the warzone is now our doorstep, not some faraway place we can all conveniently forget about and label as somewhere 'foreign' and nothing to do with us.

Alec is crying silently; I can only tell by the way he keeps raising his hand to his eyes. The camera now shows part of the Tesco Metro on Piccadilly Circus, at the top where Lower Regent Street turns into Jermyn Street. Its entrance has been partially destroyed and there's someone's shopping, left discarded on the pavement outside, with what looks like milk spilling from the plastic carrier bag. I wonder where that milk was destined for. A mug of tea in a nearby office or shop staffroom. Or maybe for the fridge back in someone's house, to be poured chilled onto their cereals tomorrow morning. Now, it's trickling down Lower Regent Street, never to see a mug or a bowl.

We sit and watch in silence for another half an hour, neither of us able to say anything. Alec speaks first.

'I've taken that photograph down. The one of the boy you put up in the kitchen. It's not healthy.'

I have trouble digesting what he's saying at first. The news crew are currently in the middle of an interview with a young American woman who works at the nearby Waterstones store, describing the loud bang they heard and the way the windows shook when the bomb went off. I turn to Alec and see him looking at me, watching to see if I react to what he's just said.

'You haven't thrown it away, have you?'

He nods.

I lean forwards so I'm no longer lying next to him. 'I wanted that there. I put it there for a reason.'

He closes his eyes, as if in pain or discomfort, and wipes a tear from his face. 'Caroline. Please. What good will it do? Having us staring at his face every morning over breakfast from now on. I can't do it.' He's talking quietly and slowly, as if keen to promote a sense of calm. Calm is the opposite to what I feel and my voice gets high and loud.

'Well I'm sorry you "can't do it" but I'm afraid it isn't up to you. That boy is integral to our lives now, don't you see? He's the reason—'

'The reason Jessica's dead, I know,' he says. He sounds almost bored now and this infuriates me further. 'Don't you feel this is all a bit predictable?'

I gape at him, confused. 'What are you talking about?'

Alec shrugs a little, turning his eyes back on the TV. 'Just you acting like it's all the fault of a man. As if all men are evil or something.'

I let this sink in, feeling my blood start to burn underneath my skin. 'Get out.' All memory of the comforting feel of his hand as he slipped it into mine has vanished. I'm enraged. 'I mean it. Leave me alone.'

He swings his legs off the bed. 'Well, if you're going to be like that...'

'Like what? Upset? Don't you think I've got a right to be upset? With you making cruel jibes at me – on a day like this!'

He turns to face me, 'I admit maybe I made a few mistakes. And I regret that Jessica found out... what she did… But I think a lot of this is to do with your own prejudices. Your own complex about your dad, and your mum's deranged response to him, and the fact you've never been able—'

My eyes widen, flooding with tears. 'Been able to WHAT?'

He sighs, 'Able to truly satisfy me. The whole idea of us… you and me as a couple… not being enough for me. For either of us. That's it, isn't it? We're just not enough for each other.'

I throw the remote control at him. It misses – hitting the door of the en suite. He doesn't say anything, just bends down to pick up his shoes from the floor and pads out onto the landing and into the bathroom. I hear him turn the taps on, which makes me suspect he's gone there to cry without being heard. Not for the first time, I've found myself wishing I could pity him more. Understand him more. If I'm honest with myself, I've come to terms with the fact we've never really been on the same page about things, even at the start. Sure, when we first met there was a spark of something. I was accompanying a friend to a corporate awards ceremony at a posh hotel in London and he was seated at the same table as us. We certainly fancied each other. But maybe that was it? As the years went on, I became scared of facing up to the fact that I just moved in and then married him because it was 'the thing to do'. Perhaps my troubled teenage years and my complicated relationship with my parents had something to do with it. A need to make my life tidy and tick off the important milestones. And if that's the case, some of the blame has to fall on me for letting myself get this far – to the point where we had a child, then lost that child, and the two of us are now so irrevocably damaged, nothing we can do can solve it.

Thinking about our marriage has made me feel even more het-up and unsettled. I slam the door so he knows I'm not in the mood for reconciliation when he comes back out of the bathroom, and then I settle back down onto the bed to cry some more by myself.

———

I think I always knew I'd gravitate back to Jessica's phone and the messages she sent him. Love messages to a boy I never knew existed. I've kept it on charge by my bed since I found it, Alec never being observant enough to notice on the rare occasions he comes into my room now. As the sun sets on another beautiful summer's day, I sit huddled under a duvet, the air-conditioning turned up to max so I don't overheat, scrolling through Jessica's messages to him. Michael Kelley. Some of them make me cry again, particularly the ones where she mentions me:

I went out shopping with Mum to get a new sports bra. Netball tournament soon. Yay for nerves and pre-match nausea!

And:

Mum and Dad are currently reading, both of them

buried in big hardbacks. Don't get me wrong, I fucking
LOVE books but sometimes I feel like I live in a library.

There are also some exchanges that one can only
describe really as 'sexting' although mercifully without any
photographic contributions from Jessica. There is one from
him though, although in the grand scheme of things it's
fairly tame – neither his face nor any explicit nudity is
shown, just a photo of his underwear-clad crotch area. It's
her response (*Hmm maybe show me what's underneath?*) that
bothers me more than the picture itself. Thankfully he
didn't acquiesce to her request. What he replied does
interest me though:

Come and meet me now. Just get a train down. It
wouldn't take long. We can go to the beach for ice
cream. Then maybe I could show you more in person?

I swipe at the screen to show more of their exchange:

JESSICA: Hmm. Tempting, Mr Kelley. Tempting.

MICHAEL: 7 Calatava Road, Southend, Essex. Want
the postcode for your satnav if you're driving? ;)

JESSICA: I don't have a satnav. I don't know if you
know this, but it's illegal for 16-year-olds to drive.

MICHAEL: Excuses, excuses.

I stare at the address and feel a swell of excitement within me. I now know where he lives. Exactly where he lives, right down to the house number.

I spend most of the night imagining scenarios where I deface his house with red paint or smash up his parents' car or maybe just send him anonymous letters simply saying MURDERER, with the characters cut out from newspaper and magazine clippings. All of this sounds highly satisfying to me, but a niggling voice at the back of my head knows it wouldn't be enough. Because, in the depths of the night, I think I realise something. All my life, I've tried to sweep things under the carpet. Pretend they haven't happened. The horrible situation I left behind me in Australia. The truth about my father's death. And more recently, the behaviour of my husband. Things I've done. Secrets, lies, regret – all of it. I've had a cerebral clear-desk policy. Never allow it to stay on the surface, always bury it underneath the fabric of everyday life. It hasn't worked. It's never really worked. So this is my chance. My chance to confront a problem, follow the mystery through to the end and *do something* about it. And that something has to involve finding that boy. He needs to know, without a shadow of a doubt, what he has done. To recognise it. To face up to it. And, in some way, to pay for it.

By the time the clock shows 6am, I know what I have to do.

Chapter Twelve

THE MOTHER

May. Three months after the attack.

I leave the house at 6am. I don't say anything to Alec as I pass what used to be a guest bedroom but has now become his general living area. I leave him sleeping, taking care not to make a noise. I don't take anything with me other than my handbag, purse, the two iPhones – mine and Jessica's – and some books – two light romances and an Agatha Christie mystery. *Never go anywhere without a book,* an old English teacher used to say to me. I've stuck rigidly to this rule all my life, through good times and bad. If I haven't got one in my bag, there's usually one in the car, hidden in the dashboard to avoid light-damage to its cover.

Once seated behind the wheel of the Range Rover, I enter the postcode into the built-in satnav and watch it plot a course from Kent to Southend. It estimates about an hour and ten minutes, so long as I don't run into heavy traffic.

As it happens, there is a hold-up – a rather nasty crash

on the A13 makes the final leg of the journey crawl by, quite literally. I come to a complete standstill at one point, with no sign of any movement up ahead. Sighing with frustration, I reach for my copy of *A Murder is Announced* and start to read, becoming quickly caught up in the story of a group of slightly eccentric villagers finding an advertisement in their local paper saying a murder will be committed at their friend's home later that evening.

Eventually an angry lorry driver behind me beeping his horn tears me out of the 1950s and back into the present day. The traffic is moving and I'm back on my way to Southend-on-Sea.

There's precious little water on the seafront as I drive down the Western Esplanade, passing shabby-looking guest-houses that wouldn't look out of place in an Agatha Christie novel themselves, mingled together with more modern-looking flats. To my left, a large expanse of grey-black mud stretches out, with only a slim line of water in the distance lapping against the end of the long pleasure pier. Memories of coming here with my parents once or twice during occasional visits to the UK float into my head, the most prominent one involving me chipping a front tooth on a stick of rock bought from one of the little tuck-shop huts. Most of them are gone now, with large sections of the space given over to more upmarket seafood restaurants or incorporated into the Adventure Island fairground.

I turn right to go up a steep hill and within minutes I'm

plunged back into the depths of suburbia. Like the seafront, it's a strange mixture of the privileged mingled with the downright shabby. Large, beautifully designed detached houses with big four-by-fours parked outside jostle for space, practically opposite poorly maintained council properties and old-fashioned townhouses. Eventually I come to a stop outside a particularly grim stretch of what I presume to be council houses, some with upturned overflowing recycling bins, discarded rusting bikes and, in one instance, a sofa with half its stuffing pulled off, as if a pack of wild dogs had been set upon it. The house I'm looking for is next door to this one and I park my car in a vacant space opposite and turn off the engine, silencing the satnav now that it's told me at least three times that I've reached my destination.

I stare over at the house: the grimy gutters that need a good servicing; the rubbish in the tiny little front garden; the weeds poking out of the concrete on the front step. Can the boy Jessica seemed so committed to really come from a place like this? If one of my friends had said such a thing aloud about one of their children's potential love interests, I would have admonished them for their snobbery, but I can't help it – I'm genuinely shocked at what I've discovered. Where the hell did she meet this boy? How could a girl from a completely different world become so attached, at least over Facebook Messenger, to someone who lives here?

Without really knowing what I'm doing, I get out of the car and start to cross the road. I have a half-baked notion of pretending to be a Jehovah's Witness or from the local church or something – just an everyday irritating cold caller

–in the hope of catching a glimpse of him. Michael Kelley. The boy who abandoned my little girl. On the doorstep, however, I find myself faltering. What am I playing at? Why am I here? My hand, outstretched for the doorbell, pulls back and I have to steady myself slightly so as not to fall. Tears prick my eyes and I walk back into the road, not bothering to look. 'This is insane,' I say out loud to myself as I make contact with the car and pull open the door, grappling with the handle and then crawling across to the driver's seat. My tiredness is catching up with me now. I probably had about one hour's sleep during the night, if that, most of it spent plotting and fantasising about finding that boy – the boy who lives in the house merely metres from me now – and making him feel all my pain, throwing it at him like it's a force, a physical force, and knocking him down with his own shame.

I take the car out of its parking space a little too quickly, hearing the tyres screech as I go zooming down the road. When I get to a junction, I realise I'm in no fit state to drive. I need to sleep. I think about pulling into a side-street and having a kip in the car, but it's broad daylight and the temperature is already soaring. Even with the air-con on, the thought of trying to sleep in this light repulses me. I need peace and quiet and darkness.

I'll go to a hotel, I think to myself. One of the nicer ones I passed on the way here. I'll get a room, just for the day, and sleep. Then I'll decide what to do.

Slowing to a more responsible speed, I turn the car around and drive carefully back towards the sea.

Chapter Thirteen

THE BOY

It's brought it all back. Piccadilly. I can't really say I've been coping. I've just sort of been existing these past few months. Drifting through school, not really paying attention, not caring that my grades are getting shitter as the year goes on. Part of me wonders what it would be like having a family that cared. Having a mother with enough interest in my grades to ground me or demand to know why I'm now getting Ds and Es rather than Bs and Cs. Why I'm staying out for hours and missing meals, if there are any meals to have, of course.

'Have you heard about Piccadilly?' Mum says as I walk through the door. She's sitting in the lounge with Tony and Mark, two weed-dealing loansharks in their early thirties who are dressed like football hooligans. They hang around the same betting shop as her, hoping to score a bit of business. She owed them money once and then suddenly her debts seemed to vanish overnight. It wasn't the only thing that had happened overnight. The next morning I found Mark, dressed only in *The Simpsons* themed underpants, rummaging around our kitchen for cereals and a clean bowl to use. He just gave me a smirk and winked, then went back upstairs to Mum's room. I tried not to think about what Mum had done in order to wipe away half a grand in owed cash. Or how many bags of the stuff they may have sold her in the meantime.

Right now she's looking at me, waiting for a response, chewing a mouthful of popcorn, one hand stuck in the bumper Butterkist bag, the other slung over the inner thigh of Tony.

'Yes, I did,' I say blankly. I don't want to talk about it with her. I wish I could. I wish I could go to her, hug her like I used to, when she was fun and smiled more. But she was never good with 'heavy stuff', she told me. She wouldn't listen. She'd just reach for the nearest bottle, then a spliff. Then sank into a half-sleep.

'Police have fucked up, should've stopped it,' says Mark, and then nods thoughtfully as if he's made an intelligent comment. I want to hit him.

'Should stop paying our fucking taxes,' Tony contributes.

'I'm going upstairs,' I say, turning away. I didn't want to stay and listen to this. 'Is there anything for tea?'

'Your mum isn't your fucking slave,' Tony says. 'Get your own sodding food. We're busy.' He edges to the side, bringing out from behind his back a see-through bag with something dark green inside it. I see him wink at Mum, and she returns the wink and starts touching his thigh. I decide to leave.

'Fish and chips,' Mum calls after me, 'if you go and get it, obviously.'

'Maybe,' I call back.

'Hey, shut the fucking door,' one of the dickheads barks.

I don't reply, but slam the door and run upstairs.

———

Upstairs in my room, I log on and try to read the BBC News updates about the Piccadilly bombing, but find I can't. My head is swimming and I keep being taken back to the night of the Stratford attacks. I'm determined not to be sick and grip hard to my desk chair, trying to steady myself. Then, when that doesn't work, I try gipping my legs, digging my fingernails into my thighs, liking the pain and feeling them dig in through my trousers into my flesh. It works. It steadies me. I transfer from the desk to my bed, taking off my clothes and getting under the covers. I must have fallen asleep for an hour or two because when I open my eyes it's much darker, the warm glow of the evening sun poking through the blinds. Slowly pulling myself out of bed, I look down and see the red marks. Scratch marks, some of them deep. Did I press that hard earlier? Or did I do it in my sleep? I touch the raw skin on the side of my right leg, feeling it tense as I lay my hand on it. It feels good. Comforting, almost, to feel something sting, feel something harsh and real.

I get dressed and go out onto the landing. My stomach is tight from hunger. I can't be bothered to leave the house and get fish and chips and I hope, even though it's pointless, that there's something in the fridge I can warm through in the microwave.

The silence stops me. I'm on the stairs, poised, trying to listen. Silence isn't good. I go down the final few stairs so I'm in front of the closed door to the lounge. I walk down the corridor to the kitchen, which opens out onto the lounge, hidden from view round the corner from anyone sitting on the sofas in the TV area. As I walk in, the tiles cool my feet, and I start to hear their breathing. And, at last, a sound. Like a quiet, dull moan, or weird singing without any beat or tune. I suddenly feel afraid. Afraid of what I might find. I'm not sure whether to take a look then leave, or go straight back to bed. I decide to go in. Twisting my head around the side of the fridge, I can see into the main part of the lounge without making myself too obvious.

Mum is lying on the sofa, up against Mark. She's on her side, he's in a sitting position. Mark looks completely asleep, his breath coming slow, causing his Ben Sherman shirt to crease slightly, in and out.

Mum's the one making the strange sound. A little, childlike sound, and when I get closer I realise she's half singing, half muttering, 'Row, row, row your boat...' Her eyes are closed and she shows no sign of noticing I'm there. And then I notice three things. First, a strange smell, mingled with the regular one of weed – a smell like burning metal or something chemical. Second, the fact that Tony and Mark both have their sleeves rolled up. And lastly, among all the half-eaten bags of popcorn and empty pizza boxes on the table, there's an ashtray filled with the ends of spliffs... and three syringes. Mum's slow, sad song is going round on a loop, and I can see a line of saliva trailing down her cheek. I'm about to go and nudge her, try to get her to wake up, but then I hear a noise behind me that makes me jump.

My brother's standing there, in the doorway. He too looks as if he's been asleep, dressed in pyjama bottoms and a Superman T-shirt. He stands in the doorway, giving me a weird look. Eventually he says, not bothering to lower his voice, 'How long have they been…?'

I just shrug. 'I've only just come downstairs. Was having a nap. I thought they were just smoking today. But apparently they brought more than just weed.' There's something in the way he's looking at Mum that's making me feel uneasy. Like he's repulsed. As if he doesn't know her at all.

'It's getting worse,' he says simply. And turns and walks away, back upstairs.

Chapter Fourteen

December. Two months to go.

MICHAEL: Can't sleep. Assume you can't either?

JESSICA: Been doing essay work. I seem to be a bit of a night owl these days.

MICHAEL: Essay work at 3am?

JESSICA: Yeah, I know, don't judge. My mum does enough of that.

MICHAEL: I thought you get on well with your mum?

JESSICA: When did I say that?

MICHAEL: It just sounded like you did. Sorry if I got it wrong.

JESSICA: Sorry – me and her are, well, let's just say complicated.

MICHAEL: I know all about complicated. My mum and I would have some serious things to talk about if she wasn't stoned for long enough to actually listen.

JESSICA: Does she smoke weed a lot? Sorry, I think I always just presumed it was alcohol.

MICHAEL: She does both. The alcohol is usually when she's feeling sad. She cries a lot when she's drinking. The weed is fairly constant. It makes her grumpy most of the time and at other times she gets weird. Sometimes she thinks we've been out telling social services what a bad mum she is, sometimes she accuses us of being friends with cops and how me and my brother want to get her into prison for being a bad mum.

JESSICA: Oh my God. I'm probably naïve, but I've always thought of it as harmless. Everyone does it, don't they?

MICHAEL: Whenever people say it's harmless, I always want them to come and stay at my house for a week. They literally have no idea. My clothes always smell of the stuff, too, and teachers keep giving me leaflets on it or accusing me of smoking it myself.

JESSICA: Do you not use it?

MICHAEL: My mind's already fucked enough without messing it up even more.

JESSICA: Sorry, that was a stupid question.

MICHAEL: It's OK. Anyway, just remember, if things with your mum get bad, at least she's not off her head 24/7.

JESSICA: She's just weak. There's so much to her I can't talk to her about. And the worst thing – one of the worst – is that she's known for years what my dad's been doing.

MICHAEL: What's your dad been doing?

MICHAEL: You still there? I don't mind if you want to talk in the morning.

JESSICA: He's been fucking other women.

MICHAEL: Oh.

JESSICA: Yes, oh.

MICHAEL: You've never thought he might be?

JESSICA: Never. I knew my mum would piss him off,

and maybe he flirted a bit with people, but I never thought he'd actually go off and cheat on Mum. But he has. I heard him.

MICHAEL: You heard him doing it? With another woman?

JESSICA: No, no. I heard him talking to Mum. They thought I was asleep, but I heard her mention to him he'd have to throw a shirt away because there was lipstick on it. And from what she said to him, it wasn't the first time.

MICHAEL: What did she say?

JESSICA: She said, 'You could at least have the decency to try to hide it. You used to make up an excuse.' And he just said, 'I thought you'd be pleased I'm no longer insulting your intelligence.'

MICHAEL: How did she take that?

JESSICA: She said, 'You know, sometimes, you really make me hate my life.'

MICHAEL: Fair.

JESSICA: It isn't fair. I'm in her life. I'm part of it. Or am I not enough? I'm so fucking sick of both of them. Of all of it.

MICHAEL: One day you'll leave them. And they'll realise what they missed when they were dealing with their own shit.

JESSICA: Yeah. Maybe they will.

MICHAEL: My mum always knew.

JESSICA: I thought you'd fallen asleep.

JESSICA: Knew what?

JESSICA: Oh, you mean…

MICHAEL: Yeah. She always knew about my dad. I think that's what makes it so difficult for her to deal with. And why I can't ever forgive her. It wasn't like she found out after or when he'd gone. She knew at the time and did nothing.

JESSICA: I'm so very, very sorry.

MICHAEL: I know. I am too.

Chapter Fifteen

THE MOTHER

May. Three months after the attack.

I end up parking by one of the huts selling sweets and soft drinks, attached to one of the seafront restaurants. As soon as I smell the scent of cooking I realise how hungry I am. It must be way over twelve hours since I've eaten. Mingled with next to no sleep, it is a marvel I am still standing upright. I go over to a young woman in the process of opening the shutter and ask when they start serving food.

'Well, not really until lunch time – but we'll have a batch of fresh doughnuts cooked in a sec. They're just in the fryer.'

The thought of doughnuts for breakfast sounds rather decadent, but I nod and say I'll take a bag of six small ones with cinnamon sugar. The first taste of the warm, slightly greasy surface and the crunch of the sugar instantly takes me back to my youth. We always used to get something like this whenever we went to a seaside town. My father had a bit of a thing about them – particularly British ones, although he preferred Brighton and Eastbourne to Southend. We started our own tradition of seaside visits with Jessica, when she was very young and still content with building sandcastles, spending hours making moats and drawbridges out of sticks, then shrieking with excitement as the sea came in and steadily washed them away. Then, when my work really took off and we became more than just financially comfortable and into the realms of 'relatively wealthy', we ended up always jetting off somewhere more exotic. More glamorous and sophisticated, perhaps, but I missed the simplicity of those early days, spent running around the sand with my little girl, wondering when the changeable British weather would send us all scurrying back to the car.

I turn my back to the sea and look at the mass of buildings facing me. One of them is a hotel, apparently called The Carriage Way Hotel, and I cross the road to go and take a look. According to its sign it's five star, although from the outside you'd never have thought it, nor with a name like The Carriage Way – something you'd expect to see doubling as a country pub. The once-white paintwork is now greying – green, even, at the edges of the windows – like something once fresh and new steadily rotting at the corners. It's got character, but not the type of character I often go in for these days.

The foyer is a rather confusing mixture of the dated and the modern. The armchairs, rugs on the floor, and elderly clientele sitting by the unlit fire, knitting and talking quietly to each other, plant me firmly in Miss Marple territory, though this is ruined by the addition of a row of pristine iMacs down the side of one wall, and a disconcertingly modern large LED TV to my right in what looks like a larger lounge area. Though slightly odd, it at least feels clean and welcoming, and I try my best to smile at the lady on the desk.

'Hi, I need to get a room,' I say, taking out my purse. 'Just for one night. One day actually, I may be going back tonight, but I just need to lie down. I have a migraine and can't drive.'

The woman looks instantly concerned, 'Oh dear, I am sorry. Oh God, on a nice day like this too. Ruined your day at the seaside, has it?' She tuts and shakes her head, then carries on enthusiastically, 'I get terrible migraines myself. Have to go and lie down in a darkened room until they go. Like someone twisting a blade in the side of your head, aren't they?'

Her accent is broad Essex and irritatingly loud, and even though I don't actually have a migraine, I can't help fearing that her voice might really bring one on. 'Yes, that's exactly it. Do you have a vacancy? Anything will do.'

'Hmm, let me see,' she says, tapping on the computer in front of her. 'Yes, we've got some superior suites available, but I suppose you won't need those if you only have a sleep. Would a standard do OK? They all have double beds, so you'll be able to stretch out.'

'That's fine,' I say curtly. I'm keen to avoid any more heart-to-hearts on the trials faced by migraine sufferers. I just want to sleep. Getting out my purse, I pay for the room and shake my head when she asks if I need any luggage brought up.

'Do you have a car?' she asks, as I turn to leave. I tell her I do and it's parked almost directly opposite on the seafront.

'Oh Christ, don't leave it there. You'll get a ticket. Like ninjas, they are, round here with their bleedin' fines. We have a car park…'

'I don't care,' I say and leave, heading towards the lift and up to the room that will take me away from all the heat, noise, and light, and allow me to sink into my own terrible oblivion.

———

I sleep for nearly eight hours straight. By the time I wake my phone says it's nearly 4pm and I'm almost out of battery. I scramble for my charger and when the screen lights up properly I see I have ten texts and fourteen missed calls from Alec. I open the iMessage app and type in:

Yes, I am alive. I've gone away for a bit. Don't worry, I'm safe. Just need time to think.

I see that he starts typing almost immediately after the message is delivered but I lock the phone and set it back on top of the bedside table. The room is nice – nicer than I expected – and surprisingly roomy for a standard double. I enjoy the cool sensation of the sheets against my bare legs as I roll off and pull off the rest of my clothes and walk towards the shower. The cool water falling down my shoulders is even better – I feel like I'm washing away the stress of the past twenty-four hours. The horror of seeing the terrorist attack in Piccadilly on the news, the argument with Alec about the boy, my sudden departure for Southend in the early morning. All of it seems to be a life lived by somebody else, and I'm now stepping out of the shower onto the soft mat feeling like a different person.

I see that Alec has phoned again when I get back to my phone, but I don't bother listening to the voicemails. The battery's still only at 16 per cent, so I sit, wrapped in my towel, reading the rest of *A Murder is Announced* in the armchair by the window while I wait for it to charge. After about an hour, I remember Jessica's phone and swap that over to give it some power too. I probably won't need it, but just in case. By the time it gets to 5.30pm and the sun is taking on that golden summer evening glow, I decide to get properly dressed and go out to find some food.

The woman at the desk has gone, replaced by a young man who smiles at me as I walk past him. The elderly ladies around the fireplace are still there – perhaps they haven't moved all day, still knitting and chatting. Must be a nice life, if you can afford it. I catch myself fantasising about what it would be like to live in a hotel; a childhood dream I once harboured. 'You'd have to earn a fortune,' my mother had said when I used to go on about how I'd get room service brought up to my room on a tray every day. I think about my finances now. Although I wouldn't be able to live in a hotel for the rest of my life – the money would run out quicker than I could recoup it – I am substantially more financially free than my parents could have ever dreamed of being, especially after pouring all of their savings into an outrageously large and unpleasantly gothic-looking house in Perth. After that, they had to live a frugal existence just to be able to maintain it. It became a weight around their necks. Until my father died, and his life insurance kicked in. And suddenly, my mother wasn't poor any more. My mind flits back to a memory of her, sitting in front of her accountant in the living room. He was trying to be as kind and understanding as possible, apologising a number of times about the circumstances and how, if she needed to stop, just to say and he'd come back another time. But she told him to carry on and he gave her a piece of paper and started to explain when she'd receive the first amount of money from his policy. She kept looking sombre, right up until he straightened up to go. Then, from where I was observing, unseen in the hallway, I saw it: the small quiver of a smile flickering across her lips. She continued to keep up the sad-widow act, though. And made sure to remind me not to get used to our sudden windfall.

'Wealth isn't something one should get used to. It can vanish like that!' She snapped her fingers in my face. 'It's unlikely you and the rest of your generation will ever be able to support yourselves. So enjoy it while it lasts.'

I suppose I've spent my life proving her wrong. Last year I earned just under £80,000, and Alec, with his marketing job, around the £70,000 mark. I wonder what my mother would say to that if I told her. I shake my head, trying to clear the thought from my mind. I really shouldn't be thinking about my mother right now.

The woman at the desk was right – I have got a parking

ticket. £35 to be paid within ten days, or risk the fine increasing. I'm tempted just to tear up the ticket and tell them to go whistle for it, but instead I stuff it into my handbag.

I leave the car where it is and decide to take a walk further down to where there are some smarter restaurants, filled with people eating what looks like gourmet seafood. One of them, named The Seaview Palace, looks pleasant and has a nice menu, so I wait to be served and when a waiter comes I ask to be seated outside. The evening is gorgeous, even if the view is still mostly just the stretching expanse of mud. The sea must have come and gone while I was sleeping.

While waiting for my food – a large battered cod, thick-cut chips, and side salad – I take out the notepad I carry everywhere, almost out of instinct. Usually, if I'm on my own having food or a coffee I'll be busy planning out my thoughts for new TV series, or puzzling through a plotting issue in my head. I like to have a good crop of ideas on the go, so that when one is finished I'm ready to power on to the next. But this notepad has been barely written in for months. It's like a light has gone out inside of me – a once-flowing stream of creativity has now dried up, leaving behind it a dry wasteland free from inspiration or enthusiasm.

I'm saved from my thoughts ten minutes later by the arrival of my food. The batter is satisfyingly crunchy, the chips a beautiful golden-brown, perfectly cooked, and for a few moments I allow myself to think about nothing other than the food and how good the sun feels on my neck as it steadily sinks lower down the horizon. And then, as I'm polishing off the last of the side salad, I see him.

A group of boys are walking along the seafront towards me. One of them is holding a giant panda, the type of thing you'd win on one of those throwing-game arcades, and the rest are eating candyfloss or drinking what appear to be Monster energy drinks, laughing and shouting. And the boy at the front, with a bottle clasped in his right hand, is Michael Kelley. I recognise his face instantly – his expression is practically identical to his smug Facebook profile photo. I sit completely still as they come up level with the restaurant, my hand frozen on the way to my mouth with a few rocket leaves dangling from my fork. I probably look ridiculous, but I don't care. I just sit and watch. His eyes meet mine for a second, then he moves on, tipping his head back to take a sip of his drink.

I drop my fork with a loud clatter, causing the couple at the table next to look over. Standing up quickly, causing more of a racket as the table jolts, I throw down two £20 notes – almost double what the meal cost, but I can't wait for change – I can't just watch him disappear quite literally into the sunset. I can't.

I follow the group of boys, keeping a safe distance, so they don't spot me. The pavement is crowded with families with prams and children running around and I have to be careful not to lose them completely. Eventually they stop, near a row of benches, and appear to be saying goodbye to each other as one group takes off up a winding steep path away from the seafront. One other boy stays talking to Michael for a minute, and I contrive a reason to pause where I am, squeezing myself up against a lamp-post as if I'm checking my bag for something I may have forgotten. And then he's alone, the other boy crossing the road and away from us, leaving Michael walking along the pavement. I follow him, picking up the pace. Then, when I'm just a few metres away, I pull out my purse, take out the last twenty I have in there and say: 'Excuse me!'

He doesn't turn round straight away. Probably lost in his own world. 'Excuse me!' I call out again and finally he stops and looks over. He faces me and I feel at once a chill wrap itself around my body as if the temperature has just dropped and we are actually standing together in a snow drift. I hold out the money and say, as brightly as I can manage, 'Hi there. I think you dropped this.'

He looks at the banknote in my hand, clearly a little puzzled. 'Er, I don't think so.'

Fuck, I think to myself. What is it with kids not carrying cash, these days? It's all bloody contactless and Apple Pay.

'Well, I saw it fall out of your pocket. Or it may have been one of your mates. You passed my table at the restaurant and it was left on the pavement when you'd gone and it definitely wasn't there before.' I smile and hold it out again.

He looks around him, as if I might be either insane or part of some elaborate hidden-camera stunt. I stand there, waiting for him to come up with a suitable response.

'OK, I mean, I don't think it's mine, but if you're offering me twenty quid and it's going spare, I'm not going to say no.' He reaches out to take it and my hand grazes his slightly as the note leaves my fingers. I can see why Jessica was attracted to him. Even if she never met him in person, he has a charisma and carefree charm that seems to fit with the messages I read during their Facebook conversations. He says thanks and turns to leave. *No,* I think. *I can't let it end here.*

'Wait,' I say and he turns back to me again. That puzzled expression is back, coupled with the ghost of amusement. 'This sounds a bit weird, but… I'm from a modelling agency. We do all kinds of things, really, but the majority of it is youth modelling – brands like Hollister and Gap – and I hope you don't mind me saying, but you're very good-looking and I think you'd be absolutely perfect for one of our campaigns.'

I don't know where the lie comes from. It just arrives, perfectly formed, ready for the moment and I thank God I've got a creative brain.

He still looks wary, as if I might be trying to trick him in some way. Of course, this must all look rather strange, but I stick to my guns. 'It wouldn't take much – just a few headshots and I can see what my colleagues think. Maybe we could have a quick chat about it first, if you like.' I don't wait for a response, just fish inside my bag for my notepad and pen and tear off a blank sheet of paper and write down the name of my hotel and my mobile number. 'I'm staying here locally for a bit – at the hotel, The Carriage Way, a short walk up there. Do you want to pop in now for a chat? Or tomorrow maybe?'

I hand him the page and he looks at it, still unsure. 'Ahh, sorry, I've got to get back home now…'

'That's OK, I'm here for a while. Tomorrow, then? Just come to the hotel foyer and we can talk.'

I think he's going to say no. I think he's just going to hand back the sheet and say sorry, he's not interested. But he just shrugs and then smiles, a wide beam lighting up his face. 'All right. Don't see why not.'

It takes me by surprise, but I try to keep my flow. 'Great. That's really great,' I say, returning his smile. 'So, what kind of time? Would lunchtime suit?'

'Ah, I have school…'

I've completely forgotten it's a school night – with all the little children running around, the whole place has a summer holidays feel. Apparently parents take their kids on trips to the seaside on weeknights during termtime nowadays.

'Oh yes, of course. How about after school? I… I could buy you dinner? There's a restaurant at the hotel.' I'm starting to worry I'm sounding desperate, but he seems to grow even more keen at the mention of dinner. 'Yeah, sure. That sounds good. If that's OK with you?'

'More than OK,' I say, trying to make the relief not too obvious. This is going better than I could have ever believed. 'So, does 5pm suit? I know it's early, but it should probably be quieter then.'

He nods. 'Sure thing.'

We smile at each other and I'm not sure what to say now, so I just nod too.

'So, I'll see you tomorrow then, in the hotel lobby.' He nods again and turns and leaves.

Chapter Sixteen

THE MOTHER

May. Three months after the attack.

The euphoria that fills me as I walk back to the hotel quickly turns to doubt when I get to my room. How on earth am I going to play this? How far am I going to take it? I have a vague idea – and many quite colourful ones – about what I could do, but now they have the potential of becoming a reality, I find myself unsure. Then there is the possibility – no, the likelihood – that he'll never show up. He is a teenage boy, consumed with thoughts about school and hanging out with his mates and homework and food and whatever else is going on in his life. He probably wouldn't want to break off from the early summer sun and go visit a random older woman at a hotel to talk about a modelling career, a career he has apparently never thought about pursuing.

After a couple of hours of fretting, I try to distract myself with something else, but the television is still full of the Piccadilly attack and I've finished my Agatha Christie novel and can't get into the two irritatingly cheery volumes I've brought. I decide to take a trip to the nearest twenty-four-hour supermarket and have a look around. I could just wait for the morning and go to the nearest shopping centre, but the thought of being stuck without anything to do, aside from scrolling through BBC News on my phone for the whole night, fills me with anxiety.

I'm relieved to find my car hasn't been clamped, though there is yet another parking ticket on it for an even steeper amount than before, with a threat that the car will be removed forcibly if it isn't taken away soon. The evening sun has turned to twilight, with a gorgeous sapphire sky that lights up the horizon as I navigate my way along the motorway to the massive all-night Tesco Extra. I gather up a good selection of chocolate bars and sweets, not caring about the sugar hit I'll likely get so late in the day, and also pick up a heavily discounted (and slightly dog-eared) copy of Agatha Christie's autobiography from a random clearance bin.

'My goodness, you're going to be busy,' says the young girl, although I'm not sure if she's referring to the book or the mountain of chocolate.

'Yes, I'm on holiday,' I say back, as if that explains everything.

Back at the hotel, I settle myself down and start reading my new book, whilst making a start on the Dairy Milk. When it gets to 4am, I finally try to sleep, and doze fitfully for a couple of hours until at last my mind lets me fall into the darkness of sleep and leaves me at the mercy of whatever dreams may lurk for me there.

Daylight shines through the sides of the curtains, bright and strong, as if affronted by my attempts to block it out and stay indoors. It's 11 a.m. and my phone is buzzing next to me. Alec is ringing. I consider throwing it out the window, then give in and click the answer icon.

'What?' I say, not bothering to make my tone sound civil.

'Christ, Caroline! I came THIS close to calling the police and reporting you missing and the car stolen.'

I groan and turn over, enjoying the cool side of the pillows on my cheek. 'That would have made you look pretty foolish,' I say. 'Woman takes her own car on a trip to escape her depressing life and texts husband to say she's fine. Hardly a riveting mystery.'

'I thought you might do something stupid.' He does sound worried, and angry too, but that's Alec all over. Angry I've rendered him impotent and inadequate – left him at home like a child told to amuse himself while the adults do some real work. It's turning the tables on him and his past behaviour, and he doesn't like it one bit.

'When have I ever said or even given the remotest suggestion that I would kill myself, Alec? Even during the worst of it. I may have felt like I wanted to die, and Christ knows it's been hard trying to adjust, but I don't think you can realistically imply I would—'

'Caroline, please,' he cuts in, sounding exasperated. 'This isn't adjusting. This is just running away from the problem. Where are you? Please, can you just tell me and I'll come and get you.'

'No,' I snap back at him. 'You can't. I'm going to Australia to see my mother.'

This shuts him up, if only for a few seconds. 'Please tell me you aren't serious?'

'I am. I need a change of scene.'

I hear him exhale. He's probably clutching wildly at whatever strands of his short hair he can get between his fingers. 'I really don't think that's a good idea.'

'It's not up to you, is it,' I say. 'I'm flying out this evening.'

'Caroline, after all you've said about her... about... what she did... might have done... that whole crazy business surrounding your father's death, and those bouts of radio silence. I mean, she barely even acknowledged her granddaughter's murder, for God's sake. She never bothered to get to know her, even though we repeatedly invited her and offered to go and visit her. You said – they were your words, I remember – you said she spent your childhood caring more about her own weird little obsessions, like the hundreds of books on bonsai trees, despite never actually owning one, and that bizarre toy collection you said she has, which in a grown woman must be a sign of some kind of psychopathy. You always maintained you had no plans to keep in touch and she could die out there alone for all you care.'

I nod, even though he can't see me. 'I know all this, Alec. It's not going to change my mind. And anyway, why should she escape the misery? We're going through grief. Why shouldn't she feel some of that agony?'

I hear him mutter something about Laini and my therapy not working, but I just talk over him. 'I'm off now, Alec. I'll message you in a few weeks. And don't even think about trying to ambush me at the airport and guess which flight I'll be on. If I see you, I swear to God I'll make such a scene in front of all those police officers with guns, you'll wish you'd never met me.'

I hear a spluttering of disbelief on his end. 'I can't believe you're doing this,' he says. 'I'm looking up the flights now. I can come with you…'

'And what would your gaggle of school mums and desperate divorcees do without you? I think I saw at least two wistful faces staring across the room at you at Denise's party.' It's not strictly true. I wasn't being that observant at the party, but I know it will unsettle him. 'Stay home, Alec. I mean it. I'm entirely serious. And if I see you coming towards me at the airport I will start shouting and screaming things – words like *bomb* and *knives* and *terrorist*.'

I cancel the call, feeling instantly bad about that last bit. I have no intention of going to Australia, and it would serve him right for him to have a wasted journey to the airport. Looking for me in departures. Wondering where I was. If I'd boarded my flight already. A flight ready to take me back. Away from one horror, and into the arms of another.

Even though I'm stationary, I feel the room starting to rock back and forth, as if the hotel has been cast out to sea. I feel my phone still clutched in the palm of my right hand and bring it close to me. Almost without thinking, I touch at the screen until I get to the contact page I need. Then I press call.

He answers almost immediately. 'Caroline? Jesus, Alec's been calling me. Are you OK?'

Even though he sounds agitated, Rob's voice has a calming presence on me – less confrontational than his brother, filled with concern rather than resentment and bitterness.

'Yes, I'm fine.' I say this trying to conjure up a sense of firm confidence that I don't feel. It doesn't sound at all convincing.

'Where are you? I can come and—'

'No,' I cut him off, 'I really don't think that would be good…'

'Alec seems really cut up.'

'Alec can fucking cope!' I start to shout now, swinging my legs out of bed, feeling my back click as I straighten up. 'He can have his little solitary cry-fest watching the news and wringing his hands about what a terrible state the world is in, when the real horror, the real figure of guilt, is staring us right in the face!'

I'm ranting. And I can tell Rob's taken aback. Silence greets my outburst for a few seconds, then he says, 'Caroline, I really think you should talk to someone. This is worrying me. It's worrying Alec.'

He's sounding all adult and responsible now. And when a few seconds pass without me answering, he cuts the call. Then when I try to call him back in a mad rush of panic and regret, he doesn't answer, and I'm left to cry in the dark alone.

Chapter Seventeen

THE MOTHER

May. Three months after the attack.

I'm feeling calmer now. After lying in the bed for nearly an hour, I feel ready to wake up properly and think more clearly about what I want to do with the time I've bought. I can stay here for weeks. Just me. I can go for walks. I can read. Go to the cinema. It's unlikely I'm going to bump into anyone I know. Because after tonight, a weight is going to lift from my shoulders. I'm going to show Michael Kelley what he did. I'm going to make him face up to what he's done. Confess his guilt. Lay out all the facts in front of him so he's going to leave this hotel with no doubt that he is the direct cause of Jessica's death. I get up and walk straight to the shower. It's going to be a big day.

I spend the morning in the nearby shopping centre and get a surprising amount of pleasure going through all the shops and buying things with abandon. I get a few cardigans, new shoes, a handbag. I rarely splash out on unnecessary gadgets and tech, but I find myself drifting through the doors of the Currys PC World store and glancing at the latest laptops and tablet devices. The sight of all their shiny screens makes me wince – a reminder of the laptop at home sitting on my desk, barely used for anything work-related for months. I'm just walking out the doors when I think of the small, budget TV screen attached to the wall in my hotel room. I miss watching rubbishy comedies and bland romances – things where the plot mechanics are comfortingly predictable, whilst keeping clear from anything too violent, too upsetting. Too close to my reality. I march back down to the far end of the store where a shop worker – Kamal, according to his badge – is sorting out some cables behind the display of soundbars.

'Hi. I think I need a TV.'

He grins, but looks slightly puzzled, 'Well… sure, you've come to the right place.'

I nod, businesslike. 'I'm living in a hotel for the time being, but the TV is crap – just fuzzy Freeview, and even that's a bit unreliable – and I'm missing the ease and quality of the one at home.'

Still looking a little surprised, he asks, 'Would the hotel let you bring in a brand-new TV?'

I hadn't thought about this, but it seems stupid now. I just give a shrug, 'I'll take the risk. Worst comes to the worst, I'll just have it sent home.'

He nods and leads me over to the higher-end TV screens. I choose a Sony OLED and opt for one of the larger screen sizes – 55 inches. It costs just under £3,000 and I think nothing of it as I hand over my credit card.

'I'd like it today. I have a car – I can take it away with me right now.'

Alec has always been a strange one with money. His marketing jobs didn't pay that much at first, and he's never shaken off the idea we should always be cautious with how much we spend. He's probably been worried that one day my writing work would dry up. Television is never a secure profession. But as my career gathered steam and the money started rolling in, with my shows getting recommissioned and sold around the world, it all seemed to have a strange effect on him. He started to look strained. Stressed, almost. Upsizing our property to a large detached house in an affluent area of Kent prompted something close to a mid-life crisis in him, even though he'd only just reached thirty-three at the time. He became more and more frugal, as if we were trying to conserve money rather than enjoying the freedoms it had brought us. He'd chastise Jessica for putting the expensive orange juice in the trolley rather than the supermarket's own brand. I'd catch him on price comparison websites, looking to find the absolute cheapest car insurance or electricity provider he could find. He would window shop for clothes when walking around Bluewater or Lakeside, then buy similar but cheaper items online on eBay outlet stores. Whenever I tried to gently remind him that much of this was unnecessary, he became prickly and defensive. 'That's the problem with our culture these days. More, more, more. What's the matter with being sensible with money?' I said, on more than one occasion, that I didn't think allowing Jessica to have Tropicana was unsensible, but he'd just go selectively deaf and not reply.

He even went so far as to buy a book (second-hand, online) called *Affluenza* by some psychologist about how modern life's must-have-the-very-latest-thing attitude to living has been causing widespread mental health issues such as anxiety and depression. He didn't read much of the book; it sat on his bedside table, and then in our library when I'd grown tired of seeing it every day. Brushed out of sight, hidden away. Like most of our problems.

As I leave the shopping centre with the TV loaded in the car behind me, thanks to the help of shop assistant Kamal and another nice Currys staff member, I get a perverse sense of satisfaction thinking how shocked Alec would be if he knew how much it had all cost. I fantasise about buying other things, maybe when I return home after my Southend adventure. Perhaps I could just bankrupt us. Put everything on credit cards, fritter the rest of our savings away and then just write weird, childlike notes in crayons to American Express and MasterCard saying, 'Dear Money People, I'm sorry, I spent it all. It was fun while it lasted, lots of love, Caroline.' They'd think I'd flipped. Maybe I have.

There is a problem with the TV when I get to the hotel. Kamal was right. 'You see, the thing is,' the dopey-looking young man at the reception desk says, nervously clenching his hands as he does so, 'everything electrical has to be checked by our health and safety department.'

'They can check it,' I reply, shrugging. 'I can talk to them, if you like. Where in the building are they located?'

He goes red, looking more panicked. 'Ah, you see, the thing is, we subcontract it all out to a firm based in Brighton and… well… given the time of day, and the fact we're not expecting another visit from them for… er… I'm not sure how long…'

I hold up my hand to cut him off and he stops immediately. It's almost comical. I reach into my bag for my purse and pull out three crisp £50 notes I got out of a cashpoint earlier and lay them neatly next to each other on the desk.

'Turn a blind eye and these are yours.'

I've never bribed anyone in my life, but this seems to be a week of firsts, and a tiny part of me finds it all rather thrilling. He looks stunned, waits for a few seconds, then says, 'Leave it with me.'

The two young men who bring the TV up to my room don't do anything other than set it on the carpet and murmur to me as they leave. It takes me over an hour to set the thing up and I could have done with an extra pair of hands to lift the massive screen onto the frame, but I just about manage. I was worried I was going to need a screwdriver or something similar, but luckily it's a fairly simple slide-and-slot affair. I sit back and stare at the gleaming mass of black screen in front of me. When the screen bursts into life once I've connected it to the hotel's superfast wi-fi (I had to upgrade to their high-speed version for only a tenner), I flick onto a random romcom and settle into the pillows.

By the time I'm finished, there's only an hour and a half to go until 5pm. Until he arrives. Potentially arrives. I'm not going to get myself too excited. Even though the thought of me and the boy, face to face, with him having to listen to every word I say, sends a jolt down my spine. I know I have to expect him not to show. He'll probably get carried away talking to his friends and forget the time, and the chance meeting on the seafront will be the last I ever see of him.

Except it won't be. I'll make sure of that. A dark thought crosses my mind – of me, camped outside his house in the car with binoculars, waiting for him to come home from school. How long can I keep this up for? I need to be firm with myself. If he doesn't come tonight, I will try to put the whole thing to the back of my mind and focus on writing my new TV project.

I know deep down it won't be that easy, but I try not to think about it as I shower, dry my hair, and then unpack a smart but rather stylish pencil skirt and blouse I bought from Debenhams in the shopping centre. Once everything is done, I stand back to look at myself in the mirror. *Yes*, I think to myself. *I've got the balance right.*

I dither in the lobby, unsure whether to take a chair in the open-plan lounge area where the old ladies seem to have a permanent residence, or if I should just stand awkwardly, aware I probably look like one of the hotel's managerial staff. I opt to stand by the racks of visitor information which hold leaflets advertising local restaurants and attractions, including the Sea Life centre and the place I ate at the previous night.

4.50… 4.55… 4.59… I keep glancing at my phone, which I hold clasped in the palm of my hand so tightly, I am probably risking the safety of its screen, but I don't care. Then I remember. Fuck. I've left Jessica's phone upstairs. The phone I need to confront him with. I want to show him the messages. To show him where they stopped. To make him face up to the fact that he asked her to be there and she did as she promised and then was left, abandoned, to die alone at the hand of a bunch of murdering sociopaths. *Fuck. Fuck. Fuck.* I can show him photos of Jessica on my phone, see his reaction, but I want the messages. I want to read them out. Have him read them out. I want him to cry, to shout, to argue, then finally face up to the fact that he is no better than a murderer.

He is here.

I don't notice him at first. I'm in the midst of getting myself worked up over Jessica's phone and have closed my eyes, using the wall to steady myself. When I open them, there he is, right in front of me.

'Er, hi,' he says, pleasantly.

I pull myself upright. Smile. Then go over to greet him.

Chapter Eighteen

THE BOY

My issues surrounding sex never actually stop me from finding it. That bit is easy. It's the guilt afterwards that's always difficult. I always go home and cry into my mattress, part of me not sure why I'm upset, the other part of me knowing exactly why.

And it's always older women. I find them on Tinder or other dating apps. It's amazing how simple it is – who'd have thought Southend would have so many sex-starved divorced women, eager to drop their knickers for an awkward, disturbed teenage boy. But it is. And they're happy to. They never use their real names and I don't use mine. I pick a woman on my phone, usually while on break at school, chat to her for a bit. Then at lunch, I'll say that I'm free later in the afternoon if she fancies hanging out for a bit. 'Hanging out.' We both know what that will mean.

Usually I go home first and change out of my school uniform. I've learned from experience that school ties and blazers put some women off – makes them think twice about what it is they're about to do. Occasionally, though, I find one who wants that. A woman once asked me to come round in my PE kit and even gave me a script. I had to ring the doorbell and ask if 'Tony fancied a kickabout over on the field' and she'd say Tony had been grounded and had to stay in and do his schoolwork, but I could come in and have a lemonade. I did as I was told, went into her kitchen and she handed me a glass of lemonade, then nodded at me, encouraging me to go on with the words she'd sent beforehand. I almost forgot them then, but they came back eventually. I had to ask, would she mind if I had a quick shower as our boiler was being fixed back home. She said I could and I walked up the stairs as she directed me, then she set the shower running and told me to undress and get in. Once I was under the warm rush of the power-shower, she stepped in herself, still fully dressed, and said, 'You must promise not to tell Tony at school tomorrow – I wouldn't want his mates to think I do this with any boy.' And then she wanted to do it against the glass shower door, which we did, whilst she kept telling me to 'do her like a MILF'. I wasn't sure how you do it with a MILF compared to any other woman, but I did what she wanted.

I saw her a couple of times until one day, when we were at it on the dining room table, my gym clothes scattered over the expensive-looking carpet, the door to the room opened and some lad, about the same age as me or maybe a year older, walked into the room and said, 'Mum?! Fucking CHRIST!' And she screamed, 'Tony, Tony! I'm sorry, let me explain.' She ran after him and I heard them shouting at each other, with him saying, 'What about Dad? What the fuck are you doing?' His voice was posh and by the look of his uniform, he went to a private school outside of Southend. I wasn't sure what to do and within seconds the boy came back: 'Hey, chav boy, who the fuck are you?' I considered saying something smart in response, but he looked muscly and I thought he might hit me. He didn't give me much time to reply anyway. 'Get the fuck out!' he screamed, throwing my boxers at me and lobbing the rest of my clothes out of the dining-room door towards the hallway. 'What are you, a pervert or something? Do you just shag random middle-aged women? You do realise she's nearly fifty? *Fifty.*' He said 'fifty' like he couldn't imagine anyone living that long. '*She's* the one who found *me*,' I just said, and he shook his head and muttered 'Prick' as I walked out the front door.

I've deleted my Tinder account now. I'm not looking for anything like that. I've tried, but the women who mess around with teenage boys don't want anything proper. Anything meaningful. And they especially don't want ones who cry. Who have to leave because their tears overwhelm them. It frightens them. So now I'm not seeing anyone. And don't plan to any time soon. Unless something crops up out of the blue – and it would have to be a very special something.

Chapter Nineteen

THE MOTHER

May. Three months after the attack.

I'm shocked by how well I've managed this. The boy is here. Right here, right now. The old ladies on the sofas are watching closely, some looking wary, as if he might behave inappropriately, disturbing their little safe haven.

It takes me a few seconds to get my words out, but eventually I reply, 'Hi,' and we stand and stare at each other for a bit, then he says, 'So where are we going to do it, then?'

I feel myself turning red, 'Er... sorry?'

His smile widens, slightly wickedly, as if he knows the effect he can have on women and isn't a stranger to using it to his advantage. 'This chat. About my glamorous modelling career.'

I understand and laugh and tell him we'll go through to the restaurant. They aren't serving food until 5.30, but we can have a drink and discuss his options. He nods. 'Sounds good,' he says, and follows me through in silence round to the restaurant area, situated in a built-on extension to the main hotel, with wide, expansive windows offering a dazzling view of the seafront. From here, we could be in the South of France, not Essex, and if I were in less weird circumstances I'd have wanted to take a photo. But I don't. I sit down at our reserved table and ask Michael Kelley what he'd like to drink. 'Do you like wine?' I ask and he shrugged.

'Your call. I drink anything.'

I look down the drinks list and tell him I'm thinking of having the house red and try to make a joke about it being early to start drinking, but it comes out wrong. He smiles again and looks around, taking in the expensive décor, the rows of neatly set empty tables. We're the only people in the restaurant, apart from a family with a small and remarkably silent child, having tea or coffee at the far end away from us.

'You ever been here before?' I ask.

He laughs. 'No, never. Never needed to. I live in Southend.'

I laugh too. 'Of course, sorry, I meant the restaurant.'

He doesn't elaborate further, just shakes his head. I think then of the run-down mess of a council house he lives in, with the rubbish and discarded sofas and kicked-over wheelie-bins lining the street. What a stupid question. Of course he hasn't been here.

'OK, well, when the wine arrives we'll start getting down to business.'

He raises one eyebrow and gives me that wicked grin again. Is he flirting with me? I'm about to start trying to attract a waiter's attention, but then he asks a question that takes me by surprise.

'What's your accent? You not British?'

'Er... no,' I say, slightly disconcerted, 'I'm not British. I'm Australian. Well, I was actually born in Saudi Arabia and lived there until I was ten, but my parents were Australian and we moved back to Perth so I could go to high school there. We did come to the UK quite a bit, though. I had relatives over here. Not too far from here, in fact. We even came to Southend sometimes, though that would have been before you were born, and quite a while before I settled in England properly. That was some time after. I had to escape Australia and the UK seemed like a good place to escape to.' I stop myself for a moment, realising I'm sounding like some kind of convict on the run. 'I mean... when I say *escape*... I just mean that I didn't want to live at home anymore.'

His eyes are glazing over and I'm aware that I'm boring him. He's looking around again, as if looking for something to amuse himself with.

'I'm impressed you noticed my accent though,' I said, hoping to get onto more neutral, lighter territory. 'My daughter always said it faded a bit every year and that by the time I reach fifty I'll sound like a Kent native.' Another silence follows this and he just looks at me. 'I live near Sevenoaks, you see.' The clarification sounds perfunctory and almost as if I'm boasting. We always used to desperately pretend we weren't posh as a family. Since neither Alec nor I are English, we always maintain it would be impossible for us to be 'posh' in the way that our friends Elaine and Jackson are, forever driving between their city home in Kensington and their huge, rambling, great country house in Kent.

'You don't sound like a stereotypical Essex boy,' I say, giving him a wink then instantly regretting it. It's not entirely the truth either – he does sound like an Essex boy, just not one of the loud, screeching, yobbish kind. More natural, less intense.

He shrugs. 'Never really thought about it,' he says.

Of course he hasn't. I doubt there are many teenage boys who ever really think about their voice or accent, unless they've been cursed with a particularly notable high-pitched screech that would make heads turn.

We pause our slightly awkward conversation to order our drinks. I go for the house red I've been considering and Michael chooses a beer. 'I'm afraid I'll just need to see some identification if you're ordering alcohol,' the young female waiter says apologetically, looking at Michael, then at me.

'Oh, surely he's allowed a beer?' I say. 'We'll be ordering food. And he's over 16, aren't you?' I nod at the boy and he nods back.

'I don't think...' the young woman starts to say.

'If you check, I'm sure you'll find that it's perfectly legal for someone over 16 to have alcohol with a meal so long as they're not buying it themselves and are accompanied by an adult. Well, I'll be paying and I'm an adult. And we'll be ordering food as soon as you open your kitchens.'

I can feel myself getting riled, but I try to keep my tone calm. The waitress doesn't know how important a meeting this is, after all.

'I'm sorry, I'm not sure, I'll have to go and get my manager,' she says, looking embarrassed. Michael shrugs, looking a bit puzzled by the fuss. 'I'll just have a Coke.'

The girl disappears off and I feel my deep-seated sense of anxiety starting to bubble to the surface. What now? I've got him here, but the very thing I wanted to show him is resting upstairs on my bedside table. Perhaps I won't need the evidence. After all, he'll probably either make a scene or walk out as soon as I mention Jessica's name. Maybe I wouldn't even get as far as showing him the messages, proving how he was the last person in the whole world who she ever messaged before the bullet that killed her ripped through her body.

'Are you OK?' he says, drawing me out of my thoughts. I stare at him for a few seconds, feeling a bit dazed, then smile to try to cover myself.

'Of course! Sorry, I think it must be the summer heat.' The comment is ridiculous, since the air conditioning in the hotel's dining room is more than adequate, and today hasn't been especially humid. He's clearly now wondering why we're not launching into a discussion about the potential modelling career I've promised him. He takes his phone out and starts tapping away, apparently messaging someone. The drinks arrive and just as the waitress is walking away and the boy's Coke is sitting on the table, condensation dripping onto the cream tablecloth, the idea hits me.

'Tell you what,' I say, 'why don't we go upstairs? To my room, I mean. Then I can order room service and you can have a beer – they won't know who it's for. And we can chat more informally.' I add a little laugh onto the end. It sounds lightly flirtatious. I don't think I mean it that way, not really, but his eyes prick up. He stares at me, a slow smile spreading across his face. 'OK,' he says, standing up straight away.

———

He takes his Coke with him, sipping it in the lift as we journey up to my room on the third floor. A voice inside my head is crying out, screaming at me, *What are you doing?* but I don't let it take hold. I'm going to do it. I'm going to destroy him. There'll be no stage-fright from being in an open public space. It will be just him and me alone in my room.

'Fuuucckkk,' he exclaims when he sees the television. I'd forgotten about it and am surprised myself when I see it sitting there, like a big sheet of black ice in the middle of the cool décor and white bedsheets of its surroundings. 'Does every room come with one of these?' he asks, sitting on the bed, not waiting for an invitation, and reaching for the control.

'No, I bought it earlier,' I say. I watch him try the channels then, realising it isn't hooked up to get a TV signal – try the Netflix button on the remote. He scrolls through the movies, as if genuinely selecting something for us to watch, pausing to read the two-line plot synopses. I'm not sure what to do, so I journey over to the side of the bed and watch him closely, looking at how his olive-tanned skin seems to continue down under his loose T-shirt. *He must sunbathe topless,* I think. *Or have a natural tan all-year round.* Jessica went through a phase of trying to maintain a natural-looking tan, trying moisturisers and sprays, only for it always to turn out looking fake or non-existent. I don't think it came from a natural vanity, more from a cruel comment from a girl at school about how pale she always looked. I refused to allow her to use tanning beds and she maintained that once she'd become an adult and moved out, she would go to a tanning salon every spring and I couldn't stop her. But of course, that will never happen, now. Pulling myself back to the present, I try to bat away these thoughts. 'You can put a movie on if you like, while we wait for the drinks,' I say, remembering I haven't even ordered them yet. 'And what would you like to eat? They should start cooking soon.'

He doesn't take his eye from the screen. 'Er... a cheeseburger? And chips?'

I nod. 'I'm sure they can rustle one of them up.' I'm about to ring down for room service, when Jessica's phone catches my eye. I pick it up and touch the home button on the screen. It lights up and her face, along with mine, and Alec's, arrive in view instantly, glowing and vibrant and alive. And then I hear the zipper.

'Shall we get started?' he says.

I turn around and almost drop the phone in shock. The boy is removing his trousers. He's got them bunched around his knees and, hampered by the skinny cut of the leg, is trying to step out of them. He eventually pulls them off completely and stands there, looking expectantly at me.

'What… what are you doing?' I stammer the words out, probably sounding more scared than I feel. I'm more astonished at his boldness. Did he really think this is what was going to happen?

'What does it look like?' he says, pulling his top off now. His body is toned. Not protein-shake and chemical-supplements toned – something more subtle and natural. He's probably one of those teenagers who can eat all day and never put on a pound, going through their youth not realising how incredibly lucky they are. I was one of those teenagers once. I wish someone had told me that by the time I hit my mid-thirties I'd find it difficult to keep the weight off and that a strict regime of low-sugar diets and gym visits would become a necessity.

He's still staring at me and with a jolt of alarm I see the desire in his eyes. I feel myself going hot. 'I think there's been a… misunderstanding.'

He has his thumbs under the waistband of his underwear, ready to pull them down, but pauses and looks puzzled. 'What? I thought you wanted to?'

I'm still in an awkward position by the side of the bed, clasping onto Jessica's phone so tight, I feel my nails strain against its metal back.

'I… well, aren't I a bit too old for you?'

He laughs. 'Believe me, I've had older.'

I don't know what to make of this and I'm scared to enquire further.

'How old are you, anyway?' he asks.

'I'm forty,' I reply, my voice coming out breathy and whisper-like, my heart beating inside me.

He shrugs, 'Fine by me.'

And he crosses the room in two purposeful strides. Pulls me to him with his large, firm hands, and starts to kiss me. His lips feel strangely cold, and softer than I would have imagined. A few seconds of shock pass and, in the confusion, I feel my mouth open, close to accepting him in. But I don't. 'No!' I try to shout the word, but it comes out muffled. I push him away as hard as I can, but my right hand is now caught up in his and with horror I realise he's trying to drag it down to his groin. 'I said no!' I shove him away so violently, he loses balance and falls back against the wall.

'I'm sorry,' he says immediately, 'I'm really sorry. I got carried away.' He stands there, looking a bit stunned.

'Get out.' I say it in a half-whisper, then begin clawing at him, pushing him towards the door. He goes. Doesn't put up a fight, like I thought he might. He still seems a bit stunned as I usher him through the door and slam it shut, pressing myself up against it, as if he'd try to break it down. He doesn't. But after a moment or two, a voice sounds just above my left ear on the other side of the wood. 'Hey, I'm really, really sorry… I just… Can I get my jeans?'

I take a deep breath, then cross the room, scoop up the clothes, open the door, and quickly throw them out, barely catching a glimpse of him standing there, looking confused and slightly forlorn, before I slam the door.

I think he may have mumbled something – perhaps 'Sorry' – but I don't hear it properly. I go back to the bed and lie down in a small ball, clutching at the covers, pulling them closer. For a moment, I think he must have gone, but then I hear something – the sound of a belt buckle tinkling and a zipper being drawn up. Then the slow thud of him walking away, down the corridor. Leaving me alone.

Chapter Twenty

THE MOTHER

May. Three months after the attack.

I while away the next morning trying not to think about Michael Kelley. I had a difficult, unsettling night, tossing and turning. Each time I moved, I dreamt I could feel someone next to me – a boy's body, with a handsome face, whispering things in my ear. That it was my turn now. He'd taken my daughter, and now he was here to kill me. Take me into his darkness, his evil, quiet midnight whisperings, leading to a place from which I'd never return.

I kill a few hours of the morning by eating a big breakfast platter I order to my room, followed by a third of Agatha Christie's autobiography. By 11.30am the light from my window has grown weak and I have to turn my bedside light on to see the words on the page. By 12.30pm, I get up and have a stretch and journey over to the window. The unusually dull light for midday is in stark contrast to the gorgeous sun and blue skies the South East has been basking in for the past few weeks. The day is still dry, but ominous grey clouds now completely cover the horizon. I don't know if it's the actual temperature or just the sight of the darkening sky, but I can't help shivering slightly and I bend down to fish the cardigan I bought yesterday out of its shopping bag.

When it gets to lunchtime, I realise I can't stand the idea of staying in my room all day. Afraid of where my mind will lead if I sit on my bed, ruminating, I set off downstairs. The old ladies who usually sit near the entrance are absent today, and the lobby feels emptier than usual. I step outside and, although not winter-level freezing, the temperature has certainly dropped a little and there's a closeness to the air that you get before a storm.

'I wouldn't head out without an umbrella and coat, if I were you,' the man at the desk says. 'It looks like it's going to chuck it down.'

I give him a quick smile. 'Oh, I'm sure I'll be fine,' I say, and head out of the main doors. Once outside, and walking down the steps towards the seafront pathway, I begin to think the desk clerk was right. This is probably foolish; it's obviously going to rain, and the wind is already starting to whip my hair up around my eyes. I don't really want to admit defeat straight away, so I decide to do a short circuit up past the seafront, around the side of the apartments and B&Bs to the left of the hotel, then snake back round, hopefully before the first raindrop falls.

About fifteen minutes later, I'm sheltering in an upmarket pub, and the young man who shows me to my table is clearly alarmed at how drenched I am. 'Got caught in the rain,' I say, with a little shrug.

'Are you waiting for someone?' he says, passing me the menu.

I tell him I'm not. 'Just me today,' I say, with a smile, and he shuffles off quickly as if I'd told him I have Ebola.

Halfway through my half roast-chicken, chips, and side salad, my iPhone lets out a little ping. It's a message. From him.

I'm sorry about yesterday. I can't stop thinking about it. Can we meet?

The words more than take me aback; they cause me to leap up, as if I've been physically attacked. Waving at the waiter to tell him I'm fine, I sit back down and look back at the phone, wondering if I imagined it, but I didn't. It's there. An unread message, joining the twenty-five unread messages from Alec. Then another ping sounds and a new message appears before my eyes.

I feel bad I upset you. Please. I'd like to see you.

Though I stay still this time, the words hit me even harder the second time. There it is, plain as day, the ultimatum. The invitation to carry on with this dangerous game I'm playing. The niggling voice inside me is telling me to stop, but another louder part is screaming out for something far harder to resist. Retribution. I type back a reply.

Certainly, we can meet if you'd like. When are you free?

Another ping.

This afternoon? I finish school at 3.15.

I want things to be different this time. Deciding to keep things away from the strange hotel setting, I message back:

I'll come to your house. 4pm.

I turn off my phone after this. I don't want any more discussion, at least not by text.

I race back through the rain to the hotel as soon as I've paid, feeling a little sick when I arrive from running on a full stomach. I see the receptionist raise an eyebrow at my soaked appearance, but he doesn't say anything. I shower, blow dry my hair, apply make-up, and brush my hair. Then, when it gets to 3.40, I gather up my keys and head out of the room.

The weather's transformation is rather astonishing. The dark black clouds that have been threatening to move in throughout the first batch of rain are now dominating the landscape entirely, like a big black rug thrown over the sun. It's like I've slipped into a different world: dark, moody, and dangerous, everything in motion, the trees gusting about, sending leaves falling everywhere.

Downstairs in the lobby, an old lady I haven't seen before is sitting by the fireplace. She smiles at me and says,

'I wouldn't go out there, my dear. It's the worst storm we've seen for years. You could be swept away.'

I smile and tell her I'll be fine and carry on out the door, though by the time I'm down the steps and heading towards the back to the car park, I'm thinking she may have been right. I was foolish to come without even a raincoat after my soaking in the rainfall earlier, let alone an umbrella. Drenched and with my hair flailing around me wildly, I throw myself into the car and try to turn the heating on. Cold air hits me in a blast and I scrabble with the controls to stop it. I decide to get going, hoping the engine will warm up quickly and encourage the heating to get a move on. I'm shivering as I reverse out of the space and head onto the road, climbing the hills away from the seafront and towards the mass of large houses that sprawls along this part of the coast. Before long, I'll be pulling into the road where all those run-down council properties are. One of them home to the Kelley family.

Chapter Twenty-One

THE BOY

After the bomb attack on Piccadilly, I've had trouble focusing. I try my hardest to act casual, confident, to smile, or at least behave as normally as possible, but it's more than difficult. It's like a dull ache is spreading throughout my whole body.

I try not to look at the news on my phone during the days after, but I end up giving in. The main headline hits me hard as soon as I see it. The final death toll has increased to twenty-seven.

The stronger the dull ache inside me gets, the more I press my nails into my thigh, digging deep, letting the discomfort give me strength. I deserve to hurt and when the blood starts to drip into the bath as I'm showering before school, somehow it makes me feel a tiny bit better.

At school, two days after the Piccadilly attacks, Ms Phelps, General Studies teacher and all-round nagging witch, asks us to debate how the growing frequency of terror attacks in Britain could have an effect on public behaviour. She goes round the class, picking on people. Some give vague shrugs; others try. I used to be a tryer. Never loudly or in a way that would make anyone notice me, but just in my own way. Now I don't give a fuck. The girl next to me tells Ms Phelps that hate crime may rise because of it, leading to people feeling scared and religious communities becoming isolated.

'That's a very good point,' Ms Phelps says, nodding. 'This may certainly lead to people exercising their prejudices. They may exercise them through criminal, undemocratic, and violent means, such as hate crimes, as you mentioned, Sayeeda, or they may start voicing opinions through social media or on the TV.'

Ms Phelps has been impressed with Sayeeda, and this isn't a good thing, since it now falls to everyone else to match this or do even better. She eyes me expectantly and I avoid her gaze. She bobs her head, clearly trying to get my attention without actually speaking. Eventually I give in. 'Er... guilt.' It's the first thing that pops into my head and I feel myself turning red as soon as I say it.

'Guilt?' Ms Phelps says, sounding taken aback at first, then she catches on. 'Oh, you mean survivor's guilt?'

I nod. 'Guilty that we've survived.'

She's satisfied with this and I would be glad too if the nausea hadn't returned, along with the need to start scratching at my leg. I've had to curb the habit in class in case someone thinks I'm playing with myself under the desk.

'Very good example. Of course, this frequently can affect family members or friends of the deceased or injured, especially those with them at the time of the attack. This is true for all tragedies, whether they're terrorist attacks or natural disasters or even smaller-scale, but still devastating murders like gang-related knife-crime.'

Ms Phelps likes gang-related knife-crime. Well, I'm sure she doesn't *like* it, but she chooses to talk about it wherever possible ever since she watched a Channel 4 documentary on the subject (which she made us watch clips of, giving a loud running commentary, talking over it, using words like 'disaffected', which made the interviews with reformed thugs rather fucking pointless when we couldn't hear what they were saying). She's gone off on one now, talking about how gangs don't realise that, as soon as one of them carries a knife, they are all putting themselves at risk of prosecution.

I start to stare out of the window and slowly lower my ruler so that it's digging into my lap, pressed up against the wound on my thigh. Nobody notices the tears that follow.

Chapter Twenty-Two

THE MOTHER

December. Six weeks to go.

I've always had a love/hate relationship with parties, and I really wasn't in the mood for a Christmas gathering that evening. It started out fine, with lots of drinks and huddles of people talking, but as the night went on Jessica started acting like a spoilt, moody teenager and Alec spent his whole time pretending not to notice. I didn't approve of this parenting act of his, but I had to admit there was something tempting about the path of least resistance. I, meanwhile, had been trying my best to be both the charming host and the disapproving mother. At one point, irritated by the sulky way the girl was huddled in a corner, I took her phone out of her hand, resulting in a yell of protest.

'You're being antisocial,' I snapped.

'So what? These aren't my friends.' She scowled at me as I stood over her.

'It's you who wanted to have a New Year's Party,' I hissed.

'Yes, when I thought my friends would be at home. Now they've all gone away and I'm the only person in my whole group with a mother who won't let her go to Paris for New Year's Eve.'

'I'm not getting into this again. You know why I don't want you to go.'

'God, you don't want me to go to London because you think I'm going to be blown up! Where *can* I go, Mum? Surely Paris is no different. There's an attack practically all the time now, in nearly every city across Europe. Is every teenager going to be imprisoned until they stop?'

People had started to stare, but Jessica showed no sign of stopping. 'It's like you want there to be a constant crisis so you can keep me shut up in here.' She gestures around at the party going on in her family home as if it were a jail cell full of rats.

'There is still a crisis, Jessica,' I said, trying to keep my voice low, steering her away from our friends the Richmonds, who are showing every sign of eavesdropping. 'They're still under a state of emergency in Paris, Jessica, since the explosion near the Louvre.'

'Yes, yes, I know, we're at Threat Level Critical. Again. And there will be another bombing or massacre and we'll all have our hashtag-pray-for-London moment or pray-for-Paris moment and then it will all go back to normal for a couple of weeks until it happens again. Don't you see, this is our lives now. This *is* normal. So we might as well enjoy what we want to do while it lasts and not let the terrorists win.'

This wasn't the first time we'd had this conversation. And part of me desperately wished I could go along with her attitude: sod the terrorists – let's just carry on with our lives, difficult as it may be. But that was for an adult to decide. Not a teenage girl.

With the quick run of recent terror attacks weighing heavily on the mind of everyone in the country over these past few months, especially the bombing of a Eurostar train at Ebbsfleet, it should have been obvious why I didn't want my only child to hop on a train to Paris with her mates. Much as I admired her spirit and enthusiasm to live her life, she couldn't understand what it was like to fear for your child's safety. She wouldn't find that out until she became a parent herself.

I tried to bring the subject back to the party: 'Go and talk to someone,' I said, casting my eyes over the drinking, laughing guests – or at least, the ones who weren't trying to listen in on our conversation. My eyes then fell to Rob, sitting by the small thin shelving unit holding travel books.

'Talk to your uncle. He could do with one of your lively debates about refugees or the EU or something.'

He acknowledged my words so quickly, I suspected he too had been listening. With a smile, he shuffled his chair over to Jessica.

'It's quite likely you'll be educating me on these matters,' he said. 'I've never been one for politics.'

I smiled at them both, encouragingly, but Jessica avoided eye contact.

'Or,' I continued, in semi-desperation, 'go and talk to Ms Parker. She's just in the dining room – I think your dad's boring her about some book he's read that he thinks should be on the English Literature syllabus.'

Jessica rolled her eyes at this. 'I'm not going to talk to my English teacher at a party at my house. It's weird. Why the hell did you invite her anyway?'

I could feel my patience waning. 'Because she was lovely enough to come to one of my events at the *Radio Times* TV festival at the BFI and we got talking – she's very nice.'

'I know she's nice! She's my bloody teacher.'

'Well go and say hello then.'

'I'm going to bed,' she spat back, getting up out of the low armchair she'd been nestling in and stalked out of the room, pushing past clusters of people.

'I'm sorry,' I said to Rob, once she'd gone. 'Difficult phase. Can I get you another drink?'

Rob accepted more than one extra drink from me as the clock ticked closer to midnight and the big countdown. Jessica hadn't returned, and I didn't bother going looking for her. My mood didn't improve when Alec and I ended up having a muttered argument in the kitchen. He'd been serving people champagne in some scuffed old glasses we keep at the back of the cupboard and never use, and I was trying to show him which ones he should be using. I got so annoyed with him that I decided to step away from the gathering altogether and went out into the garden. It seemed we weren't the only couple having a quiet marital – so too were two of our neighbours who lived a few doors down along Oak Tree Close, Janet and Richard Franklin. Janet was berating her husband in a hushed voice – something about how she was 'sick of it, just sick of it' – and although my interest was piqued, I didn't get to hear the end of the discussion. The two of them noticed me at the same time, their heads swinging almost comically over to where I was standing in the freezing night air.

'Goodness, you both must be cold,' I said, making a show of pulling my cardigan closer to me and shivering.

'Cold?' Janet asked, as if she hadn't ever heard of the word. 'Oh yes, very. Richard, go indoors before you catch a chill.' She spoke to her husband as if he were a child. He didn't seem happy about this, but obeyed, leaving me alone with Janet. I'd only invited her and her husband to be polite; I found her an insufferable busybody, but she'd asked Alec and me over to one of their garden parties in the summer, so I thought it would seem rude not to include them. Over the painful minutes that followed I listened as she tried to make small talk with me, she apparently unaffected by the cold and me doing my best not to let my teeth freely chatter.

'Such a lovely… um… party,' she said, awkwardly.

I replied with a polite smile.

'It's nice to be able to mark Christmas in some way. We were going to go up to Oxford Street and do a bit of shopping, but… well, now we're back to dodging terrorists…' She shook her head. 'Terrible, isn't it? So many awful things in the news this past year.'

After my conversation with Jessica about Paris, this was the last subject I wanted to tackle. 'Yes… I suppose… awful,' I said. With anyone else I'd have been embarrassed about how inarticulate I was being, but Janet didn't seem to notice.

'Does your husband have to go into London every day? Gosh, how you must fear for him on the tube.'

I started to explain that Alec didn't use the tube, but walked from Charing Cross to his office, but I'd barely got three words out before she cut across me. 'Who was that pretty little thing your husband was talking to earlier? Colleague of his? Or… close friend?'

There was something about the little pause before 'close friend' that made my eyes snap to her face with renewed attention. 'What?'

'Very pretty, yes,' Janet said, and there was a cruel glint in her eyes that suggested to me she'd been working up to this little nugget of info. 'I actually thought it was a bit inappropriate, how familiar she was, but I suppose that's what it's like in the world of advertising. I mean, I've seen *Mad Men*, of course, so I have some idea what those high-flying types get up to. I don't know how you stand it.'

So many of Janet's words were so clangingly preposterous, I would been tempted to laugh at her – if she hadn't just hit upon a weak spot. A very sensitive weak spot, one which had been pricked earlier when I too had seen Alec flirting with no fewer than three other women. Any of them could have been the one Janet was referring to with evident relish. I felt a sudden need to get away from her, get away from everyone. With a sick feeling in my stomach that I was giving this awful woman exactly what she was after (proof she'd been right in her suspicions), I told her to excuse me and walked away quickly, back into the house.

I scanned the room, looking for Alec, listening out for his voice, his laugh. I didn't know if I wanted to confront him or just see for myself if he was still embarrassing himself – embarrassing both of us. He was nowhere to be seen.

It was when I tried to climb the stairs that Rob stopped me. 'Caroline, stay down here and have a chat,' he said, trying to steer me away and stop me going upstairs.

'I just need to—'

'No, I think you should stay down here for a bit,' he said. There was something in his face that made me go all shivery again, as if I was still standing in the cold night air. That was when I knew. I pushed past him, marching up the stairs, not caring who saw me acting oddly. I could hear him as soon as I reached the landing. Him and whoever he was with.

The whoever part became clear very soon. The lovely English teacher, Ms Parker, came out of our guest bedroom looking dishevelled and a little flushed. Alec followed a few seconds later in time to see the face-off between me and the terrified-looking young woman, who didn't know what to say. In the end, I didn't have to say anything. Because that was when the screaming started. 'Fuck you! Fuck you!' Jessica was shouting wildly and lashing out, arriving like a ball of fury as if from nowhere. She pushed round me and struck Ms Parker across the face, messing up her recomposed hairstyle, her clip ricocheting off the walls, deep-red folds cascading across her face. Her make-up was smudged and she looked like a state. Jessica stood over her, shrieking like a banshee. 'Get the fuck out my house!' she shouted. Ms Parker shot a terrified glance my way and ran down the stairs, apparently in a bid to escape the fury of my daughter.

'What's going on?'

Rob was at the bottom of the stairs and watched as Ms Parker struggled to pull her coat on, then looked between me and Jessica, the latter trying to get past me, presumably to continue shouting at her teacher.

Jessica didn't answer, nor did she continue her assault on Ms Parker when she reached the bottom of the stairs. As the embarrassed woman fled the house, leaving the front door swinging open behind her, Jessica collapsed on the stairs and cried. Cried and cried and cried. I tried to comfort her. I tried to make her stand, coax her away from the worried onlookers, our friends, our neighbours, people I'd have to see again and feel the burning embarrassment of this whole horrid ordeal. But Jessica couldn't be comforted.

'Her! That… bitch… and him!'

She spluttered as she pointed at her father.

'Do you need any help?' Rob was stepping around anxiously, as if he wanted to help take control of the situation, to clear up his brother's mess, but unsure where to start. Meanwhile, another of our busybody neighbours, Angela Stoke, made her way through the guests and over to me, laying an oh-so-understanding hand on my shoulder. 'Is everything OK, Caroline?'

'Yes!' I snapped at her, and she instantly looked wounded. I tried to soften my voice, 'Thank you, Angela, just… just give me a minute.'

I needed to either get the party back on track or ask them all to leave. I decided on the latter. Mortifying as it was, I needed to be with Jessica rather than faking merriment. Alec was still standing halfway up the stairs, useless and ineffectual, his face still sporting a vague look of shock. I turned to Rob and said, 'Could you take Jessica up to her room? I'll be up in a sec.'

Rob nodded and put his hand out to Jessica, crouched on the bottom step, but she flinched and said, 'Get off me.'

'Jessica, please darling,' I said, trying to sound calm and soothing, but she didn't stay to listen. She picked herself up and ran up the stairs, disappearing off in the direction of her bedroom.

'I'm sorry,' I said to Rob. He gave me a weak smile. 'Don't apologise. She's upset; it's fine. Please… just go.'

I turned round to the guests watching, some staring openly, some milling around in the lounge awkwardly. 'I'm sorry, everyone, for this, but we're going to have to draw the party to a close.'

Of course, that evening wouldn't become the worst night of my life. But it still killed me a little inside.

Chapter Twenty-Three

THE BOY

The wound on my leg is starting to hurt when I walk. It's a good kind of hurt. Reminds me it's always there, and if I forget it's there for a moment, there's always that sting of a reminder as my other thigh rubs up against it when I sit down.

A rumour has been going around the school that the Piccadilly bombers' network started in Southend. It's bollocks, of course – the whole story was started by a local journalist on Twitter who decided to make a connection between a drugs raid in Rochford (cocaine hidden in cuddly unicorns, according to Dexter in my maths class) and the searches that the anti-terrorism cops are doing in East London. Total shit, but even so, everyone's talking about it, with one boy even claiming he could smell gunpowder coming from his mate's neighbour's house. 'They don't even use fucking gunpowder,' I said to him. I was feeling tetchy anyway. The whole thing at Piccadilly had shaken me badly and I was only just about managing to keep a calm and quiet front. Some lunchtimes I went into the toilets and just cried in one of the cubicles, staying in there the whole fifty minutes until the steady flow of boys going in and out stopped. I'd just sit there, letting the tears fall. Sometimes I'd listen to what the other guys were saying. It's a myth that only girls travel to the bathroom in packs. Boys do it too, and most of the time they're talking about the same things – they moan about their parents, their brothers and sisters, their homework, their teachers. They bitch about each other or the member of their group that isn't there. Quite often I just tune out and let everything around me become background noise. I sit there and sway, sometimes scratching at the cut on my leg so it goes red and feels raw for the rest of the day.

At home, the subject of the terror attack in Piccadilly has gone off the radar, not that it was ever really on it. Mum likes to gossip and moan about things going on in the world she doesn't really understand, but never stays on one topic for very long. When she bothers to cook – when she's not getting off her face with drug-dealing pricks in the lounge – she spends the whole time laying into some reality star she 'can't fucking stand', or blaming the government for her 'fucking shit life'. Sometimes I try to escape, but she points at me and tells me how useless I am and to clear the fucking table of all my shit so we can sit down like a proper family for once in our miserable lives. If I'm feeling angry, I tell her all the stuff on the table is her stuff – an ugly mixture of *Hello* magazines, cigarette boxes, bags of weed and stale bourbon biscuits – but usually I don't bother. I'll only end up getting a smack round the head or she'll start crying and disappear off upstairs for hours, leaving the frozen pizza she's thrown into the oven in there until it's full-on cremated.

I had to go through one of her 'breakdown nights' about a week after the Piccadilly attack. My brother was out and Mum didn't have anyone round, but the quiet in the house unnerved me. It's never a good sign. I'd spent most of the evening playing *Minecraft* in my room, but at around 9pm, with my stomach crying out for food, I went out onto the landing and I could just hear her quiet sobs coming from her bedroom.

'Mum,' I said, careful not to make her jump. She flipped off if you made her jump.

She was sitting on her bed, a large joint alight in her hand. She was puffing on it between sobs, coughing slightly with each breath. In her other hand she had a photo frame. I knew which one it was before I got a proper look. Its glass was smashed – clearly she hadn't replaced it since the last time she'd thrown it against the wall. When she saw me, she jerked upright, looking startled, then relaxed back into her slump, her eyes down towards her lap.

'What do you bleeding want?' she muttered, taking a big sniff and dabbing at her nose with the sleeve of her jumper.

'Er... do you need anything?' I asked.

She laughed. A horrible, screeching cackle. There's no smile on her face when she stops though. Just a curled lip and dead, dark eyes, dulled by the weed. 'Need? What do I need? Christ, you've got no fucking idea, have you?' She threw the frame on the floor. The glass finally disintegrated and came away from the wood, the flimsy photo flopping out onto the carpet.

'Pick that up and put it back over there.' She gestured to the chest of draws over in the corner of her room.

I stared at the photo and the frame on the floor. I could just make out his grin filling most of the picture, the light from her cold fluorescent bulb distorting the rest of his features.

She looked at me then, and her curled lip stretched into a sneer. 'What? You scared? Still scared of Daddy?'

I felt the blood rushing to my head, the deep, quickening pounding of it pushing against my cheeks. I was going red, I knew it, but she probably couldn't see. She was only a few puffs of that shit away from passing out. I tried to ignore her as I bent down to pick up the photo, trying not to look at his face. I went and put it in her knickers draw, then went back to pick up the frame and glass. That's when she said, 'Do you miss it?'

I froze, bending down to scoop up the sharp fragments. 'What?'

'All the attention. All the fucking love he poured on you. His two boys. His two little men. You were his favourite though, weren't you? Do you miss all that love? Love I can't give you.'

I stood back up and looked straight at her. 'It wasn't love,' I said. I was trembling, but I got the words out. Then I turned and walked out of the room, leaving the broken glass scattered round the floor. *Let them cut her*, I thought. *Let them rip the soles of her feet to fucking shreds. She deserves it.*

That was nearly a week ago now. Last time I looked in, the glass was still there.

———————————

The storm causes a power cut at school and we are sent home. When I get in, Mum says back in her day they'd have just lit a fucking candle and carried on. I could say I'm surprised to hear she'd been in school long enough to witness a power cut, but don't fancy one of her outbursts.

I've been moping around since I got in, lying on the sofa watching videos on my phone, trying not to let my mind start to spin into upsetting directions. I'm just starting to drift off to sleep for an afternoon doze when I hear a screech. Mum's been going in and out of the kitchen, getting first a cup of tea, the some vodka, then coffee.

'Door!' She screeches at me from over at the kitchen table where she's slumped reading some gossip magazine, her spliff sticking out of the corner of her mouth.

'Didn't you hear me?' she says, when I don't respond. 'Get off fucking Facebook and answer the door.'

'I'm not on fucking Facebook,' I shout back at her. It's true, I wasn't on Facebook. Although of course I've used the Messenger app, I've never liked the idea of sharing stuff on there or Instagram or any of the other sites. I don't even look at what others post about. Like my brother says, most of it's for 'total show-off pricks', especially Instagram.

My mother screams again. 'You're doing my fucking head in these days,' she says, going to get up.

'OK, OK,' I shout, pulling myself off the sofa and going

to the front door. It's a courier delivery – the guy was turning away to leave when he saw me just in time. He hands me a parcel and I sign for it. He turns to go, looking at the broken sofa outside the front and muttering 'Christ' under his breath. I bolt back inside and start to climb stairs.

'Here, hang about, who was that?' Mum calls out. 'Is it my stuff?'

She has a habit of spending the little money we have on bulk batches of make-up and hair stuff, sent over from China via online sellers at a fraction of the cost you'd pay for them in Boots.

I hear the thud of something coming from my brother's room and he sticks his head out. 'What's going on?'

'Nothing,' I say and walk past him into my room.

'Hey, I asked you, is that my stuff?'

'No it's not your fucking stuff,' I shout back at her, and slam the door.

I put the package down on my desk. It's small, and the little wrapped-up parcel inside is even smaller. I pull away the wrapping and take out the metal heart. I thought a heart-shape might be a bit tacky, but it seemed appropriate and the shape was perfect. It barely cost a thing – the next-day postage cost more than the little photo frame itself – but I don't care. I quickly go over to my bed and pull out a shoe box and retrieve the bit of paper I was looking for. I saved it from a copy of the *Daily Mirror* I found at a bus stop. Her face is splashed large across the front, along with other victims of the Stratford attacks. The front-page one is too large for the little heart-shaped frame, but the one inside is just right. I cut it out neatly when I saw it and saved it.

Now, at last, I have something I can do with it. After a bit of snipping at the edges, I have the photo in the perfect shape and inside under the glass covering of the little frame. Jessica's face stares out at me, smiling, almost laughing. I don't know where the photo was taken. I've seen it though, on her Instagram feed, so I presume the paper just took it from there.

I sit and hold the photograph for nearly an hour as the rain and wind smash into my bedroom window. Then, as I wipe away my tears, I pull my pants down and position the frame so that the point of the part that finishes in a spike rests against the red, sore mark on my thigh. And I press. The pain feels white hot and as good as a cold drink on a hot day. It sends shivers through me and I realise I am crying again, but they aren't normal tears. They just slip out of my eyes without the need to properly cry. I keep pressing and pressing until I feel something wet and see the blood dripping down the side of my leg, soaking the grey material of my tracksuit bottoms with a dark red stain. I can't help but cry out a little as I pull the sharp point of the heart out from my skin, seeing the small flap of the wound peel back as I remove the frame and put it on my desk. The pain is both terrifying and welcoming, beckoning me in, offering me something else to focus on instead of the thoughts in my head – or at least it can stop them hurting when I think about them. I sit back and properly cry; sob, like a small child. For a minute, while the pain is running through me, it's like she is here. Like she hasn't died. Like tomorrow I will get a message from her checking we are still on to meet at Stratford station and we'll discuss what we're going to do when we finally meet each other.

I could sit here thinking about her for hours, but a noise pulls me back. It's a shout, coming from the road outside. It sounds like a woman has shrieked, 'Fuck!'

Shouting in the street isn't unusual around here, but I get up and go to have a look outside. It's getting very dark now, even though it isn't yet properly evening, and it takes me a while to see who's made the noise. A woman is in the middle of the street. She's flailing around, trying to pull herself up on the open car door. She must have slipped getting out. I watch her scramble up, her clothes and hair completely soaked. Then she brushes her hair out of her eyes and looks up. Directly at our house.

Chapter Twenty-Four

THE MOTHER

May. Three months after the attack.

The road is being pummelled with rain so hard it looks like a carpet of fireworks. I drive the car faster than I should down the street until I get to his house. The broken sofa is still there, its material clearly soaked through, darkened by the weight of the moisture.

I inch the car carefully into the only spare space, aware it would be tight if any of the neighbours opposite tried to get theirs out, then turn off the ignition and get out. I'm halfway across the road when I remember Jessica's phone. It's in the glove compartment. I turn back and just manage to get my hand under the handle of the car door when the throb of cramp hits my leg, causing me to lose my balance. I grab hold of the door as it swings open, and the change of angle twists me back and I'm sent toppling into the middle of the road, landing on my side with a horrible jolt that I feel reverberate across my body. 'Fuck!' I shout; I can't help myself. The whole thing is so awful. I shouldn't be here. I'm out of my depth. I don't know what I'm doing. I scrabble around, trying to get into a position to pull myself up, my right hand scratching on a small fallen tree branch that's presumably been thrown to the ground by the storm. The wind is still raging, making it hard for me to straighten up, looking towards the house I had planned to enter. Once I'm steady I lunge forward into the car. Eventually I'm in and reaching for the glove compartment. I scoop up Jessica's phone, then pause. Should I just go now? I have a chance. Another chance, one of countless chances I've had to put an end to this strange, dangerous game. But a small voice inside me keeps telling me that to leave now would be giving him another chance. Giving him the permission to carry on living his life as if my daughter never existed, never mattered, never died.

'Are you OK?'

The voice can just about be heard over the roaring wind. I turn round and close the car door. He's standing there. Michael Kelley. I stay completely still and for a while there's just the two of us, standing in the rain. We both must look a sight. He's in a vest-type sports top and grey tracksuit bottoms that are steadily growing darker as the rain hits them. One of his feet has a sock on it, the other is bare. I, on the other hand, am coated in water and dirt from the road. I can see my wrist is bleeding and I'm dimly aware of a leaf stuck in my hair, fluttering in the corner of my vision.

'Yes,' I call back, 'I just tripped.' I stagger towards him. I've done something to my ankle during the fall and feel it protest as I put weight on it and reach his side of the road.

'I've been trying to call you but I just get your voicemail,' he says. He looks happy and worried at the same time, as if he's not quite sure what's going on but is quietly optimistic about where it might lead. 'You should come in. My mum and brother are around, but they shouldn't bother us.'

I nod and allow myself to be led into the house. The scent is the first thing that hits me; a rather nauseating combination of cannabis and tobacco, mixed with something like burnt toast. I feel myself growing stressed immediately. The look of the place doesn't help matters. The stairs, which are so close to the front door there's barely a hallway at all, are coated in a stained, scuffed carpet. The banisters are laden with coats and hoodies and there are shoes – some of them football boots caked in mud – lining the short corridor towards what I presume is the kitchen. I glance into the doorway to my right and see a lounge with an average-size television and tatty-looking sofas.

'Do you want to go and sit down in there and I'll get you some water?' Michael says. 'Then we can go up to my room?'

I nod again and go in, letting myself fall onto the nearest sofa. It's more comfortable than I expected and I feel the pain in my ankle ease a little. Michael goes into the kitchen, which turns out to connect to the lounge as an open-plan affair, and I hear the chink of glasses and the tap going.

'Here,' he says, 'have a drink of this.'

The water does me good – I can feel the fog in my head lifting slightly as I drink, and I'm surprised by how earnestly he is looking at me. This whole thing has rather caught me off guard. His caring, attentive side would be rather sweet to witness if he were any other teenage boy. But I can't let myself be thrown off course this time.

'I can get you a plaster for your wrist,' he says. 'Let's go upstairs to my bedroom. There should be some in the bathroom up there.'

'OK,' I say, setting the water down on the only bit of space on the coffee table. The rest of it is covered with old issues of gossip magazines and cigarettes. I wasn't really sure what to expect when I walked into this place but now I see it, it all feels horribly inevitable. I've spent my life quietly wondering if I'm a snob, like my parents – parents who used to act like they were better than everyone else simply because of the car they drove or the newspapers they read or the ridiculously huge house they owned. My mother used to look down her nose at other people's jobs and hobbies, even though she didn't work herself, and make comments about my friends' 'uncultured music tastes' or tatty clothes. Even our wealthy neighbours didn't escape the firing line, with our jet-ski-owning neighbour – a charming young man named Bernard – being branded as 'common' due to his 'uncouth pursuits' or 'irresponsible wasting of money'. All this from a woman who spent untold amounts of money collecting rare children's toys. Now, looking at the Kelley household and feeling my discomfort and revulsion all too keenly, I wonder if I've absorbed more of my mother's views than I realised.

The upstairs of the house feels even more cramped and untidy than the downstairs. There's stuff everywhere – boxes of junk obscuring walkways. Some of them clearly contain clothes, others stacks of CDs. I even spot two stereo players that are obviously beyond repair stacked on top of each other outside of the bathroom. Why the hell don't they just throw this stuff away? It's like they've just moved in, or were in the process of moving house or having a big clear-out but stopped halfway.

'Turns out we don't have any plasters,' Michael says, coming back out from the bathroom. 'Er… I'm sorry. You can use this though.' He's got a clump of tissues in his hands. I take them, ignoring my concern about the cleanliness of the whole situation, and dab at the blood on my wrist. The scratch is long, but not deep and the bleeding is already stopping.

I follow him into his bedroom and he closes the door. It's quite small, though not as packed with stuff as I would have thought. In fact, compared to the rest of the house, it's borderline minimalist. Just a bed, a chest of drawers, a desk, and what looks like an old office chair, and a little pile of video game magazines in the corner.

'You don't have a window,' I say, looking round. 'I wouldn't cope without a window.'

He shrugs. 'Not much to see around here anyway. It's not like I'm on the seafront, like you in that hotel of yours.'

'It's not my hotel,' I say.

He laughs. 'Yeah, of course, you know what I mean…'

He's been sitting on the bed, but now he gets up and starts pulling at his gym top. I feel myself go tense. *Not this again!*

'I… think I made myself clear before…'

I feel my breath constricting, not out of fear of what he

might do, but more the emotional mountain I'm already struggling to climb.

'It's drenched. I'm just getting a dry one,' he says.

As he rifles around his room for a new T-shirt, I put my hand in my pocket and grip Jessica's phone. Then I straighten up and walk towards him. 'I need to talk to you…' The world moves a little. I'm worried I'm going to lose my balance. Now. Now is the time. I need to say something now. I pull out the phone, and prepare to tell him why I'm there, tell him who I really am. But the movement causes me to sway forward, and a wave of nausea crashes through me. 'I'm going to be sick,' I whisper.

Panic flickers on his face, 'Shit, you OK? Fuck, you've gone, like, grey.'

'Bathroom,' I murmur, and he says some instructions and points. I clatter through the doorway out onto the landing, fearing the vomit will surface before I get there.

I only hear the sound of the shower after I open the door. It swings back to reveal the naked figure of a teenage boy, probably a year or two younger than Michael, standing in the bath, one leg oddly raised so that it's resting on the edge of the tub. The water is pouring down him and he looks up in surprise. The sight roots me to the spot, the feeling of nausea still present but ebbing away, as if the sudden distraction has spared me from its strength. I'm about to say sorry and slam the door when I see a gush of red and realise what the boy's doing. He's got a razor blade in his hand and he's cutting himself. The inside of his leg is red and sore and I see an angry-looking open wound along his inner thigh. Blood is trickling down his leg, carried by the spraying water, and I can't help but gasp. He's frozen in his strange act, and the two of us look each other in the eye.

Eventually he speaks. 'Close the door,' he says. He doesn't shout, he doesn't ask who the hell I am, but says it so urgently and forcefully, I obey him instantly.

I'm gasping for breath on the landing and Michael must have heard me as he comes out of his room, looking confused.

'I'm OK,' I say, trying to regain composure. 'There's... someone in the shower.'

He relaxes. 'Ah, sorry. My dick of a little brother. Utter psycho. Didn't freak you out, did he?'

I raise my hand to my head, feeling the scratch on my wrist sting as the skin stretches across it. I pat the pockets of my trousers with the other hand and feel the comforting bulk of the two iPhones, mine and Jessica's, pressed up against the fabric. 'Only a little. Let's go back to your room.'

'Aren't you going to be sick?'

I give my head a tiny shake and wipe my brow. 'No... I think I'll be fine. I need to talk to you about something.'

Chapter Twenty-Five

THE BOY

I first started using my brother's Facebook page about two months after he stopped using it. He suddenly went off the whole idea of social media altogether, saying it was just for twats and how he couldn't be bothered to pretend his life was any less shit than anyone else's. Instead of deleting his profile, he just deleted the apps off his phone. He never really uses his laptop – a broken old thing that Mum got off a friend – unless it's for schoolwork, so as soon as his phone was cleared of Facebook, he was never bothered by that Messenger-app ping ever again.

I used to have it, but deleted my account soon after joining. I don't like people much, especially the other kids at school, so I couldn't make myself very enthusiastic about a site that made it possible to connect with others. Until I discovered Jessica.

We'd been talking on another web forum for some time, which then led to us talking on the forum's phone app, Circle. But for some reason, it kept messing up on Jessica's phone – she said she wouldn't get my messages, and she asked to befriend me on Facebook instead. I told her I didn't have it and she found it funny:

Red Flag Number 1. Never trust a guy who's not on Facebook.

So I told her I'd use it, but only under my brother's old account. That worried her at first (*Are you sure he doesn't use it?*), but I assured her he honestly didn't, and then changed all the passwords just to make sure. He was now effectively locked out of his own Facebook page and we were free to chat as much as we liked.

It's weird, me talking to you when you have a different name and a different boy as your profile pic.

She said.
I typed back:

I can change it to something like just the sky or a cute dog if you prefer?

She didn't care that much.

It's fine, your brother's kinda cute… Maybe I've picked the wrong Kelley sibling… ;)

I knew she was joking, but it hit a bit of a sore spot. I'd always been conscious of the fact that Michael was notably more attractive than me. I'd mentioned this to one of my only friends at school, Annabelle. She's gay, so I'm not sure she was the best judge, but she did make me feel a little better: 'Evan, you're so handsome, just not in the flashy, surfer-boy way that Michael is. You're intelligent good-looking.' I decided to take this as a compliment.

Jessica and I chatted for ages. About pointless things, mostly, but sometimes we got onto heavy stuff. Jessica would talk to me about her problems and coming to terms with things in her life. She'd complain that her mum was useless, always looked grumpy and was a constant nag, and how her dad always treated her better, talking to her like an adult rather than a naughty child. Until she discovered her dad's habit of shagging other men's wives. I told her she was one up from me by just having two parents, full stop. My mum was useless at many things, too, but a different sort of useless than Jessica's dad seemed to be. My mum was in a different league.

I can't believe she did that, Jessica wrote when I told her what my mother had done to me and my brother when we were very young. What she had let happen under her own roof and how – even though it went on for years, maybe earlier than I can remember – the authorities never knew, never investigated, never did anything but ask why we kept missing school and send letters when we didn't attend. And then it stopped. Very suddenly and without any warning, all of it was over. Dad vanished. Disappeared forever. And we just carried on as if nothing had happened. I only have very vague memories of it, but I can sort of figure out what age I would have been – probably about six or seven.

She must have known. Known all about it. How could she not have?

Jessica was right, of course. She did know.

I replied:

Yeah, she knew But she just didn't care. Or if she did, she just cared about the drugs more.

Chapter Twenty-Six

THE MOTHER

May. Three months after the attack.

I was going to do it. I really was. I was going to confront him with the phone and show him everything – all of Jessica's messages – and then leave him, shocked, not knowing what had just happened. But seeing his brother crouching in the bathroom like that unsettled me and now, when I close the bedroom door, I stay still for a moment and he just stares at me.

'What are you doing?' he says, looking puzzled. *He does puzzled well*, I think. That kind of boyish confusion, as if someone's just spoken a foreign language to him in a very quiet voice.

'I need to show you something.'

He nods. 'Yeah, you said that. What?'

I take a deep breath. 'There's a reason I knew your address. A reason I spoke to you on the seafront. A reason all of this is happening right now.'

He keeps staring back, waiting.

I pause, gathering my thoughts. Just as I'm about to continue, the door knocks me forward and I'm jolted towards Michael, almost falling onto the bed. A woman appears in the room. She looks a fright. Scraggly peroxide-blonde hair with more than an inch of roots showing, skin spotted with blemishes and a large cold-sore cracking around the side of her mouth. Her lips are dry and badly chapped, even though it's summer, and whilst it doesn't look like she's wearing any make-up, the area around her eyes is deep and shadowy, making the rest of her look gaunt and ill. She's dressed in a bright-pink tracksuit, speckled with stains of food and liquids of different shades. In one hand she's clasping what I think at first is a roll-up cigarette then, smelling the smoke coming from it, I realise it's probably something less legal.

'Who the fuck are you?' She more or less screams the words at me and I can't help but flinch, pulling myself further back so that I can sit properly on Michael's bed while this woman bears down upon me like a witch from a fairy tale.

'Mum, get out!' Michael shouts back at her now.

'Holy fucking Christ,' she exclaims as her eyes fall over her son, sitting there in just his boxer shorts. 'Are you two shagging? Here, how *old* is she?'

'Fuck off!' he shouts again, his voice hitting my eardrum hard, and I move away from him now, caught between these two shrieking members of the Kelley family. I just want to go. Get back to my hotel room and burrow under my sheets. I shouldn't have come here.

'Jesus, I thought it was your brother who liked the MILFs. How old are ya?'

I start as I realise she's switched to talking to me.

'Erm, I should go.'

'Yes, you fucking well should. This isn't a bleeding bed and fucking breakfast.'

I scramble to get up and start grabbing around on the floor for my cardigan.

'You are one vicious cunt,' Michael shouts at his mother. 'You do fucking nothing for me and Evan but still manage to butt in whenever we have a little bit of fun or look like we might actually enjoy something. We were only fucking talking, anyhow!'

'Oh leave it out,' his mum sneers back. She grabs the door and opens it wide, gesturing to me. 'Here, out, now! Clear the fuck off.'

I don't wait to be told twice. I bolt out of the room and down the stairs, managing to get my arm tangled in my cardigan as I almost fall against the front door. I can hear Michael calling for me to stop but I keep going.

I'm in the car and reversing out of my parking space within seconds and as I put my foot down on the accelerator and drive way too fast down the road, I see a glimpse of him running out of the house reflected in my wing mirror. He stands there in the rain, watching me drive away. I can't take my eyes off him. He looks so pathetic, standing there in the rain like a lovesick loner in a teen movie.

I'm not sure how I feel. About him, about any of it. It's becoming too much to handle. One big, tangled mess.

And then there's a loud noise. And a lot of pain. And then darkness.

Chapter Twenty-Seven

THE MOTHER

May. Three months after the attack.

Someone's asking for my name. It sounds like I'm back at school. The voice has that strange, patronising quality, as if I'm being told to introduce myself to the rest of the class.

'Can you tell me your name?'

Who is this woman and why does she want me to tell her my name? It's none of her business. And then I feel someone rifling through my pockets and hear another voice:

'Found her purse. Her name's Caroline Byrne.'

What the fuck's some man doing with my purse? I need to get up. But I can't. There's a stabbing pain in my neck that runs all the way down my shoulder and into one of my arms.

'Caroline, can you hear me? My name's Jessica.'

Jessica? It's Jessica? She's here? I think I say it out loud.

'You're here?' I'm pleased I've managed to say it out loud, and I start to cry.

'I'm a paramedic. You've been in a car accident. Are you able to open your eyes for me?'

It's not Jessica. Not *my* Jessica. I stop listening to her now. All I can think of is my Jessica. I see her face flutter before my eyes. I think she's in Spain. It looks like one of our holidays. Maybe Majorca. In the villa. Haven't been to that villa in years. I want to go back there now. Back to the villa and be with Jessica. I need to sleep.

I wake up slowly, then in a big rush. At first there's nothing, no sight, no sound, but I can feel I'm conscious. Then there's a disorientating roar as sound fills my ears. People talking, machines bleeping. Movement. Wheels. The sounds of curtains. There are people near me. I can hear someone saying something that doesn't quite fit: 'I told her she should just book it off as annual leave and go, but you know what she's like. Won't give herself a moment of joy. The trouble is, she's already blown him off before with that wedding reception thing and if she keeps doing it he's just going to lose interest in her.' The woman stops and another woman starts talking and I open my eyes to look at them. 'You see, the trouble is, she's just never willing to put herself first for once and...'

The woman talking has noticed I'm awake. I look up at them, not saying anything. Then they both smile. They're in nurses' uniforms and one of them has a clipboard in her hand. She's much older than me, probably in her fifties, whereas the other barely looks twenty-five.

'Oh, hello dear,' the older one says. 'Lovely of you to join us.' Then she turns to the younger nurse. 'Go and get the doctor, love.'

She moves around the other side of the bed so she's closer to me. 'Can I get you some water?'

I nod, and try to pull myself up, but one of my arms is in a cast and the other feels weak and wobbly.

'Stay still, dear,' the nurse says, and holds the cup to my lips. 'Small sips. There we go. Danielle will be back with the doctor very soon.'

Sure enough, the young nurse is approaching my bed, accompanied by a tall, thin woman with dreadlocks and bright pink glasses. She beams at me and says in a warm, cheerful voice, 'So glad to see you awake, Ms Byrne. Do you mind if I call you Caroline?'

I try to smile in response but feel some sore skin stretch across my lip, and abandon the attempt. 'Caroline's fine,' I say.

'Good. Now, it's important we just go over a few things first, just to check how you're doing. My name is Dr Newton and you're at Southend University Hospital. Do you know why you're here?'

I try to think and a sound flashes through my head, as if I'm hearing it again. A loud smash, then a screech, then another crash. 'A car accident,' I say hoarsely. Dr Newton nods.

'That's right. Do you remember where it was and what you'd been doing up until the moment of the crash?'

I try to think back, but find it more difficult than I expect. I have some images, some scraps of information, but it's as if they're flickering just out of reach, like a movie being shown too far away. 'There was rain. Lots of rain. I was driving down a road. I'm not sure why... why I was there.'

Dr Newton nods and then writes something down. 'OK, Caroline. Things may feel a bit confusing to start with. That's perfectly normal.'

I nod, then wince at the pain.

'Try to remain as still as you can for now. Can I just ask you some questions that may seem a bit random, but I just need to cross them off my list, OK? Can you tell me who the current British Prime Minister is?'

The name arrives immediately and Dr Newton nods.

'And what month we're currently in. I can assure you that you've only been asleep for two days and we're in the same month we were in before the crash.'

I have to think for a moment, then the answer comes to me. 'It's June.'

'Good good. Not that we'd know it, from all the storms.'

Dr Newton seems satisfied and comes over to examine my eyes and does some checks with a light, like an optician.

'What's the last thing you remember before the crash?' she says. I decide I like her voice. It's the most comforting thing I have right now and I don't want her to go away, but I'm struggling to find much to say.

'I don't know. It's all a bit hazy. Very hazy. I just remember rain. And the road being wet. But I'm not sure where I was. Why have I been brought to Southend Hospital? I live in Kent.'

Dr Newton bites her lip a little, then looks down at her clipboard. 'You don't remember coming to Southend?'

Anxiety starts to course through me.

'No, I don't…' I try to control my voice, but it comes out in a cry. 'Why am I here?'

Chapter Twenty-Eight

THE MOTHER

May. Three months after the attack.

I am told to relax, to try not to worry about my memory and that there will be an MRI and various other tests booked to check on my brain function. But the words 'perfectly normal' keep on being said, over and over, as if that makes the whole thing any less frightening. Dr Newton is called away before long to assist with an emergency situation happening on one of the beds down the ward and I am left with Danielle, the young nurse, who explains the meds I am on and the injuries to my arm, wrist, and back. 'Dr Newton will be able to tell you more when she comes back, but I understand it's nothing major. You'll have some aches and pains but she said she's confident you'll heal.'

Of course this is comforting, but the physical damage done to my body hasn't occurred to me until now as a thing I needed to worry about. I'm more worried about why I was in a crash in another county, away from my home and my family.

'Your husband should be back soon. He just drove home to have a shower and change his clothes.'

I feel instantly better. 'He's coming? Was he with me? In the crash? Is he OK?'

Danielle makes calming motions. 'Don't worry, he's fine, he wasn't with you. You were in the car alone. His number was in your emergency contacts on your iPhone.'

Thank God I'd bothered filling out those details. Alec had pestered me about it for weeks before I finally caved. I realise that I'm remembering things now. The conversation I had with Alec about the phone, back in the autumn, when I upgraded to the new model. We were in Bluewater shopping centre and had stopped to have a muffin in the Starbucks there and he kept saying that one day, if I was in an accident, it would be useful to the emergency services if they could have all my details at hand. It could save them hours trying to track down family or discover if I was on any medication that may conflict with whatever treatment they needed to give me.

'I think I need to go back to sleep for a bit,' I say to the nurse, feeling my eyes starting to close of their own accord.

She smiles. 'That's all fine. You need your rest and just listen to your body. The morphine will make you feel drowsy for a bit, but we'll go through your recovery steps once you're feeling more awake.'

I nod, even though I'm only vaguely aware of what she's just said. Sleep carries me off and I go willingly.

It feels like I'm spinning down a long, dark tunnel that's steadily growing lighter and lighter. Then the light is blinding and I wake up and someone is staring at me.

'Hi, darling.'

A man's voice. Alec's voice.

'It's you,' I say, then start crying. I'm not sure why, I'm just so pleased to see him.

'It's me. I've been so worried about you. When they said you'd woken up… God, I can't tell you how relieved I was.'

I gesture to the water with my one working hand and he gets up hurriedly, as if he should have thought about it himself, and helps me take some sips.

'Why am I here?' I say. It's the thing I most want to know above anything else. I don't care about fractures or the degree of bruising or any of the other things I'm sure they're clamouring to tell me. I just want to know what's going on.

'You've had a car accident.'

I tut. I've only been awake minutes and I'm already tutting at him. I try to stop myself feeling annoyed, but the happiness at seeing him is fast being replaced by an all-too-familiar feeling of irritation.

'I know that. I mean, why am I in Southend?'

Alec looks pained and stares at me through his deep, sad eyes. 'Well, I was rather hoping you could tell me that.'

I stare back at him, completely at a loss. 'I didn't tell you I was coming here? You didn't know where I was?'

He shakes his head. 'No. Well, to be completely honest, you told me you were in Australia.'

'What?' I'm completely baffled by this. 'Why the hell would I go to Australia? On my own?'

Alec shrugs. 'To see your mother? At least, that's what I thought.'

'And I didn't want you to come with me?'

He looks awkward again. 'We've been having a few issues. It's not exactly a happy time. You going off to Australia alone would have been a bold step but it would have… made sense. If you wanted a bit of space.'

I rub my eyes with my hand. The tiredness is threatening to return, but I need to stay awake. I need to work out what strange hell I am in.

'That's a whole lot of space. Couples don't need thousands of miles if they need a break.'

Alec's rubbing his eyes now and I think he's crying. 'Caroline, I need to ask you something very important. It's about your memory. Dr Newton says she's aware of some amnesia and that it can happen in major accidents and they'll be able to tell very soon what's causing it, but I need to ask: how far back do you remember? Do you… do you remember what happened to Jessica?'

I stare at him, then down to his trembling knees. And then something clicks and I realise I know what he's talking about. It's all here in my head.

'Jessica's dead,' I say, nodding a little. And he nods too. Then I start crying fully, and he does too and comes close to me and holds me as best he can and we just stay like that for what feels like ages.

'I was worried... I don't think I could bear it if I had to see you go through all that again...' He withdraws from the embrace and gets a pack of tissues out of a rucksack by his feet. He shakes one free of its folds and hands it to me and I dab at my face. After blowing his nose, he straightens up and asks: 'Do you remember how she died? And when?'

I nod, slowly. 'Stratford,' I whisper.

It's strange, I think, how a place name can begin to take on a whole new meaning once an atrocity happens there or something that passes into the public consciousness. Like Columbine, or Amityville.

'Yes,' he says, nodding too, 'Stratford.'

We sit in silence for a moment, then he says, 'The day you left, or the night before, there was another terrorist attack. Do you remember that?'

I shake my head. 'I don't think so. Where was it?'

'There was a bus bombing in central London. ISIS claimed responsibility. It was in Piccadilly Circus – it killed twenty-three people. Both of us were very upset by it. It brought back memories, of course.'

I nod, understanding what he means, but I have no memories of what he describes.

'I knew it had affected you – I could see it. We watched the news together. We'd been arguing and you were already very unhappy – well, we always are – but something about seeing the new attacks on the news must have caused you to react in a fight-or-flight kind of way. I presume that's why you just took off in the night?'

I go to rub my eyes with my right hand then wince as I

feel the joints protest and I remember I can't move it. 'But I don't understand why I said I was in Australia…'

He sighs. 'Maybe it was just to get me to back off. To make sure I didn't follow you. I thought about it, of course. I was even going to drive to the airport, but you made some threats and said you'd make a scene if I did, so I decided it would just be better to let you go. Let you have some space. I think… I think you may have started to hate me, recently. Or maybe before that. And I think I'm to blame…'

I see a few tears slip from his eyes and he dabs at them. I try to shift in my bed to face him properly, but I find my whole body feels limp and reluctant to respond. I'm still extremely groggy from the painkillers they're pumping through me but I try to focus my gaze on Alec's face.

'I'm sorry.'

He smiles. A genuine smile. For a second, he's the kind, beautiful man I married. Or thought I married. Before things started to fall apart. Before our daughter became a pawn in a warped game of his, forever punishing me for having a successful career while he floundered around in the shallows of his. Forever trying to make out I was a bad parent just to make himself feel less insecure. Forever suggesting, in subtle little ways, that it was my fault he cheated, my fault he felt the need to look elsewhere for intimacy, because I wasn't up to the job. And then, amidst that already cluttered collection of issues, he suffered the worst thing a parent can suffer. And became the broken shell he is now – one that walks around shouting and crying and blaming the world for his troubles.

'I can't talk about this now,' I mutter quietly, now trying

to divert my gaze from his tears. 'But I don't... I can't understand why I went to Southend.'

Alec shrugs. 'Didn't you go there as a kid? There's a photo in that old album you found in the loft when we were moving out of the old house. Most of the pics were of you in Saudi, but a few were in England. I could have sworn I saw Southend pier in there. I'm fairly sure you said you had relatives of your father who lived down here.'

I nod. 'Uncle Tom and Auntie Cathy. Both dead now. And I only came a couple of times. There were other places that meant more. Like Somerset; we went there at least three or four times when we visited England. It was my dad's favourite place. Why didn't I go there?'

Alec shrugs again. 'I don't know. But I'm sure you will soon. The doctors are fairly confident your memory will come back. It will happen in bits at first, apparently, but it's very normal after a trauma like you've been through.'

I try to smile in response but I'm scared I'm going to cry again, so I close my eyes and eventually hear Alec tell me I should get some more rest. As if on command, I feel myself drift off. Sleep feels strange and surreal and as I fall deeper into its clutches, an image keeps flicking in and out of my brain.

A teenage boy, in the middle of a road. Standing there in the rain.

Chapter Twenty-Nine

THE BOY

I didn't cut for over a week after that woman walked in on me. I hadn't even meant to then, but I'd got myself so worked up whilst standing under the cold water, I ended up hunting for the old razor Dad used to keep on top of the bathroom cabinet. It felt so good and so bad all at once and I couldn't stop crying once I'd started. Taking the top layer of skin off, where it had begun to start healing at the sides, made my whole leg feel white hot with the pain. And as always, I thought about Jessica as I did it, and her face in my mind looked into my thoughts and she knew this was for her. I kept telling her over and over that this was for her.

I know deep down she wouldn't want me to hurt myself. We talked about self-harming, as the teachers call it, quite a bit sometimes, usually when we were still chatting on the Circle app, but then not as much once I'd moved over to Michael's Facebook account. We'd got to know each other by then. We'd covered a lot of the heavy stuff earlier on. She confessed that, on some nights, when she thought about things – her 'demons' – too much, she used to pinch her arm, really tightly. Sometimes she'd be all bruised in the morning and would have to wear long-sleeve tops. I told her I'd never properly tried. But I did confess other things. Like issues I have about sex. How I sometimes do it with random older women. And how I felt alive when doing it, then awful and confused afterwards. She told me not to worry. How she had her own issues with sex and that it was only natural.

And then, on the day I told her all this, I typed out a reply that made my hands shake. I wanted to say it, to get it out, for it to not be the monster inside my head anymore. I said that sometimes, when I was trying to sleep at night, I would think about those times when Dad would come into my room. His hand over my mouth. Stop my cries getting too loud. I would think about those times and I'd imagine I wasn't me any more, but I was someone else, standing some way away, watching myself as if from someone else's eyes. And that would make the blood rush through me so strongly, I would eventually end up crying, or being sick, and in the morning it would feel like I'd been through it all again. But I couldn't stop. I couldn't stop the thoughts coming at night. And how I'd never be free of them. Her reply made me cry:

> You are free. We're both free. And we'll make memories
> so good, they'll cover up the bad.

I should have told her I loved her then. But I was too upset to think clearly. And I've regretted it every day since.

I don't think I believe in heaven. Or the afterlife. Or ghosts. But Jessica, if I'm wrong about all that, I really hope you can in some way hear what I think and feel. Because I want you to know that, if I could go back in time, I'd change everything. I'd turn up. I'd have been there. And I wouldn't have hidden anything from you. I would tell you all my demons, the same way you told me yours. I would give you all of me. Every piece that's left.

Chapter Thirty

THE MOTHER

May. Three months after the attack.

Alec is starting to unnerve me. As the days go by and my memory starts to return, I remember all of my anger towards him, bit by bit, and each day I wake up feeling more conflicted. He's being kind. Kinder than he's been in a long while. And while I'm trying to find the right way to accept this from my hospital bed, I'm also having to reconcile it with the puzzle that's slowly being built in my head – and how much I hate the picture that's steadily emerging. A picture of both of us caught in deadlock, for years; a stalemate that's truly stale.

I've had MRIs and blood tests and talks with physiotherapists. The upshot is that there's nothing wrong with me, really. Aside from damaged muscles, strains, cuts and bruises, my body is in pretty good shape, including my brain. The memory loss is something they need to keep an eye on, they said, and advised me to keep a diary for the first few weeks in which I should write things as they come back. If things stop coming back, and there are still major gaps, this might be a bad sign and they'll do more tests. I still have check-ups and outpatient appointments to go to, but for now, I'm free to go. And Alec's got everything organised.

'We're going to your hotel, first, to get your things, then we'll drive home,' he says, as he walks me slowly out of the hospital, his hand on my good arm, guiding me as if I'm a child who might lose her way.

'I know,' I say. 'You've told me three times.' I don't mean to sound prickly, but I'm not sure how else to cope with his fussing. The truth is, I've forgotten how to reciprocate kindness.

'I thought you might have forgotten,' he says, then gives a little chuckle, to show it's a joke. *A rather unfunny joke*, I think to myself.

'Well, I'm pleased you're finding my near-death experience so amusing,' I say quietly, meaning it in a semi-humorous way myself.

He sighs. 'You know I didn't mean it like that.'

'It's OK… I didn't either.'

We fall into one of our trademark, tension-filled silences. In the car, we drive through the empty streets, the rain still pouring, hammering a steady thud on the windscreen. I want to ask if it ever stopped raining whilst I was in hospital, but I can't be bothered to croak the words out. My mouth is still so dry and it hurts my back to keep having to take sips of the water bottle Alec's brought. After a while, the silence seems to get too much for him and he tries again to make conversation.

'The hotel has been in touch. They know we're leaving and are just coming to get your things, but they said something about a TV.'

I don't reply. I can't think of anything to say.

'Apparently you've got one. A TV, that is. A very big one. You bought it and bribed a member of staff to let you have it in your room. He's in a lot of trouble, according to the woman on the phone.'

'I'm sorry to hear that,' I murmur.

'So you remember buying the TV?' He sounds hopeful, but also a tiny bit something else, too. Suspicious?

'No.'

He sighs and changes gears as he moves off onto a quieter road, heading downhill. I see signs pointing in the direction of the seafront and before long we're there, gliding along the edge of the road just before the sand, with little huts and restaurants valiantly staying open in spite of the awful weather.

'We can stop and have lunch, if you like?' he says, and without waiting for an answer he swings the car into one of the vacant parking spaces facing the sea. I'm quietly thankful he has his umbrella in his car and I don't protest as he helps me across the road and we walk slowly towards the nearest seafood restaurant.

We're greeted by a smartly dressed middle-aged woman, holding a clipboard in a managerial sort of way. 'Sorry, I hope you haven't been waiting long,' she says, even though we've literally just stepped through the door. She conjures up two menus as if from nowhere and motions us towards the nearest table on the right. 'You're our first customers of the day, so food shouldn't take long. Do you want to peruse the menu or do you know what you're having?'

Usually I'd have told her we need time to decide, but for some reason I can't shake off a strange feeling of vulnerability and nerves, so I just nod and say, 'Large cod and chips, please.' Alec orders the same and two Diet Cokes, and then we sit in silence again watching the miserable weather ruin the seafront view.

'Hello again,' a male voice says. I start out of my daydream and see a young man standing by our table. He's holding our drinks and as he sets them down he beams at me and says, 'Couldn't resist coming for seconds?'

I stare back, baffled, then something stirs in my head. 'I've… I've been here before?'

The young man is still smiling, but something falters in his expression. 'Er… yeah. A few weeks ago. I never forget people's faces.'

Alec's staring from the boy to me then back to the boy like a gormless child, and just to cover the awkwardness I say, 'I'm sorry, of course, I remember now. Thank you very much.' I mean it as a dismissal and reach for my Coke and start drinking. The young man lingers for a few seconds more, then retreats, leaving me with Alec and his confused expression.

'You've been here?' he says.

'Apparently so.'

'And you can't remember?'

'No.'

He shakes his head, 'I don't think they should have let you come out so quickly. If there's still major holes in your memory...'

'What do you want me to do?' I hiss, exasperated. 'Pretend I can remember so you can go on acting like everything is fine? Like we're on some jolly holiday jaunt?' I don't succeed in keeping my voice low and can now see the staff looking over at us.

'I only meant—'

'There's no point me lying in a hospital bed for days on end, exposing myself to MRSA and dire hospital food when I've been medically advised to go home. I'm sorry if I've interrupted your nice little time without me...'

'Nice little time! Are you joking? I've been literally going out of my mind with worry about you, Caroline. Do you know how many times I phoned and texted you? If I hadn't had your rude and rather nasty replies and rebuttals I would have gone to the police. I just wanted you back home.'

'Why? Because home's so fucking fabulous at the moment? Treading on eggshells around each other, wondering who's going to kick off next. Fighting over stupid little things then retreating to our separate rooms to cry into our pillows. You going out to shag other women who seem perversely turned on by the thought of screwing a sad grieving father, when you should be in your own home supporting your own wife? It's no wonder I wanted to get out. We don't *do* anything. We don't *exist* for anything. We just sit around waiting for terrorists to blow up another bus or gun down another load of children, and then we can sit and cry and feel terribly sad. And then nothing changes. So I don't think anyone could really blame me for running away. I can't think why I picked this dump of a place to run off to, but maybe it was just better than the slow suicide of living with you.'

When I've finished, I look into his eyes and for a second think he's going to cry. Then he sniffs and the tears don't fall.

'I'm sorry you feel that way,' he just says simply. Then we sit in silence until the food arrives, him on his phone, probably tapping out emails, blaming his loopy wife for why he's not been in work for days.

Ten minutes later I'm crunching through the batter of my cod when he finally says, 'I want to talk. You say that we don't but I always want to. But you never do.'

I look at him for a beat, then focus back on the chips I'm in the process of stabbing. 'Christ, what a man thing to say.'

'And what's that supposed to mean, exactly?'

'Nothing.'

'It sounded kind of sexist to me. If I'd said you were behaving like a typical woman – which I would never say – you'd be all over me with accusations of misogyny and…'

'You're right, I'm sorry.'

He shrugs, 'I just thought it should work both ways…'

'I said I'm sorry. Do you want it in writing?'

'I thought you'd given that up? Writing, that is.'

'Fuck you.' The words jolt me as I say them. We've never been the sort of couple who swear at each other. I've always tried to keep the peace. Biting back every shriek, every stab of anger I've wanted to hurl at him.

'Why are you getting nasty?' he says, sounding properly hurt.

I feel my eyes flare in anger, my body tensing, all my aches and pains suddenly very present.

'I'm leaving.' I get up, the screech of my chair ear-splitting in the empty restaurant. I snatch his keys from the table.

'Caroline, stop.'

I walk past him, heading for the door. 'You can get a taxi back,' I say.

'What about the hotel? And you can't drive, Caroline.' I ignore him.

'My husband's getting the bill,' I say to the boy by the entrance.

'Caroline, give me back the keys. If you drive off in my car, I swear it, I'll call the police.'

I freeze and turn around to face him. He's standing, still at the table, his phone clasped in his hand, as if brandishing a weapon.

'Oh come off it. Wife steals husband's car? They'd laugh at you. And the doctors said I can start driving as soon as I feel able to perform an emergency stop.'

'Yes, but not in my car.'

'Why the hell not?'

'Because it's a fucking manual!' he shouts.

I stare at him. Then, after a quick glance at the waiter near the door, who is busy looking at his shoes, I walk back to Alec.

'What are you talking about?'

'You can't drive a car with manual transmission, Caroline. You can only drive an automatic. Always have. You only have an automatic licence.'

I stare down at the keys in my hand. Then back at him. 'I forgot,' I say, pathetically. I don't know what it is – the emotion after the row or the realisation I'm trapped, dependent on the sad, weak man I married, or just the cocktail of pain meds I'm on – but I start to cry. Huge, gasping sobs. And I sink to my knees and suddenly there are two members of staff around me and Alec trying to help me up. But I can't get up. I just stay here, lying on the floor, writhing and crying, wishing the ground would open and send everything tumbling into darkness.

Chapter Thirty-One

THE MOTHER

May. Three months after the attack.

I'm out in the pouring rain again. Alec's helping me to the car. I'm sobbing. My clothes are wet and through the blur of tears I can see marks on them – no doubt dirt from the restaurant's floor.

Once I'm in the passenger's seat, I manage to stop crying. 'How far are we from the hotel?' I say in a tiny voice.

'Only a few minutes. Walking distance if it were nice weather and if you hadn't…'

'Hadn't been smashed up, bruised, and broken,' I say bitterly, finishing the sentence for him.

'You're not broken,' he says after a moment.

I don't reply, just watch the dark-grey horizon across the water as we drive down the seafront. The deep-black thunder clouds look so dramatic; it's rather mesmerising, like something apocalyptic or otherworldly. As if the end is coming.

Alec's got the hotel address in his satnav and I glance at the route laid out on the car's built-in screen. We are indeed almost there.

I think, for the first time since I've woken up, about what I might find there. What Alec might find. Clues as to my disappearance? Why I suddenly set off for Southend? I think Alec's clearly hoping for something – he's looking tense now and parks the car on a slope in a road away from the seafront.

'They advised me to park around the back,' Alec says, undoing his seatbelt and, unprompted, helping me with mine. 'They said it would be easier. With the TV.'

'Right,' I say. 'That makes sense.'

'How big is it? Will it fit in the boot? Or should we lay it over the back seats?'

'I don't know, Alec. You know I don't know.' My hand pauses on the door handle. 'Were you just testing me? You were, weren't you? You're suspicious. Of me. You think I'm making all this up? Malingering or something?'

He looks momentarily panicked. 'I haven't said anything of the…'

I pull myself away from him and get out of the car. 'We haven't finished talking about this,' I say, giving him what I hope to be a hard look.

'I didn't think we had,' he mutters.

He leads the way, back down a sloping road towards the seafront and makes a sharp turn. 'I think this is the main entrance,' he says. I don't know why he's sounding so vague – maybe this is his way of trying to get me to answer a question without actually asking one. As if I'd suddenly take control and lead the way, forgetting my attempts to deceive. Is he really that suspicious? Can't he, in the midst of all this, just be prepared to trust me and comfort me and deal with my flaring temper as and when it manifests?

We stop to let a group of elderly women pass us and make our way to reception.

Alec cuts across the young man at the desk, midway through his welcome speech. 'Sorry, we're not guests. Well, she is.' He gestures to me. I don't know what to do, so just smile back at the confused boy. 'It's a bit difficult. I spoke to the duty manager, a woman named Kristen, a couple of days ago. My wife was – is still, sort of – staying here and we've come to collect her things, but we don't have her key.'

'Right, no problem sir,' the young man says. 'If I could just see some ID from your wife.' He looks at me, now. 'Oh, yes, I remember. You're the lady with the TV.'

I hear Alec take his breath in through his nose. I think the thing with the television's pissed him off, somewhat. 'She's the one,' he says in reply. I just stay silent.

'Yes. It's been a bit tricky. Although we, er, always try to help our guests out wherever we can. I think—'

Alec holds up his hand, rather rudely I think. 'I've been through all of this on the phone with your manager. Can we please have a duplicate key to the room so we can take the TV away and get out of your hair? I also need to settle up anything my wife hasn't already paid for. Could you prepare a bill?'

The young man looks a little irked by our presence now, but starts tapping at his computer and within a minute has produced a print-out of the charges, and offers Alec the card machine. Once our debts are paid, another young man is conjured out of nowhere and leads us to the lift and then up to the room.

'I've been told to assist you with the television,' he says. 'Apparently it's very large.'

'So I've heard,' Alec says.

A quick scan of the key card unlocks the room and the man steps back so we can enter first.

'Christ,' says Alec and freezes, causing the young man behind me to bump against my sore shoulder. I step to the side and see what's made him stop.

'I bought *that*?' I say, staring at the sleek black monstrous creature situated opposite the bed. 'That must have cost a fortune.'

'It must have been on your private account. I'd have been notified if it was on the joint one.'

'I must have had some serious Netflixing to do,' I say, then let out a short, weird laugh. Alec turns and looks at me as if I'm insane. The hotel boy is now at my side, looking both awkward and terrified, and the urge to laugh rises in me again. This whole thing is ridiculous.

I walk past Alec and go round to the bedside table and notice with relief an iPhone lightning charger. I plug in my phone and see the Apple logo arrive dimly on the screen. 'I've been doing a lot of reading too, it seems,' I say, resting my phone next to a stack of books. I pick them up, one by one. Light fiction, mostly, along with Agatha Christie's autobiography.

'Shall I take one end of the TV, and you can take the other?' The hotel boy's getting impatient, it seems.

'Sure,' Alec says. He's looking at the books on the bed. He seems to be turning away to return to the TV, but then stops. And goes over to the books again.

'What is it?' I ask. He's staring so intently, as if he's working something out. He doesn't say anything for what feels like years, then finally looks at me, his eyes wide, and says, 'Agatha Christie.'

I don't understand what he's getting at. 'Yes, I know. It's her autobiogra—'

'I can see what it is,' he snaps. Out of the corner of my eye I see the boy jump a little. Alec looks back down at the book, back at me, then his mouth twists into a sneer that isn't like anything I can remember seeing on his face before. It makes him look ugly. And, even in his worst moments, Alec never looks ugly.

'I can't believe you'd do this.'

'Do what?' I say, exasperated. 'What are you on about?'

'She disappeared, didn't she? Agatha Christie. Took off one day and wasn't seen for weeks. Vanished into thin air. And then turned up in some random, godforsaken place, claiming she'd lost her memory.'

I can't do anything but simply stare at him. His meaning hits me hard.

'What's the point of it?' he asked. 'Why are you doing this? Is it to punish me? Surely there are more effective ways of doing that?'

'Alec, you're talking nonsense. I promise you. Utter nonsense.'

'No, Caroline. I've found you out. And you can't stand that, can you?'

'I was in a car crash! I could have died!'

'A pretty convenient car crash, wasn't it? What did you do? Drive into oncoming traffic deliberately? Or are you just a shit driver and when you woke up you took advantage of me, the doctors, everyone around you…'

The hotel boy straightens up, seems to teeter for a moment, then walks out of the room and closes the door. He's had enough of us, apparently.

'If you truly believe that, there's nothing I can say.' I'm aware of the tears bubbling to the surface again.

'Oh no you don't. Don't start getting upset. You're trying to shut down this discussion, trying to distract me. You always were manipulative, spiteful…'

'No, that was *you*. You were manipulative. You were spiteful. You were like it all the time with Jessica, proving to her you were dad of the fucking year while always making out like I was stupid or too busy with work to care. You stole every happy moment and made it yours, shoving me to the sidelines. And do you know what I think it was? Deep-rooted male insecurity!'

Alec's face is a picture of outrage, 'Oh here we go. Here's comes the self-righteous sexism. One dose of concussion and suddenly you wake up a psychiatrist with a hang-up about gender.'

I ignore his jibes and attempts to distract me and warm to my subject, 'No, everything I'm saying is true. You've always had a problem about me earning more money than you. Always felt disempowered, emasculated. I think that's why you go off and sleep with as many people as you can get your hands on, because you can fulfil your warped, backward-looking view of what a man is supposed to be like. And it's why you always made me feel guilty for having a successful career. Because you were *jealous* of it. It's the reason for all the games you'd play, the little digs you'd make sure I'd pick up on, the little asides to Jessica about "busy Mummy never getting things right", the lying to your friends about how important you are in your office and downplaying my achievements. You're weak. That's all you are. Too weak to realise that a *normal* man wouldn't care about all those things.'

He's turned white now. Then he says something very quietly through clenched teeth: 'You disgust me.'

The words hit me. The cruelty of them is startling, dizzying, and, rendered temporarily speechless, I pick up a book from the bed between us and hurl it at him. It hits him on the shoulder, then falls pathetically to the floor.

He looks at the now dog-eared novel, then looks back at me. At first I think he's going to cry, then, when I think there's no room to astonish me further, he does something that has me backing away. He starts undoing his belt.

'What the fuck are you doing?' My voice is getting tight. I'm staring at his moving hands – they're pulling down his zipper now. And his trousers are coming down. He's stepping out of them.

'It's what you want, right? You said I should have been

paying more attention to you. How you've been jealous of all those other women while not getting any yourself.'

'I didn't say that… I didn't mean that I wanted…' I'm still staring at him, transfixed. He's unbuttoned his shirt now, his bare, still well-defined torso coming into view. He casts the shirt aside and kicks away his jeans from around his feet. Then he rounds the bed. Walking towards me. And something in my mind stirs. A weird, rippling sense of déjà vu. I've been here before. In this situation. With a man coming towards me.

'Please,' I whisper. Then I see his face change. The anger has gone. And now he's worried. As if he's just been jolted out of a dream.

'Jesus, Caroline. I'm not… I didn't mean… I wasn't…' He looks around, down at his own unclothed body, apparently ashamed. 'I was just making a point.'

'Consider the point made,' I say, regaining some conviction in my voice.

He sits down on the bed and puts his head in his hands. 'Everything's so fucked up.'

I don't say anything to this as there isn't really anything to argue with. He's right. Everything is so fucked up. I haven't got a cure for it. And there's nothing I can say that will make it any less so.

After a minute of sitting in silence, he gets up and says, 'I need to charge my phone. I've got work emails I need to reply to.'

The unspoken implication is that I wouldn't have any. I don't protest as he walks past me to unplug my phone and attach the cable to his. I wait for him to come back, but he stands by the bedside for some time. Then exclaims, 'What the hell is all this?'

He's looking down at my phone, scrolling through what appears to be a mass of notifications on the home screen. I get up to have a better look and see they're all text messages from an unknown number – or at least one that doesn't have a name next to it in my contacts.

'I don't know,' I say, reaching out for the phone, but he holds it out of my reach.

'Where are you? I'm sorry she chucked you out. She hates me shagging women at home. She's a bitch.' He looks up at me, something glowing in his eyes – something that looks horribly like triumph. 'Care to explain?'

I'm completely dumbfounded. 'I... what? Let me see.'

He steps away again, flicking through more: 'I saw the crash. Are you OK? Then a bit later, Came to hospital again today. Took ages to find you but I did and there was a man sitting by your bed holding your hand. You were talking to him. He your husband?'

I stare at the message. I'm astonished. And then my mind flicks back to that fleeting sense of déjà vu moments ago. And I'm suddenly horrified. Have I had someone in this room? A man? Am I having an affair? 'I don't know what that is,' I say, finally.

'What the actual FUCK, Caroline? Do you think I'm stupid? Do you think this is helping us? What, you decided you'd have a holiday away with some guy, fuck him a few times, blow a load of cash on a five-star hotel, not to mention that monstrosity,' he gesticulates wildly at the television, 'and then what? You're going to leave me? Is that what you want? Us being miserable on our own, rather than miserable together? Christ, say something!'

I'm crying now, shaking my head, mumbling something even I can't understand, until it finally comes out in a rush: 'I'm sorry, I'm so sorry, I don't know…'

'"I don't know" is no longer good enough,' he spits towards me, pacing the room now. 'Fine! If this is what you want, if you NEED dirty weekends away in fucking Essex in order to get your shit together, be my guest. You know what? Stay as long as you like. I was scared, Caroline. First I thought you were missing, then I thought you'd fucking DIED and sat by your hospital bed praying you'd be OK, and now I find out you've been fucking random men…'

'A bit rich, coming from you!' The anger gives me the propulsive energy I need to fight, to claw back some sense of weight in the argument, otherwise I'm just going to end up cowering in tears while he shouts at me.

'Oh that's cheap, even by your standards.' His lip curls in disgust.

'How is it any different? How?'

'So you're admitting it, huh? Is this your confession?'

I glare at him, unable to verbalise what I want to say next, my brain teeming with so many thoughts, I can't get one to the front of the queue quick enough. Then, suddenly, he stays completely still, as if a thought just occurred to him. 'Is it Rob?'

That makes me jump. Physically jump. And he notices. I really don't want to get onto the subject of Alec's brother right now. 'Don't be ridiculous.'

'I'm not being ridiculous. I've always wondered about the two of you.'

'I'm not doing this again, Alec. I'm not getting into your strange sibling jealousy thing…'

He lets out a short laugh. 'Sibling jealousy? Oh here we go again, Caroline the psychotherapist, eh? It's exactly the sort of thing he'd do, too. I've always known he was a cruel bastard deep under. Always wanted what I had as a kid, stole my girlfriends when I was a teenager, did what he wanted with them and made sure I knew about it, taking whatever I owned…'

I raise a hand to stop him. 'If he did all that stuff when he was a teenager, that would have been nearly twenty years ago. Move the fuck on, Alec. And second, you don't *own* me. Women aren't something that can be stolen or kept. You should know that.'

He mutters something that sounds like 'Unbelievable' and then gets up and starts to walk away.

'Where are you going?' I call after him.

'If you want all THIS, you can have it. If you want to cry yourself to sleep miles away from home, then fine, that's your choice. Maybe one day you'll realise that your grief isn't more important than anybody else's. That other people hurt too.' His voice breaks as he finishes his speech, then he marches over to the door, opens it, then leaves, slamming it purposefully behind him.

I collapse onto the bed, but I don't cry, although my eyes are still moist. I just shift into a position that doesn't hurt my arm and listen to the sound of the rain raging against the window, sending a curtain of water splashing across the glass. *Maybe I should stay here,* I think. *I'd be near the hospital, get to see the same doctors. Work out what's going on. Discover why I came here in the first place.*

My thoughts almost start to slip into sleep. Then a loud thump on the door startles me out of them.

'Caroline.'

It's Alec's voice, from outside in the corridor. I don't reply.

'Caroline! Open the fucking door!'

'Why? I thought you were leaving?' I call out to him, aware we must be disturbing – or thoroughly entertaining – any guests spending the day in their rooms.

'Because I left most of my clothes inside your room.'

Again, a stirring occurs in my mind. Like something tripping a very tiny switch. Someone leaving my room in a state of undress. Me opening the door to them. The thought unnerves me a little and I try to shake it off, but the feeling lingers. Taking in a deep breath, I slip slowly off the bed. 'I'm coming,' I say. Then walk over to the door and let him in.

Chapter Thirty-Two

THE MOTHER

Seventeen years to go.

My wedding to Alec was a nice day in many ways, but it would have been a lot better if I hadn't had to deal with his childish insecurities and petty sibling rivalry. We'd opted for The Chesterfield in Mayfair – a venue more expensive than I would have liked but Alec, always weird and illogical about money, seemed to think it made a good statement getting married somewhere so grand. That and the fact that one of his colleagues at the firm he was working at had also got married there a year or two previously and had recommended it. I think the idea of Alec saying, 'That's out of our price range,' probably made him feel rather ill. So The Chesterfield it was, and I just went with it.

After the ceremony, the reception chuntered along like these things do. People pretending to be nice, pretending to be having a great time, when all they really wanted to do was get back home and watch *Brookside*. When the time finally came for the best man's speech, I could see Rob wasn't in the best of moods. He'd accepted the role gracefully and with good humour, although I think he had probably guessed he hadn't been Alec's first choice. He'd wanted a slightly more senior friend from work, hoping it would give his career-ladder aims a boost. I told him that would be embarrassing and on no account was he going to use our wedding to get ahead in his job. We'd had a row, he'd stormed off for a few hours, then when he came back he conceded that his brother would be the more natural choice as a best man.

'Ladies and Gentlemen,' Rob began, 'beautiful women and beautiful men, the latter being just me, of course.' Polite laughter. 'Thank you for joining us to witness the union of these two annoyingly happy people, my dear brother Alec and his enchantress of a wife, Caroline. I could fill this talk with long and painfully embarrassing stories about my dear brother – of course, a best man is contractually obliged to provide some, and I'll be waiting at that table over there afterwards to offer some to anyone who cares to listen for the rest of the night.

'But I didn't want this speech to be like that. It's a very short speech and it has only one anecdote. One day, when he was sixteen, my little bro had girl trouble and came home a bit upset. I tried offering some advice, as I was already a bit of a ladies' man at the tender age of eighteen, but he told me to sod off and the job fell to our late father to cheer him up. He said to him, "Son, throughout your life you'll be faced with many decisions thrown your way by beautiful women. Some will be easy. Some will be hard. But you've always got to think – am I willing to risk everything to make this experience worth it? And I mean your street cred, your money, even your life. If the answer's yes, offer up your heart and give her everything you've got."

'He was a wise man, our dad. I think today, my little brother has found the perfect woman who transcends those warnings and meets those requirements. Alec is right to offer up his heart to Caroline. He's not risking his street cred – he's substantially gaining some, marrying a woman so wonderful. He's not risking his money, since she has more than he has.'

He paused for laughter, and was rewarded. I laughed a little too, just to seem good humoured, but inside my heart gave a little jolt. *Alec won't like this,* I thought to myself. I glanced his way and I could see him looking down at the table in front of us, his eyes cold and stony.

'And, although I'm hoping it won't come to it, I'm sure he'd be the first to offer up his life to save hers. So please, join me in a toast to Caroline and Alec.'

Everyone drank.

It didn't take long for the confrontation to happen. Alec and I had been talking to our next-door neighbours, thanking them for coming along to the wedding, when Rob sidled over.

'Hey, little bro,' he said, patting Alec on the back. 'Did

you well up at my speech?'

Our neighbours smiled calmly, then used the interruption as an opportunity to wander away. Alec said nothing at first. Just pursed his lips and stood next to me. I wasn't sure if he wanted me to take over and defuse the situation, but eventually he spoke, in little more than a whisper:

'Why did you do that?'

I saw Rob's brow crease. 'What do you mean?'

'That story. About Dad. You knew I wouldn't want to hear that.'

He shrugged. 'It was a nice thing he said.'

Alec was getting redder and redder and I worried the whispering was about to turn into shouting. But he carried on talking quietly, with whispers that steadily grew into hisses as he got into his stride: 'You know exactly what I'm talking about. He said that to me after I'd been sent home from school, having it off with a girl behind the bike sheds, without realising that an entire Year 11 boys' football class could see, including two teachers. I was dragged onto the pitch by my collar by one of them, who then lectured me on "the sins of the flesh" and then shamed me by making me "beg the Lord for forgiveness" in front of all those laughing boys.'

Rob laughed. 'Don't blame me for the crazy Catholics of our youth.'

Alec leant forwards and pulled his brother in closer by his tie so that he was a couple of inches from his face. 'You

KNEW I wouldn't want to be reminded of that on my wedding day. You KNEW that would upset me. Imagine if you'd lost your virginity like that. Would you want that to be on your mind shortly before your wedding night? You did it on purpose. You twisted Dad's words so it made it sound like he was giving me heartfelt advice on romance. You did it to wind me up.'

Rob tried a casual laugh, pushing his brother away. 'Not that it worked, of course. Come on, mate, let's not be like this. I'll get you a drink...'

'Yes, let's go outside,' I started to say, feeling I should be doing more to stop this developing into something violent, like one of those soap-opera weddings that end in tears and the blue lights of ambulances. Before I could get any more words out, however, Alec had shoved his brother away and disappeared off. Rob turned to me, clearly a bit rattled. 'Sensitive soul, isn't he?'

I decided to treat the whole thing lightly and just rolled my eyes and laughed a little. Then the two of us went to get more drinks, and I left my new husband to wander around the small hotel garden, pissed off, drunk, and alone.

'Well, for what it's worth, I thought your speech was very sweet,' I said, smiling.

'My pleasure,' he said. I could see him examining my face, as if checking to see if I was upset. I smiled more broadly to show him Alec's behaviour hadn't ruined my day. It was too predictable to do that – I'd known he'd have some kind of strop. I was just glad it was because of something his brother had said and not me.

As if reading my mind, Rob said, 'I'm sorry, it's my fault he's cross. I should have thought about it more, I suppose.'

I made a dismissive gesture with my hand, 'Oh, he often is these days.'

'I thought you guys should be still in the honeymoon mode. Considering you haven't even had the bloody honeymoon?'

I let out a half-laugh, half-sigh. 'Yeah, you'd think so, wouldn't you? But even that seems to be a stress. The flights and hotels and things like that. Anyone would think he was a teacher organising a school trip, not a luxury getaway with the woman he loves.'

He put his hand on my arm. 'Men are dicks. Don't let it get you down.'

He kept his hand there for longer than seemed entirely normal. I glanced around. We'd gravitated towards a quiet corner, with not many guests in sight. A quick scan of those I could see told me eyes were not upon us.

'Well… sometimes I can't help but wonder…' I said, feeling a flutter in my chest. Something like excitement. Or a warning.

'Wonder what?' Rob asked, his eyes holding contact with mine.

'Whether I maybe chose the wrong brother.'

He stared at me and I stared back. Then I laughed.

'I'm joking, of course,' I said, suddenly feeling a rush of panic. A feeling I'd exposed more of myself, my feelings, my insecurities, than I ever meant to.

'Of course,' he said, copying my laughter. But we both knew there wasn't anything funny in what I'd said.

'I'd better get back to Alec. Check he hasn't made a member of the catering staff cry over their wine-pouring skills. See you around, Rob.' Trying to make my smile as natural as I could, I drifted back off towards the main function room, my heart still pounding.

Chapter Thirty-Three

THE BOY

The news of the Piccadilly attacks has filtered out of the main headlines now, even though the threat level is still at 'Critical', meaning they think another attack might be imminent. There's still a couple of stories, but just stuff about the 'ongoing police raids' of houses in Ilford and Barking. They're still worried there's a wider network of terrorists, apparently – that this could be the first of more to come. But for now, other things going on in the world are starting to take top billing.

Previously, I would have thought that would be a good thing. A relief. A break in the madness. I thought the days of me coming home from school and dreading what the news would tell me – though still being unable to look – would stop for a bit. Let me breathe. But today something happens that completely fucks my world. Bigger than anything I could have expected.

ITV'S INSIGHT DOCUMENTARY TO NAME KEY MPs IN CHILD SEX RING

The headline makes me freeze. And then the photograph accompanying it makes everything start to spin. A man, in his forties. Still fit, some girls might say. Still got it. His dark-blond hair hasn't yet gone grey. His face is still thin. His teeth still white. I remember his teeth to this day. How they glinted. How he smiled. How he was one of the few men who didn't wear a mask. I know who he is. I don't have to read his name. Seeing his face is enough. I vomit all over my desk.

I don't know if I passed out or if the world started spinning too fast for me to see. But at last the screen comes back in front of my eyes again and I can read the article. Bits of it.

> Three Conservative MPs and a number of other prominent figures are to be named tonight in an episode of ITV's investigative news and current affairs documentary series *Insight*. The programme, which has reportedly been two years in the making, will allege Nathaniel Jones, MP for North Forrest, Peter Catton, MP for Heldford, and Ernest Kellman, MP for Rowland Park, have participated in the organised sexual abuse of children and committed further sexual offences against other vulnerable people over a number of

years. Mr Kellman, pictured, was seen walking to his
central London home earlier today in the company of
Jacob Wakefield, QC, and two advisors from Allerton &
Quinn Consultancy Services, Millbank. When asked for
a comment, Mr Kellman replied, 'It's all nonsense.'
According to the programme's producers, the report
will include 'details of a wide-reaching paedophile ring,
operating amongst high-profile members of Parliament,
in association with the trafficking of women for sex
and, in the case of two of the MPs and other unnamed
individuals, an alleged assault relating to their days at
Oxford University.'

I'm not able to read any more. The images I've tried for
years to push away are flooding to the front of my mind.
They're everywhere. Every part of my brain is full of that
room and that door – the door that would open to let in
another man. And then another. Until the night ended and
I'd wake up to find Dad driving me home. Telling me not to
talk about the nightmares I'd had. *Real boys don't talk about
nightmares,* he would say. *They just deal with them.*

My eyes flick back to the three men at the top of the
news piece. Three smiling men, with the photos taken from
event shots or TV debates. I couldn't swear to seeing two of
them. I might have done. There were so many of them, and
usually they covered their faces. But the blond man... his
face has always been with me. And now I know I didn't
imagine it.

After a few hours of sitting there, my old laptop finally

going into sleep-mode, my back aching from being in one position for a long time, my mind does finally turn to her. Jessica. Because I know, if she were alive, the first thing I would have done would be to message her. Send her the link to the news article. Tell her everything.

Chapter Thirty-Four

THE MOTHER

May. Three months after the attack.

'Are you sure you want to do this?' Alec asks as he hands me a sports bag filled with things from the wreckage of my car – some jumpers, a couple of magazines, some comfortable shoes. I zip up the top of it to protect the contents from the rain, now spitting but threatening to start again.

'I want to stay,' I say. 'I need to clear my head. Recover in peace. Find out why… find out a few things for myself. I think it's better for the both of us, don't you?'

He looks down at the floor. His expression is sad, troubled. Hurt. 'I didn't mean all the things I said. I think we both lost it a bit in there… and I don't think you should be on your own after your accident. What if you have a relapse?'

I hold up a hand. 'Please, Alec. Just go. I'll be fine. And

if I have any concerns, I'll get a taxi to the hospital or phone for help.'

He looks unimpressed. Then nods. 'Your room is paid for for another week. If you still want to stay after then, well…'

'I'll pay for it from then on.'

He grimaces. 'I wasn't talking about the money. I meant if you want to come home.'

I look at my shoes.

'OK. Well… bye.' He goes to kiss me, then stops and pulls himself back. 'Oh, there's another phone in the bag. It was in the car.'

'But… mine still works. I don't need another one.'

'I know yours still works. I think we've covered that,' he snaps. Then he shakes his head. 'It's not a new phone. I think it's Jessica's. You had it with you in the crash.'

Then he turns on his heel and walks away. Back down the rain-drenched street, away from the hotel.

I stand and watch him go, lingering a while after he's disappeared from sight. Then the rain starts up properly again, announcing its arrival with a cacophony of wind and water, threatening to destabilise me from my position on the hotel steps. I pull my cardigan close around me and walk back inside.

'I'd like food in my room tonight,' I tell the man in the desk. 'Is there a menu I can take up with me to choose from?'

He smiles. 'No problems, there should be a room service menu in the drawer of the desk in your room, but if there's anything else you'd like that's not on there, do just call the number and I'm sure the kitchen will be able to accommodate most things.'

'Thank you,' I say, returning his smile, and take the lift back up to my floor.

Inside my room, I put the bag on the bed and take out the clothes, along with the other bags of belongings that had been packed up for me, ready to take home. I like the room, I decide. Although not homely, it feels comfortable and clean; a nice space for me to get my thoughts in order, reboot, reset, put some distance between me and the horror of the accident.

When I get to the bottom of the bag, my fingers touch something smooth and solid. I take it out. It's an iPhone. The one Alec mentioned. Jessica's iPhone. I try to turn it on but the screen stays blank. I fish around in one of the other bags, presuming I'd have brought a phone charger with me. I'm correct – there are two. I plug both into the sockets next to the bed and watch them for a few minutes until the Apple logos appear on the screens. Jessica's phone starts up properly first and it takes me a moment to suss out the passcode – her date of birth – and then start scrolling through her photos. Pictures of her friends, shots clearly intended for Instagram of blueberry pancakes and smiling friends.

I lock the phone once more and, finally, take a deep breath and turn to mine. On the screen I see the cascade of messages, some from a few friends who have heard about the crash, a couple from O2 telling me about a soon-expiring offer to get priority Beyoncé tickets (as if I cared), and a whole host of others from that number I don't recognise.

> I saw the crash. Are you OK? I didn't talk to the police in case I got you in trouble but I saw them and the ambulance and the medic people.

> Going to sneak out tomorrow and come to the hospital. Please just message – say you're OK.

> Am at hospital – can't find you. This is stressing me. Please text.

> Came to hospital again today. Took ages to find you but I did and there was a man sitting by your bed holding your hand. You were talking to him. He your husband?

> OK, I get that you probably don't want to talk anymore. But I really want to see you.

> Please. Answer me.

I stare at the messages, first completely baffled, then with a mounting sense of pure horror. I was having an affair. Here. In this hotel.

For a minute, my heart beats fast against my chest as I accept my own infidelity. Then, slowly, steadily, things seem to fall into place. Alec and I weren't happy. The Piccadilly terrorist attack, as he'd described, must have triggered some emotional response, sent my post-trauma panic senses sky-rocketing. I must have just taken leave of my senses, come down here, picked up a man in a bar somewhere, maybe even another guest in this very hotel, and shagged him. And, by the looks of things, he's got quite attached. Very attached. Borderline desperate, some could say. Although, to be fair, if he witnessed the crash, he too must be pretty shaken up. But why didn't he come to the hospital with me? Why didn't he run to the scene? Surely any normal adult, under those circumstances, would throw caution to the wind and rush to help?

I ponder this for a long time. After a while my shoulder starts to ache and my stomach is twisting up inside of me. I need food and rest. I dial the number as the man on the desk instructed and ask for a lasagne and chips. I don't bother to check the menu but the woman at the other end seems unfazed and simply checks if I want it to contain meat or vegetables.

When the food arrives, I plug the TV back into the wall and turn it on, startled by the sheer brilliance of the picture as I try out content on the in-built, and already signed-in, Netflix and Amazon apps. Halfway through both the lasagne and a documentary about the survival skills of seals and otters, a thought hits me like a dart, slicing through my sluggish, crowded mind. I pause the film, put the dish on the bedside table and grab my phone.

I saw the crash.

It's there. The key to everything. Whoever this man is, whoever I was having an affair with, was standing nearby. Or looking out of a window, maybe. I can't remember the name of the street where the accident occurred, but I understand, from my conversations with Alec, the hospital staff and, briefly, the police, that it was a suburban street, away from the main seafront. Although it isn't definite, it seems very possible: the man must live on or around that street.

I turn off the TV, take the lasagne on its tray and place it outside the door, then start getting ready for bed. I'll need my strength for tomorrow.

Chapter Thirty-Five

THE BOY

Michael's been acting strangely ever since that woman walked out of our house. Or rather, got thrown out by Mum. She's been off her head most days since, which usually means Michael keeps out of the house. Part of me thinks it upsets him seeing her completely pissed or high, but the other part of me thinks he'd prefer to be out of shouting distance so he doesn't have to clear up her sick if she doesn't make it to the bathroom in time.

I don't really spend time with his mates – they leave me alone most of the time – but even I have missed seeing Nav and Asher hanging around outside either before or after school, waiting for him. Nav asked me at school if Michael really has flu – apparently the story he's told people to cover his absence. I didn't know what to say, so just nodded. One of the few times I've seen Michael in the kitchen getting food, he's looked as if he's about to cry, or has been crying.

'What's wrong?' I say one evening, when he drops his Coco Pops, scattering them across the floor.

'Nothing,' he snaps.

I watch him as he tries to sweep them under the dishwasher with his foot, then he gives up and shakes what's left into the bowl on the counter top. 'Is this about that woman?' I don't know how, but for some reason, I know before I say the sentence that it's likely to make him flip. And he does. With a few strides, he's got his strong hands at my throat, pushing me up against the wall. 'Don't. Talk. About. It.'

I should stop, quit before he hits me properly, but I gabble out, 'Was she in the crash?'

He presses tighter on me then, as if he's going to strangle me. Then I see his face. The tears coming pouring down his cheeks. And he cries. It's the first time I can remember him crying since he was, like, ten. He's properly crying, and he's loosening his grip and I'm sliding back down the wall and, weirdest of all, into his arms. He just falls onto me. And without thinking about it, I hug him. I hold him in my arms, clutching him tight around his shoulders, and let him cry into me, as if I was the older brother and he was the little one.

After about a minute or two passes, I'm not quite sure where to go from here. I'm pleased he's not trying to hurt me, but I'm not used to this kind of closeness with him. But he's still crying, and doesn't look like he's going to stop. Something tells me this isn't just about some random woman he's shagging. So I ask him.

'Is this about Dad?'

The reaction is instant. He pulls away from me, out of the hug and pushes me backwards. 'What? Why you saying that?'

'Because…' I'm trying to get my thoughts together but they're starting to swim around my head, 'because when I'm upset… usually, in the end, it's got something to do with Dad. Not always. But usually.'

He sniffs and wipes his eyes roughly with the back of his hand. 'It's just… she was going to tell me something… something she seemed to think was… like… important. And then that bitch came in and threw her out… no reason to… and I can't… I just… I just think, why didn't she do that when I really needed her to? When *we* really needed her to? When he used to lead those men up the stairs to our bedrooms… Or take us out to the van… while we were sleeping… to some horrible, horrible, place… Why didn't she fucking come in screaming and shrieking then? She just let it fucking happen.'

He's ranting, shouting and crying at the same time, and I don't know what to do. I've never seen him like this, as if he's close to losing control, as if all the torment I know must be there is rushing to the surface.

I reach out to try and put my hand on his shoulder, but he flinches and pulls it away, but I try again, desperate to calm him down. He's stronger than me, but he's not putting up much of a fight, and after a few attempts I've got him again in my arms, and he's back sobbing into my shoulder. 'It's going to be OK,' I say, because it's what people say in films when someone's crying on them. He doesn't respond. He doesn't need to. We both know it's a lie.

Once he's all cried out he coughs a few times and pulls himself away from me, gentler this time. Then something makes him stop. He looks down towards his legs and says, 'What the fuck?'

I look down. There's a dark, reddish-brown mark on the light grey of his tracksuit bottoms, just above the right knee. Then he looks over at my legs and I hear him take his breath in. 'Christ... you're bleeding... what *is* that?'

I'd been cutting upstairs earlier in the evening when I'd got back from school, before having one of my half-sleep, half-nightmare naps. I'd pulled on a T-shirt and boxers to go downstairs. I should have chosen different clothes. The white material of the left leg of my boxer briefs is a shocking red around the side of my crotch, and there's a large trail of blood dripping down the inside of my thigh, down past my knee. I can tell immediately that the cut's opened up. And now I can see the blood, I can also feel the pain. The throbbing, aching sting of it, coursing through the whole area, through my leg and up into my stomach, as if I'm becoming inflamed, zone by zone, until eventually all of me will be ablaze with agony.

'That's... not fucking normal.' Michael's backing away as if scared.

'I'm... it's... it's nothing. Just a cut.'

'Pretty big cut. You should put a plaster on it or something. Let me see...'

'No!' I shout. I do the only thing I can think of: I run. Out of the kitchen, away from my brother, and up the stairs. I only stop once I'm in the bathroom with the shower running. I don't bother getting undressed, I don't bother waiting until the water has heated up, I just climb into the bath and let it fall around me. Drop by drop, it soaks into my clothes, coats my skin and, slowly, I watch the blood fall off into the stream of water at the bottom of the bath and float towards the plug-hole.

Now it's my turn to cry. And I don't have anyone to hold onto.

Chapter Thirty-Six

THE MOTHER

May. Three months after the attack.

I sleep better than I've done in days. Compared to a hospital, the noises of a hotel are barely noticeable. I decide to go down to breakfast so I shower gingerly, taking care with my movements so as not to cause the throbbing pain in my joints to worsen. I grab the pharmacy bag of medications and then journey down in the lift to the foyer. A member of hotel staff greets me on the way into the restaurant quarter and I'm shown to a small table and told I can either order something off the menu or help myself to the continental breakfast buffet on the other side of the room. I opt for the buffet and pile my plate high with toast, some cold meats and cheese and an apple, along with a large glass of fruit juice. I didn't realise how starving I was until I smelt the food and as soon as I'm back at my table I'm wolfing the food down as if I haven't eaten in years. Hospital food does this to you, apparently.

Once my stomach is no longer empty, I rifle around in the medication boxes for the pain meds and begin popping the blister packs. I can see members of staff looking at me, but I don't care how it looks. I'm sure they probably think these are pills to keep me stable, rather than various forms of codeine, ibuprofen, and paracetamol. I had hoped for something stronger, but the doctor didn't seem to think it was necessary. Once my plate is cleared, I take out my phone and send the text I've been quietly composing in my mind ever since I woke up.

Hi. I'm out of the hospital and want to meet. Is there somewhere nearby that would suit?

I'm aware the phrasing sounds distant and probably a bit formal, but I want to keep it plain and neutral enough until I find out who's at the other end of the number. A reply comes back almost instantly.

YES. NOW? At the hotel? I'm on my way.

Shit, I think. Maybe I should have made it clear I'd prefer to meet away from here. This already feels like my sanctuary, my place of shelter. Although one glimpse outside is enough to make me glad about not having to brave the elements – the sky is the darkest I've ever seen it for nine in the morning. It looks more like night rather than day and the horizon shows no sign of brightening.

I'm standing by the entrance to the hotel when someone takes me by surprise. He must have come round the side of the building, like Alec and I had, from where the car park loops round to the back. It's a teenage boy – he can only be sixteen or seventeen at the most – and his face lights up when he sees me. I give him a weak smile and move to the side to let him pass, but he stops in front of me. He seems to be waiting for me to say something, but I just stare at him.

'God, I'm glad you're here – was worried you wouldn't show.' He embraces me, his arms going round my shoulders, his hand resting against one of the large bruises on my shoulder, and I wince and pull myself away. I bump back against the concrete of the hotel wall and I jar my hurt arm, the pain sending crackles through my vision, my head spinning. I can't speak for a few seconds, only gasp, trying to steady myself. The boy is evidently alarmed, trying to help me get my balance back. 'Ah fuck, I'm sorry,' he says. 'Did I hurt you? Do you have, like, injuries?'

I don't know what to say, so I just nod. My tears can't be held back any longer – they start to run freely down my face, a rush of pain and confusion.

'Oh God, don't get upset. I'm sorry if I hurt you. I'm really sorry.'

'It's OK,' I manage to whisper.

'I've been so worried. I can't sleep. I can't concentrate at school. I can't do anything.'

With heart-sinking dread, I start to piece together what's going on here. It can't be true. It can't be. This boy is… well, a boy. Almost a child. Can barely be older than Jessica. He can't know me. I wouldn't… I just… couldn't. Could I?

'Shall we go up to your room? Not to do anything. Just to talk. I want to talk.'

I look at him, baffled. 'Talk? What about?'

It's his turn to cry now. 'Are you angry with me? I'm sorry I didn't come to you – when that car smashed into you. I was scared. I was really scared. I just ran away, went back to my room, hid under my duvet. I thought you might be dead, but then I came to the hospital and there was a man there, holding your hand and I didn't... I didn't want to make things, I don't know, bad for you...'

I'm still staring at him. Unable to talk. Unable to really comprehend what is happening.

'If I fucked up, I'm sorry. The guy just looked so unhappy, I thought it would make things awkward. And you might not like it. You seemed pretty mad when my mum chucked you out my bedroom.'

I can't help it. Something explodes out of me, a laugh and a shriek and a sob, all at the same time. The ridiculousness of it. The absurdity of what he's saying is so outrageous to me, my mind is rejecting it as a fantasy. It can't possibly hold an ounce of truth.

'I can't do this,' I say, tears obscuring my vision, my body starting to shake.

'Please, just wait...'

'No. Stop.' I dodge his attempts to embrace me again. 'Whatever is going on here... it isn't. Or at least, isn't any longer. I could be your mother. Christ, I'm probably the same age as your mum, or older!'

He nods. 'A bit. But it doesn't matter.'

'Fuck!' I shout, then freeze. A family – a man, a woman, and a little boy – are standing at the top of the steps to the hotel, staring at the scene unfolding before them, my shrieked expletive still swirling around us, as if caught in the howl of the wind. Eventually, the little boy says, 'Mummy, why's that lady crying? I don't like it.'

It jolts them out of their statue-like state, and the mother pulls the child close, as if I'm a danger to him and might suddenly attack, and says, 'Be quiet, Jimmy,' and they edge round us and disappear off into the entrance to the hotel.

'We can't stay here. I can't stay here with you.' I too am turning to go back into the hotel, away from all this weirdness, but he stands in my way and blocks my route. 'I'm not letting you go again. I'll always be wondering.'

'Wondering what?' I say, starting to lose my patience. He's acting like one of those lovesick teenagers in those silly books for fourteen-year-old girls. His words sound odd, even slightly comical, in his Essex accent and I realise how different I must sound to him, my once broad Australian vowels now more or less softened and ironed out after many years living in suburban Kent.

'What you wanted to speak to me about. Can't we go for a walk, or something?'

I stare around us at the stormy weather and gape at him.

'Yeah, I know it's not great, but if you don't want to go back into the hotel, we need to go somewhere.'

'I do want to go back into the hotel, just not with you.'

'Please, this has been killing me for ages now. I kept thinking you'd die and I'd never know. You knew my address. You came to see me. You wanted to tell me something. What is it? Please!' He's starting to shout now. Inside the hotel I see the family who just passed us talking to the receptionists. They're all craning their necks to look at us.

'Fine,' I hiss. 'Let's go for a walk.'

I march away from him, down the steps, wincing with every stride as the pain in my shoulder throbs angrily. I just need to get him away from the hotel, away from my safe haven, and try to take control of the situation. He may be shockingly young. He may say things that will upset me and anger me and disgust me. But he may also be the key to working out how I got into this mess in the first place.

Chapter Thirty-Seven

THE MOTHER

May. Three months after the attack.

When I was a little girl in Saudi Arabia, my father spent his time living the high life in the oil industry, profiting from the rising prices in the trade and doing business deals that always sounded both complex and boring. My mum and I were left to amuse ourselves, with me going to an international school for a short while, being taught by a loud, irritating American woman, while my mum drifted around whatever hotel or flat we were staying in at the time. But sometimes, when my dad got home from work, we would journey to Half Moon Bay near Khobar and I'd run along the beach, scooping up the silk-like sand, enjoying the feel of it moistening my fingers. I don't remember anything very fun about my early years there, but the beach trips stick in my mind. I was free. Joyful. Content. My parents around me, not arguing – or at least not in earshot. And then it all went to pot. We moved to Australia. Our local beaches were full of shrieking families and teenagers smoking. I could no longer be the girl running free along a stretching coastline. I was an anxious, cynical, borderline-depressed young teenager, living in an alienatingly large house that didn't feel like home, miles away from anything very interesting, with two parents who hated each other.

Walking along the Southend coastline now, I think back to my childhood moments of beach freedom. The wonderful rush of the air gushing through my hair, like it is now, although the wind in Saudi was notably warmer than it is here in Essex. And, back then, I didn't have a teenage boy following me like a lost dog.

'Please, can we just stop and talk,' he says, keeping up the pace next to me. I slow down, though more from the pain rather than out of respect for him. I didn't want to talk, but I knew I needed to.

'Let's cross the road and go into that little thing over there,' I say, catching my breath. 'I don't know what it is, a bus stop?'

He shrugs. 'I dunno. Never seen a bus there.'

I don't reply, or even wait for him, just cross the empty road and walk towards the alcove built into the side of the hill overlooking the seafront. The white walls that look like they haven't seen any fresh paint since the 70s are cracked and stained, and spiderwebs loop around the upper reaches. At any other time I would feel extremely uncomfortable, but right now I am already so far out of my comfort zone, I barely register it.

The boy settles next to me and I try to look at him but

my shoulder aches so much, I settle for facing straight ahead at the sea.

'Look,' I say, trying to choose my words carefully, deciding how much I should tell him. 'The crash sort of… confused me. I forgot some things. And I need your help.'

I feel him stir beside me, his hoodie brushing against me. I can smell his cheap aftershave. It probably isn't even aftershave, just some supermarket Lynx knockoff – extremely sweet. Almost nauseating. Could I ever have had sex with a boy like this?

'OK. What sort of things do you want to know?'

I sigh. 'Well, the point of me staying here is for me to try to work out what's going on – what I've done or been doing and, to be completely honest, the arrival of you kind of horrifies me… I expected at least someone in their thirties.'

His feet start scraping on the ground. He's tensing. 'What? You don't… you don't remember me?'

His face is a mask of horror. His sharp-cut jaw is pulled inward, his eyes glaring at me.

I decide to just come out and say it. 'I don't, no. I don't really remember anything.'

'What… nothing?'

'I don't even know your name.'

He looks at the floor. 'It's Michael,' he says quietly. Then his face contorts. For a minute, I think he's going to start shouting. Then he bursts into tears. I am completely at a loss what to do. I just sit there and stare at him as he cries in front of me. Then the mother in me takes over. I take him in my arms and he's sobbing into my hurt shoulder but I don't care. I feel how lost he is. How confused he is. And I know how he feels.

'Let's… let's just sit down,' I say, and we settle back on the narrow seats and he sniffs and inhales. I hand him a tissue and he blows his nose enthusiastically and sniffs some more.

'You can keep that,' I say. 'And stop crying. Come on. We'll work this out. I realise this is probably a bit strange for you. I can assure you it is for me.'

He nods, the tears still running. 'It's not strange, it's great. Or it was until you were in that crash and I ran off like a fucking child.'

I hold up my hands. 'Don't blame yourself, honestly. It must have been horrifying. You shouldn't have had to see that. And I didn't die. Things could have been a lot worse.'

'It's just… Every day is just so fucking shit, all the time. Nothing ever fucking changes. And then suddenly you tell me I could do modelling, but you're clearly coming on to me and invite me over, and you get angry… and then you tell me you've come to tell me something, like it's something important… and I think, for a moment, maybe this is it…'

'It?'

He sniffs and nods, 'Yeah. It. The moment it all changes. Like, you tell me something that changes everything for ever?'

'What, did you think I was there to tell you you'd won the lottery or something?'

He lets out a small laugh, 'Not likely – never bought a ticket. But I could tell it was something really important.

The way you said it. The way you looked at me. I think about you all day every day. And I feel shit about it all, as I left you and you could have died.'

'Right,' I say, buying time as I digest this. His reference to modelling also puzzles me. Did I lie to this kid, tell him I was some kind of modelling scout, merely to get him into bed? The extent of my psychological breakdown before my brush with death is fast becoming so bizarre, it feels like the plot of one of my more outlandish screenplays. Key words of what he's told me are sinking in. And what also strikes me, crucially, is the absence of some words.

'Michael. Please tell me, honestly: did we have sex?'

His eyes meet mine and I see sadness and worry deep within them, as if it's something physical, something you can point to. 'No. I think I fucked up. I started things way too soon. You seemed… I don't know… you seemed put off. Each time I thought you wanted it, you then seemed scared or angry.'

Relief floods through me. I'm not entirely sure what difference this makes or if it helps get to the bottom of what's going on here, but at least I haven't done that. At least I haven't stepped over that personal moral line.

'Don't feel bad about the crash,' I say gently. 'I told you, it isn't your fault. Any of this. I clearly just… went a bit mad. Acted out. Lost it a bit. I shouldn't have put you in that position.' I'm trying to make sense of it as I say it, aware of the innocent, slightly adorable, young face staring at me. 'There's something I should tell you. I don't know if I told you this before… before I was in hospital… I can't remember…' I take a deep breath and then say it, as calmly and slowly as I can. 'My daughter died earlier this year. It was... the worst thing. The very worst thing a parent could go through.'

He looks bewildered and his eyes widen a little. He's probably realising how far out of his depth he's been swimming all this time. I can't have told him this before.

'I'm... I'm sorry,' he says, quietly. 'How did she die?'

'She was murdered.'

He's pressing his knuckles against each other, apparently a nervous habit. If he were older or tougher looking, one would expect them to make cracking sounds, but the small bones in his hands don't make a sound. 'Fuck. That's... that's really bad.'

His response is rather pathetic, and on another day I might have flared up. Reminded him that being banned from driving for life due to speeding is 'really bad', or a conviction for high-level fraud is 'really bad', or even beating someone up so they have to press charges for assault would count as 'really bad', but having one's daughter gunned down by a masked sociopath wasn't 'really bad', it was earth-shatteringly cataclysmic. A transcendental avalanche of horror that nobody's words or attempts at sympathy could ever do justice to. But I don't say all this to him. I just nod.

'How old was she? Did they find the guy who did it?'

I nod. 'They did. He's dead too now. And she was sixteen.'

'Well, at least he's dead. How did he die?'

'The police shot him.'

'Fuck. Was it, like, a kidnapping? Did he try and get money or something? Or was he a pervert?'

The insensitivity of his words hurts me inside, but I don't let him see. I just shake my head. 'No. He was a member of ISIS.'

'What… you mean…?'

'He was a terrorist, yes. She was killed during the attack on Stratford train station earlier this year. You probably heard about it.'

I hear his gasp. 'Christ, yeah, of course. Everyone was talking about it at school. And we go to Stratford. My friends and me. When we have the money to. It sort of… put us off for a bit.'

'Well, I can understand that,' I say, brushing my silent tears away.

'They killed people in Westfields too, didn't they? They set off a bomb.'

'Yes. She wasn't there though. She was in the station. I don't know why she was there. But for some reason she was. In the wrong place at the wrong time.'

Something shifts in my mind slightly as I say this. I can't grasp what it is. Just a strange sense of familiarity, that same feeling of déjà vu, and it lingers around me for a moment, then eventually dissipates.

'I'm sorry,' he says, putting a hand on my arm now. 'I'm really sorry. I…'

He stops. A buzzing sound is emanating from his pocket, a persistent vibration against the material of his fraying skinny jeans. 'Fuck, sorry,' he says, taking out a cheap

Motorola smartphone, 'it's my brother.' He answers the call and goes to stand by the alcove entrance. Although he's facing out towards the sea and the onslaught of the screaming wind, I can still just about catch his words into the phone.

'When? Now? Just now? Is she awake? No, don't call an ambulance, just put her in the bath. Cold water. Yes you do fucking care, otherwise you wouldn't have called me. Do it now. I'm coming.'

He cancels the call. 'Fuck!' he yells at the wall, then sits back down inside and buries his face in his hands.

'What was that all about?' I ask.

'It's my mum. Well, that wasn't, that was my brother, but he's at home with my mum and she's taken something. I think it's just too much drink, but she does other stuff too. Sometimes she mixes things. I need to get back. Help him deal with it.'

I stand up. 'Come on. I'll get you a taxi.'

He looks confused, as if he's never heard of such a thing. 'You mean, a car?'

'Yes, of course I mean a car.'

'I... I can run there in about twenty minutes.'

'In this weather? If those clouds are anything to go by, it looks like it's going to start gushing it down again any second. Give me your phone.'

Silently he offers it out, still looking bewildered.

There's no lock on the interface and the functions are very simple. I've never realised how sophisticated an iPhone is until now, navigating this cheap machine's clunky graphics to Google 'Southend Taxis', pick a nearby company and click the number to call. I arrange for a car to be sent to the hotel and am told it should be there within ten minutes.

'Come on. Let's get back to the hotel and we'll get the taxi.'

He's still baffled, 'What, you mean... you're coming too?'

I straighten up, feeling my bones click and complain. If I get a moment before the taxi arrives, I must go up and get more painkillers from my room.

'Yes, I'm coming too. Because there's more I still want to ask you. A lot more.'

Chapter Thirty-Eight

THE MOTHER

May. Three months after the attack.

The taxi isn't waiting when we get back to the hotel, so I take the lift to my room to pick up some more painkillers, leaving the boy sitting in one of the armchairs with a collection of old women, all of them eyeing him warily as if he might suddenly do something antisocial or violent.

As I'm coming back down, the secretary on the desk stops me. 'Sorry, we're just letting guests know that there'll be a function in the main dining area – a party for the Southend and Shoeburyness Adult Entertainment awards. So dinner will stop serving at 6.30, but you're welcome to go in any time before then.'

I stop and stare at him. 'Adult Entertainment?'

He looks embarrassed. 'I know, it's an unfortunate name, but we've been assured it doesn't mean anything dodgy. Just stand-up comedians, musicians, that kind of thing. I think they got annoyed at the amount of children's party entertainers and teen bands entering and clogging up the shortlists, so they inserted the "adult" word.'

I'm aware the taxi is probably waiting around the back of the building by now, so I just nod and try to extricate myself from the discussion. 'Right. OK. Thanks for the warning.'

'Can I not put you down for a table? You can have dinner early? Table for two for you and, er, your friend?'

His eyes flick towards the armchairs. From this angle, we can just see some legs, evidently belonging to a teenage boy, and some trainers that have seen better days, protruding from one of the chairs, resting up against the coffee table. They're jiggling up and down slightly, causing the copies of *Essex Life* to jerk close to the edge. There's a small smile playing on the man's lips.

'Er, no. He's my… my son. I'm just putting him in a taxi. To the train station. He's going to boarding school.'

I don't know why I'm making up such a detailed story, but there's something in the receptionist's face that's making heat flood to my face.

'Oh, really? That's nice,' he says, a little archly, with a slightly raised eyebrow, then turns back to his computer.

I consider telling him that I don't like his tone, but I can't waste any more time. I leave the main desk and walk over to the sofas, raising the lad out of his seat by just a tilt of my head, indicating that we're leaving. We exit the hotel in silence and, bent double against the wind and rain, rush as fast as my bruised body will permit round to the side where there is indeed a clearly marked taxi waiting for us.

'Never seen weather like this,' the driver says as he pulls out onto the road. 'Bloody washout. It keeps getting worse. And they've had all them floods across some parts. Heard it on the news just now.'

He flicks the radio on, but instead of news we're treated to the chorus of 'Hold On' by Wilson Phillips. I glance to see what effect this has on my young friend next to me, who was probably born over a decade after this track first arrived in the world, but he's busy tapping away on his phone. Probably messaging his brother.

'Any news on your mum?' I ask.

'She's woken up, sort of. But keeps going back to sleep and… being sick. While she's asleep. I think my brother finds that a bit scary. It's not very nice.'

No, it isn't, I think to myself. And definitely not something two teenage boys should have to deal with.

'Is your father… around?' I was going to say 'home' but decided to be a little more vague.

'He died. Well, disappeared. Mum's always said he died. Said he pissed off the wrong people and they bumped him off, but I think she's just watched too many shit films.' He lets out a short laugh.

'What type of thing did he do? For work, that is.'

Something changes in his face slightly when I ask this. It becomes slightly surly, a closed-down look that makes it clear he's controlling his expression, almost like he's trying not to get upset. 'He did all sorts. I think it was a building firm, something like that. He used to run jobs for them. Find things for them. Near London.'

I don't want to press the subject. It clearly upsets him in

some way and I can fully understand the feeling of having some nosy individual prod at one's most sensitive points, carrying on with the questions until finally you just want to shriek at them. He's sniffing again and for a moment I wonder if he's going to cry, but he controls himself with a short cough and straightens up, pressing his feet into the back of the seat in front of him, causing the driver to grunt pointedly.

Before long, we start slowing down on a road of what look like rather grim council houses and I figure this is where he must live. I offer the driver my debit card and he taps it on his contactless machine and hands it back.

'Down there,' the boy says. 'That's where it happened.'

It takes me a second to realise what he means, then I have a nauseating realisation that I've inadvertently returned to the site of my car accident.

'Your car was turning out of the road down there when – smash. That other big four-by-four – a huge fucker – kind of totalled yours. It was horrible.'

I stare down the empty road, awash with water gushing into the drains and some small branches that must have come down in the winds. 'It was horrible to experience,' I say. 'Although I don't remember much of it. Just the sound, really. Nothing much else.'

The road does feel faintly familiar, although I'm not sure if it's a true memory, fighting to get back, or if it's my brain filling in the gaps with all the emotions I'm feeling.

'If you can't remember it, shouldn't you still be in hospital?' he asks.

'Probably,' I say. An impatient huff from the taxi driver. 'Come on, we'd better get out.'

Michael leads the way to his front door, my hair getting more or less soaked in the seconds it takes for us to scurry to the front door. Inside, I cast an eye over the rubbish in the hallway. Discarded junk mail, free local newspapers, takeaway boxes. A rather horrible, musty, stuffy scent hits me as I walk further in. Then another boy comes into view, stomping down the stairs. He looks tired and stressed, dressed in pyjama bottoms and a faded *Star Wars* branded T-shirt. He looks about the same age as Michael. I wonder if they might be twins, although they're not identical. This one isn't as classically handsome – more normal looking, with less evidence of a toned physique, just an unremarkable build, neither fat nor ultra-skinny, and light-brown hair.

'She's in the bath still,' he says to his brother. Then he sees me and his eyes widen. 'Why's she here again?'

'Shut up,' Michael says, then turns to me. 'You can stay down here while I sort out my mum.'

I shake my head. 'No, I'm here to help. I'm happy to. If she's unwell, we'll get her sorted.'

I'm not quite sure why I'm taking the role of 'competent adult' here. Maybe it's because I just can't stand the thought of these two boys having to deal with an unwell, unstable parent on their own. I *am* the only competent adult.

Michael looks unsure. 'It can be a bit… not very nice. She can be not very nice sometimes.'

'Lead the way,' I say, in a businesslike tone.

We journey upstairs. Although the lights are on, the

stairway and landing are dark and dingy. The bathroom is also in need of a good clean.

Michael crashes in, the door knocking against the bath, causing a dark mass inside it to flinch and murmur 'Fuuuckoffff.' I stare at the woman inside. She's lying in water up to her shoulders. She's in old, dark jeans that have tears along the sides and what looks like a black jumper with a white graphic of a kitten's face on the front.

'The cold water woke her up,' Michael says. 'But now she won't get out. I tried dragging her but she scratched me so I told her she can stay there.'

I glance at the boy and see red-raw nail marks on his arms. *Christ, is this what these boys have to live with?*

'I thought she'd gone back to sleep,' he continues. 'But when I said I was going to call an ambulance she started effing and blinding, so she can't be that ill.'

I look at her pallid, sickly looking face. She's younger than me. Early thirties at the most. She must have had her boys young. Very young.

'We really should call an ambulance,' I say. 'If you think she's taken pills. Do you know what they could have been?'

Michael looks panicked now. 'No, please. Please don't. She'll be furious and it only makes more problems.' His face is earnest, pleading. 'We'll just get her dry and into bed. She'll sleep it off.' He looks over at his brother. 'Did you clear up the sick? Where was it?'

'She threw up in the bath once. I let the water out and started again. And she was being sick in her sleep in her room. But I've put her duvet cover into the washing machine. We haven't got any washing powder, so I'll get some tomorrow.'

Tears almost fill my eyes at the thought of the boy stripping his mother's bed of vomit-covered sheets and going out to buy detergent. My little girl never had to do anything like this. I would be the one clearing up sick. Her dad would run out to buy washing powder. If either of us were unwell, she wouldn't be expected to care for us.

'We can lift her together,' Michael is saying.

The other boy nods. 'OK.'

I'm pleased to be exempted from this arrangement and I don't argue. After ignoring the doctor's insistence that I shouldn't exert myself, the pain in my arm and shoulder has risen considerably. I feel for my box of tablets in my pocket and, while they heave their dripping mother out of the bath and into a teetering standing position, I go over to the sink and turn on the cold water and scoop some into my hand. The tablets leave a bitter taste in my mouth and I rinse out a filthy-looking glass so I can take in more water.

'…the fuck? The fucking posh bitch… she here again?'

So she recognises me too. What did I do here, in this awful house? How did I find myself within its terrible walls? I feel ill and disorientated with the confusion of it. The need to get out of the grim bathroom overwhelms me.

'I might go and wait downstairs,' I say, as the boys half drag their mother out onto the landing and towards what is presumably her bedroom.

'OK,' Michael says, and they disappear through the door. I hear a *thwump* sort of sound – they must have dropped her onto the bed – then the sound of Michael ordering his brother to get her wet jeans off and find a towel.

Feeling guilty that I should be helping them, I head downstairs. The dingy open-plan kitchen-and-lounge area makes me want to sob. I had imagined collapsing onto the sofa and waiting for the pills to do their work, but the thought of sitting amongst this mess horrifies me. Within a few seconds, I locate a roll of big pink recycling sacks that the council delivers, and start shovelling the detritus – pizza boxes, cartons that look like they once contained Indian takeaways, empty crisp packets, kitchen roll, promotional Dominos flyers – into the one of the bags, wincing each time I have to use my bad arm to steady myself.

By the time the boys return, I have cleared most of the kitchen work surfaces and the small, unstable kitchen table and put on the washing machine, having found an old, dust-covered box of Ariel tablets in a Lidl bag next to the back door. Two and a half bags of recycling lean up against the sink while I sit in one of the cheap chairs and wait for the pain to subside.

'God, what have you been doing?' Michael says when he comes in.

'I thought I'd tidy up a bit,' I say. The other boy is looking at me warily, as if I'm exhibiting threatening behaviour.

'I've never seen it looking like this,' Michael says.

'I haven't finished. There's more to do. I just needed to sit for a bit.'

He nods and sits in the only spare seat next to me. The brother hovers awkwardly, his hands in the pockets of his pyjama trousers. Eventually he says, 'I'll leave you guys to it,' and wanders away. The sound of him climbing the stairs follows, then the closing of a door.

'How's your mum?' I ask.

'She'll be OK. She started telling us to fuck off and leave her alone when we were getting her into dry clothes. Usually better than not talking at all. She's sleeping now. Unless she dies in the night, things will be back to normal tomorrow. Not that this isn't normal.' He kicks a leg of the table and it wobbles precariously.

'Does... does she work?' I ask.

Michael lets out one of his short, hollow laughs. 'She borrows money, then offers the guys favours when she can't pay it back. My dad left her some in a bank account. Evan found the statements once. I think about five grand. But we barely saw any of it. After she'd bought us computers and some new clothes to make herself feel better, she pissed the rest of it up the wall – mostly weed, vodka, and machines.'

'Machines?' I ask, confused.

'You know, betting machines.'

'Ah,' I say. 'I understand.'

Silence falls around us. The hum and rhythmic thump of the washing machine is somehow comforting, mingling with the rush of the wind and rain still continuing outside. We sit there for a while – it feels strangely comfortable, cosy even, us both at the table in the kitchen, sheltering from the storm. Although it's only the afternoon, the light outside is once again diminishing, as if night is falling.

'I've never known weather like this during the summer. It's quite astonishing.'

He nods. 'Our school's flooded. Or part of it is. They say the site's unsafe for us. A tree's come down near it too. It's like the end of the world.'

I'm struck by a memory of desolate weather and ruined landscape depicted in the film *The Road*, both deeply depressing and strangely beautiful. Maybe this is the end. Maybe the water will wash everything away. And all the hatred and sorrow in the world can be cleared and we can all start again.

After a few more beats of silence, Michael says: 'So. Your memory. How you going to get it back? Is there anything you do remember?'

I try to think back. It physically hurts me to fish around in the ruined clutter of my mind, but I've managed to find an anchor point to the past, although it's only in fragments. 'I can remember the attack on Piccadilly Circus. That's a few weeks ago now. I remember being very upset about it because it brought… it brought back…'

I see him work it out before I can say it. 'Your daughter?'

I nod.

'But I don't remember it fully. Or what happened around that. I think I went to a friend's birthday party, but I don't recall much of it. It's like trying to see underwater. Just vague shapes. And I don't remember anything about Southend. Maybe, if I try, I can remember travelling here, or maybe getting to the hotel. That's becoming clearer. But I still don't know why I picked this place. Or what I did here.'

'Or me,' he says in a small voice.

I knew I would have to tackle this head-on soon, and it might as well be now.

'Michael, I don't know why I got myself involved with you... Part of me is worried that I somehow led you on or, I don't know, used you unfairly. And I know you want answers too. From the sounds of it, it was me who sought you out, but I can't think why, or what I'd want to talk to you about.'

He's watching me intently. His eyes are so earnest, as if willing me to go on, but I have little more to say.

'I thought you were after some kind of... I don't know... hook-up. My brother does it sometimes with older women, but he usually finds it online. And I could tell you were staying here by yourself – I don't know, I figured you'd left your husband or something – and you, well, just wanted to shag someone. And I hadn't got laid in a while so I thought, why the fuck not, and we met at the hotel, we went up to your room... but like I said, as soon as I tried to start something, you got, well... weird.'

He stops, looking as embarrassed as I feel.

'And then?' I prompt him.

He takes a breath. 'And then you kicked me out. But then you came to my house. And before Mum told you to leave, you were about to say something. Explain why we met. Why you already knew where I lived. It was like... like this big thing you were going to share.'

I stare at him, genuinely lost for words.

'Are you sure you don't remember it?' he says, looking more hopeful, leaning in towards me.

I wish I could offer him something more, but I just shake my head. 'No. I'm sorry. I don't.'

I think he's going to cry and I reach out and put a hand on his. 'Listen, Michael. I'm not in a very good place right now. I don't know, maybe I wasn't in a right state of mind when I said all that… maybe there isn't a big secret I wanted to share.'

He shakes his head now. 'No, I'm sure there was. You seemed upset or stressed, but you were certain of it. And you had something in your pocket, something you kept touching.' He shrugs, 'I don't know. I just think… if you left your home and your husband… surely there'd be a proper reason why?'

I turn my gaze to the dusty, stained floor, unsure how to respond. 'I think,' I say, trying to clearly articulate the situation for myself as well as for him, 'I think I came here because I just couldn't go on with how I was living at home. It was just getting so awful. Toxic. Both me and Alec, my husband, stuck in this terrible place. Our grief about Jessica manifesting itself in different ways. We became strained. I think I must have just not been able to stand it any longer.'

This makes sense to me as I say it. It sounds like the truth. A line from Michael Cunningham's novel *The Hours* comes to me, where a woman has to explain why she left her child and husband: 'It was death. I chose life.' I choose not to share this literary reference with Michael.

'I know that doesn't explain about the thing you think I may have said to you—'

He cuts me off, 'You *did* say to me.'

'OK, OK.' I hold up a hand, and then wince with the

pain. I let a few beats of silence pass before continuing, more for myself than for him. 'When Jessica died, it kind of ripped me and my husband apart. I think some couples come together at times like that. We've had little to do with the other survivors and families of victims of the Stratford attacks – just a few trips to these horribly sad meetings they organise. But I understand some of the parents of other teenagers who died have said that having each other has got them through it and may have even strengthened their love for each other. It sounds strange to say it, but maybe I can understand why it could work that way. It's been rather the opposite for me and Alec. Things are broken and nasty, and I think I must have run away to escape that. Get some fresh air. New experiences. And maybe I got a bit carried away. Lost my senses a bit.'

He just nods. I look out of the window again at the smashing rain. And then, in the reflection, I see someone standing in the archway that leads through into the lounge. A face, watching us. The brother. I jump slightly.

'Evan, what the fuck?' Michael says. 'You eavesdropping?'

The boy doesn't reply. Just stands there. Face white. Michael seems to notice something's wrong.

'What is it? Is it Mum?' I can't work out if his voice is one of panic or irritation. I wonder how many disasters involving their mother these boys have had to endure.

But the boy is looking at me. He's watching me, closely, as if terrified of my very presence. Then he runs away – literally runs out of sight. The sound of him rushing up the stairs follows immediately after.

'Jesus, what's his problem?' Michael says.

'Maybe he's upset about your mum,' I venture, but Michael shakes his head.

'We're used to it. It's not the worst she's done. And anyway, Evan's a grade-A nutcase.'

'Oh really?' I say, unsure if I should sound interested or concerned.

'Yes. He's… he's had trouble figuring stuff out. Since our dad went when we were younger… stuff… he finds stuff trickier than I do.'

I don't say anything, but nod as if I understand.

'I think it's because… things have always been a bit weird here. I think it's all because of… well, our dad was a cunt and… I just think…'

Something in his tone makes me look at him quickly. His eyes have gone all shiny and a tear is threatening to spill. I have a really horrible sense of dread, as if someone somewhere is turning out all the lights, and is getting nearer and nearer. And then I know what he's telling me. And it shocks me. Really shocks me. And I'm someone who's been through one of the worst things a human can ever experience.

'Michael,' I say softly, 'are you saying your dad was… that he behaved improperly towards you and your brother?'

He's crying fully now, and seems cross with himself about it, as he frowns and rubs away the tears. 'Fuck,' he says under his breath, 'I'm sorry.'

'Don't say sorry. You don't need to be sorry,' I say, and put a hand out onto his, but he flinches and pulls away.

'He used to take us places. To terrible places. And…'

I get up, walk round to his side of the table and embrace him. And he cries in my arms. I don't care about the pressure of his strong frame on my shoulder. The pain, in any other circumstance, would have been too much to bear, but for this poor, broken boy, I can bear it. I need to. And he needs me. All I can do is stroke his hair, like I used to do to Jessica's when she was upset, and tell him everything's going to be OK. Even though it's not.

Chapter Thirty-Nine

THE BOY

I t's Jessica's mum. My brain won't let me properly believe it, but it is. She's here. In the lounge. And she's telling Michael about what happened. And I'm going to be sick. I run as fast as I can to the bathroom and throw up in the sink. I haven't eaten much today, but there's enough for it to be pretty instant and horrible.

Jessica's mum. Jessica's mum.

How did she get here? Why is she here? So when she found me in the bathroom cutting – she was Jessica's mum then. And I didn't know. And she didn't know I was cutting my skin raw because of her daughter. Because of what I did to her. That it was me that killed her. Me that couldn't toughen up and go and meet her and, because of it, she ended up gunned down by some masked terrorist. And her mum didn't know any of it.

Or did she? It can't be a coincidence that she came to this house. Of all the thousands of houses in the world – even just Southend by itself – why the fuck did she end up here? It can't be an accident. It just can't be. She's here because of me.

———

Once I've worked all this out, I get into bed. I need to sleep. My body feels like it's dragging me down. It's not even night-time but it's no good, I can't stay awake. Staying awake means facing this. Thinking about this.

I sleep for hours. Not fully. That horrible half-sleep. The kind I had when I first saw that horrific headline on the BBC News website. The Stratford attacks. The rising body count. Mobile phone footage of people running, screaming. The front of Stratford shopping centre blown open. Things on the floor. Things that were once people. The sound of gunshots in the distance. And Jessica. Somewhere within them. Or maybe she'd died earlier. Maybe she was one of the first. I didn't know. But as I slept, I kept imagining her blood pouring out onto the floor, soaking everything, then lapping against the sides of my bed until it reached me, it found me, it covered me, it started choking me…

The banging wakes me. Someone is stomping around the house. And by the sounds of it, it's coming from Mum's room. I get out of bed and walk out onto the landing. It's definitely from Mum's room. I tread quietly, almost on tiptoe, to her door, so I can see the reflection in the mirrored doors of her wardrobe. A guy is on top of her, pulling her round to face him.

'Where is it?' he hisses in her ear. Then he slaps her. She doesn't move. So he hits her again. Then he turns round to the chest of drawers and starts flinging out clothes and old magazines and bits of paper over the already cluttered floor.

I think about going in there. Hitting him. Punching him. Killing him. Smashing his head again and again into the wall until it cracks into a thousand pieces of skull and brain. I'm drawing my breath in, trying to get the courage to enter the room, when a noise downstairs stops me. Someone is walking through the lounge and about to come up the stairs. I rush back to my bedroom and close the door quickly. I hurriedly pull on some pyjama bottoms and a T-shirt, then crouch back by my door, listening, listening as I hear someone – Michael, I think – running up the stairs and then going into Mum's room. Doing what I should have done. Doing what I wasn't brave enough to do.

'What the fuck, mate?' I hear a man's voice shout – not Michael's, it must be the stranger. Then a woman's voice, 'Michael, get off him!'

There are more shouts. Some I can't make out, something that sounds like 'She took it out my fucking coat!', but then it all becomes a garbled mass of shouting. Then a crash and a thud and a shriek. Then a lot of sounds, like a tumbling and crunching. And then silence. I come out of my room now and look out onto the landing. Michael and her, the woman, Jessica's mum – they're standing there, looking down. Down the stairs. As if there's something shocking at the bottom of it. They don't say anything to me as I walk past them. Still nothing as I stand at the edge of the top stair and look down. Then, when I see what they see, I hear the woman let out a sob. A man's body is lying at the bottom of the stairs. Twisted. On its side. Not moving.

Chapter Forty

THE MOTHER

May. Three months after the attack.

I end up staying the night. I'm not sure how it happens, it just does. Michael and I go into the lounge and sit together on the sofa, against the drab, stained cushions and old magazines, watching a rerun of *Blue Planet II*. 'TV's not up to the standard of yours,' he jokes as he puts it on.

I don't notice when it becomes night. The darkness outside has been so all-pervading for so long, I don't feel it creep up on us. A day, stolen from me in confusion, tears, and never-ending gloom. I am both starving and tired. When it gets to 9pm, Michael messages a friend of his who works at a local takeaway and he pops round with a feast of stuff. I offer to pay for it but Michael just says, 'Nah, Jimmy owes me.'

The food is fried, greasy, and smells delicious. Chicken wings, kebabs, pizza, and three huge portions of chips, spilling out of their polystyrene boxes. I gorge on the food, and so does Michael, neither of us talking as we munch and watch some weird sea creature illuminate its fins at the bottom at the sea. After an hour of David Attenborough, Michael suggests I sleep in his room. I'm feeling slightly nauseous. 'No,' I shake my head, wincing as my muscles tighten, 'I'll just get a taxi back to my hotel.'

'No, please... stay here,' he says. 'I can make you up a bed. Hold on.'

He runs out of the room and up the stairs. Seconds later, he is back down with a duvet and a pillow. 'Here. If you don't want to sleep in my bed... with me... you can sleep down here. I'll make up a little bed for you.'

I try to protest again, telling him it isn't appropriate and that I should be getting back, but he is adamant. His eyes bore into mine. Pleading. Desperate.

'OK,' I say, 'OK, I'll sleep down here.'

It is all too much. The conversation about Jessica. The suggestion from Michael that his dad has inflicted some form of abuse on him and his brother. And the fact that I somehow knew to come to this place to tell this boy something important, something that keeps drifting from me, just out of reach – all of it is weighing on my mind in the heaviest way. I just need to let sleep take the pain away, both physical and mental.

I fall asleep almost instantly after Michael leaves the room, but wake with a start when I hear the front door close. Someone has entered the house. The pain in my shoulder has spread to my neck. I shouldn't be here. I need to be back in my safe, calm hotel with my pain meds and enormous television, recovering in private. I feel like I am close to panic, so try to breathe slowly, and gently swing my legs off the sofa. They collide with something soft.

'Ahh, what…?'

It's a boy's voice. In the darkness, I realise it's Michael. He's lying on the floor nestled amongst a collection of coats and cushions.. Has he been here all night?

'Sorry. I thought you'd gone to bed,' I say.

He rubs his eyes. 'I couldn't sleep. Came down here to be with you.'

I sigh. 'Oh God, Michael. This is all a bit of a mess.'

'What is? The lounge?'

'No, not the lounge,' I whisper, even though it is a tip. 'I mean *this*. Me. God, what am I doing here?' I rub my eyes with my hand, trying not to cry.

His eyes are stilled closed. 'I need to sleep. Can we talk about this in the morning?'

I am about to reply when I hear a thump upstairs, as if someone has dropped something on the floor. Then another clunk. And then a man's voice.

'What's that?' I say.

Michael doesn't reply. He just sits up, clearly listening.

'I heard the front door go a minute ago. It woke me up,' I say. 'I think someone went upstairs.'

Michael gets to his feet in a rush, staggering slightly. 'Fuck!' he shouts.

'What? Wait! Hold on.' I try to get up quickly but my

shoulder sends a shooting pain down my entire right side. 'Christ!' I yell, and Michael turns then.

'Are you OK?'

'Yes, I think so. What's going on?'

'I think one of the cunts is here,' he says, viciously. He's angry. Pure fury. Looks as if he's going to hit something. Someone.

'What... what do you mean?'

'A man. It's what they do. She borrows money or buys drugs and when she can't pay... Fuck's sake!' He kicks the rickety coffee table in anger, sending takeaway boxes flying, and lets out a shout when his bare foot collides with the wood.

'Calm down,' I say, even though I feel anything but calm.

'He needs to leave. She's not in any kind of state to chuck him out on her own...'

He makes a move for the door and I follow him, trying to keep up with his pace up the stairs. On the landing he marches down towards the room we left his mother in hours before. It's clear, as soon as we approach it, that a commotion is occurring inside. We hear a man grunting, raging, shouting, 'You fucking junkie!' Through the slightly open doorway, I can see him pulling out drawers and going through the detritus of clothes and tissues and carrier bags on the floor. Michael bangs open the door fully and I get a proper view of him. He's a young man – probably in his late twenties, early thirties, clean shaven, tattoos dotting his neck and upper forearms. His body is extremely toned – you can see it through the thin grey hoodie he's wearing.

He clearly spends hours pumping all kinds of machines in the gym. If he tries to defend himself, I'm not sure what use either Michael or I would be. When he sees the door open, I brace myself for him to charge at us, but he just yells, 'What the fuck?', then carries on searching through the stuff on the floor, as if he's dropped something. In the seconds before Michael rushes into the room and launches himself at the man, I see something that makes me feel very, very sick. The boy's mum has blood on her face. Her nose is bleeding and there's a clear red mark on her cheek that looks like it's been dealt by a strong, merciless hand.

'Get the fuck out, you cunt!' Michael is yelling at the man, pushing him. He doesn't retaliate immediately, instead puts up his hands to defend himself. Then Michael directs a well-aimed kick to his groin. The shriek the man lets out is blood-curdling. He clasps his hands over the zone of pain, hopping from one leg to the other. Michael seizes this moment of vulnerability, dragging the man by the wrist to the door and out onto the landing. 'Come on, fuck off!'

Although apparently still in pain, the man clearly objects to both being dragged and being called a cunt, and he takes a swipe at Michael's face with his hand, slashing the boy's cheeks with his nails, so a small drop of blood falls onto his bare chest. 'She took my gear. I *know* she took it. And if she doesn't pay, she has to learn the hard way.' He then slaps Michael across the face. 'Run off back to Mummy, you little rat,' he says, sneering.

'Michael!' I shout, running to his side. He's been knocked back by the force of the slap, but I'm just grateful it wasn't a punch. I don't fancy picking up teeth from the carpet. 'We need to call the police.' My mobile is gone from my pocket – probably on the sofa where I was sleeping, no doubt out of battery. I look around helplessly but I don't know what to do. Then I see Michael take his hands away from his bleeding face and throw himself at the man in front of him. He topples. Shakes. Grabs about him wildly. Then falls down the stairs, clattering all the way down.

In complete silence, Michael and I look at each other, then edge towards the top of the stairs, and look down.

The man is lying twisted on the floor at the bottom of the stairs. Weirdly, the thing that most catches my attention is a piece of junk mail, one of several littering the space between the door and the stairs. It's touching his nose, poking into his nostrils. Normally, one would bat such a thing away from such a sensitive area. But he doesn't move.

Stairs can be dangerous things.

It's my mother's voice. It creeps into my head like a snake. I don't want to think about that now. I can't think about that now. That's not what's happened here. It can't be. It just can't be.

I pull myself out of my daze and dully become aware of a third party on the landing. Evan has come out of his room and is standing beside me, looking down the stairs too. Then he turns to his brother: 'What happened?'

Michael appears to be incapable of speech, so I make an attempt: 'He… he fell…' I stammer, unsure what else to say. Then common sense takes over. Again, I remind myself I'm the adult here. I should know what to do in a situation like this. 'We need to call an ambulance.'

Neither of the two boys says anything. Eventually, I

slowly and gingerly descend the stairs towards the strange mass of limbs lying by the front door. His top has ridden up and I can see the perfectly carved lines of his smooth chest. His body reminds me of what Alec's used to be like when we first met. Toned and athletic. He hasn't become overweight in his journey to middle-age – his body has just shrunk into something slim and unremarkable.

I crouch down on the floor so that I'm nearly next to the man and feel for a pulse. Ludicrously, part of me expects to find the body already ice cold. It isn't. It's warm and, to my immense relief, the pulse is evident almost immediately.

'He's alive,' I call back up to the boys on the stairs. Slowly, like I did, they traipse down, Michael first.

'What now?' he says. 'Should we really call an ambulance? Did you see what he did to my mum?'

I struggle to stand up, using the banister as support. 'I know. But if we don't, we could be in major trouble.'

'Really?' Michael seems unconvinced.

'Yes, really. As in prison.'

He nods, as if prison is a far-off country he's vaguely heard of.

I'm about to step over the body of the young man when a hand shoots out and grabs my ankle. I scream. And Michael leaps into action, kicking the mass on the floor. 'Stop it!' I shout, shaking my foot out of the man's grip. He's standing up now and swaying dangerously. 'What the fuck is this? You fucking attacked me.' He tries to hit Michael, but the boy dodges and the man slams against the wall. I notice one of his trainers has come off, and since he has sock-free feet, I can see a red-ish purple bruise on the skin.

'For Christ's sake, will you all please be still!' I yell. To my surprise, they all obey. Michael has his hands raised against himself in a defensive motion, in case the bigger, stronger man aims another punch at him, and the latter continues to sway, but ceases to throw his fists around. Evan, meanwhile, sits down on the fourth stair up and watches the strange tableau with a blank expression.

I turn to look at the man – the stranger, the drug dealer – and, with more courage than I thought myself capable of, speak to him: 'Why are you here?'

He turns his head towards me. 'What?' he says, looking completely baffled, as if I've spoken to him in Chinese.

'Why are you here? Do you just come in and attack random single mothers at any house that takes your fancy?'

'What?' he says again. 'Who the fuck are you? The police?'

Part of me is tempted to say yes, but I decide it's probably unwise.

'That bitch up there has stolen my fucking coke,' he says, rubbing his side where one of Michael's kicks landed. '*And* a whole bag of weed. I thought she could do with a reminder of what happens to cunts what steal.' He crunches one of his knuckles and raises his chin in a kind of upwards nod.

'She was unconscious and you attacked her.'

He looks mock shocked. 'What? No, no. She walked into her door when she was going to fetch my cash. That's all.'

314

He grins now. A vile grin. One that makes his face look fox-like. Cruel.

'Christ,' I say, 'I'm going to call the police. Michael, Evan, go back into your rooms.' I'm going into mother-in-emergency mode now, a role I was good at, once. 'You,' I say, pointing to the man, 'can either stay and wait for them, or leave. I don't think we'd be able to stop you. Although by the looks of the swelling of your ankle, I don't think you'll get very far.' I nod down to his bare foot, noticing he isn't placing much weight on it. 'It can't be a break, or you'd be screaming, but I think it's sprained.'

'Who the fuck do you think you are?' he shouts again, but I ignore him and turn to the boys. 'Go back upstairs, both of you, now. See if your mother's OK. I don't think he's going to manage to climb the stairs in his condition, but if he does, stay in your rooms.'

'I want my fucking gear,' he shouts.

'Too bad,' I say. As the boys retreat upstairs, following my demands like well-behaved dogs, I go into the lounge and start rooting down the side of the sofa to find my phone. Amidst a sandpit of crumbs, fluff, old coppers and something that feels suspiciously like a used condom, I find my iPhone. As I predicted, its battery is dead. 'Shit,' I say to myself. I start chucking stuff – magazines, empty pizza boxes – off the table and the sides of the sofa, looking for a landline. I finally locate one in the kitchen, but the cord has been broken – apparently chewed by something, maybe a rodent, from the looks of this dump – and there's no dialling tone. I feel like sitting down on the sofa and crying. Then I hear the front door slam. Seconds later, I hear someone on the stairs.

It's both brothers. They come and stand in the lounge, as if waiting for further instructions. 'He's just left,' Michael says.

'I guessed,' I say. 'We couldn't have held him here. Not without tying him up.' I let out a little laugh as I say this. I can't believe I'm in a situation where I'd even contemplate saying that sentence.

'I could have done that,' Michael says.

'Honestly, it wouldn't have been a good move,' I say. I rub my eyes and try to focus on the two boys in front of me. Both of them look back at me, like lost sheep looking for their shepherd, and it's clear what I've become to them: I'm a mother. A functioning one, a responsible one, one that deals with disasters and tells the young members of the family what to do.

'We need to phone the police,' I say.

They both look uncomfortable. Neither of them speaks.

'That means I need to use one of your phones. Mine's dead.'

They now share a glance.

'What's going on?' I say, growing exasperated.

'I don't think we should call them,' Michael says.

I stare at him. 'What? A minute ago you were trying to kick that piece of shit to death and now you want him to get away scot-free with what he's done.'

More silence.

'Can someone please explain!' I half-shout. This is getting too much.

'It's like I said,' Michael mutters, not meeting my eye. 'We can't call the police or an ambulance, because they'll work out what she's been taking. What she takes all the time. The weed, the coke. The pills. She has heroin here, too. All kinds of shit. Needles. She keeps them in her old make-up bag. And we'll be split up and won't be able to live here.'

I see what he's worried about now. 'Right. I get you. But… well, I'm not sure if that would really happen.'

'It will.' Michael says this adamantly. 'I know kids it's happened to.'

'But… you're not exactly kids…' I'm not sure what I'm saying, but I carry on. 'Michael,' I say, and go forward to rest a hand on his shoulder. 'This man did something terrible. Coming into the house, smashing up her room, attacking her in her sleep. We need to make sure she's OK or take her to A&E, then speak to the police. No matter what your mum has done or what drugs she was on, she's still a victim here. She's innocent.'

The boys share another look. I get the feeling there's something going on here. Some part of this strange saga with their mother I don't know about.

'She's not innocent,' Michael says quietly.

'She is when it comes to this,' I say, keeping my hand on him. 'She was passed out. I presume he had a key and let himself in?'

They both nod. 'Lots of them have keys,' Evan says, his voice small and croaky.

'God,' I say. 'And you live like this? With random men just letting themselves into your house?'

'Yes,' Michael says, simply.

I don't really know where to go from here. 'Well, maybe I could just report him anonymously…'

Michael is looking like he's going to cry again now. 'Please, can we just… I dunno… just forget about this.'

I shake my head. 'I can't… I can't just pretend none of this ever happened.' I try to brush my hair out of my face, but use my bad arm by mistake. Pain shoots down my shoulder. I wince and take a sharp intake of breath.

'Are you OK?' Michael asks. It's him touching me now, his hand gently resting on my good arm. 'Do you need anything?'

'I need to go back to my hotel. I didn't bring enough painkillers. I didn't think I'd be staying the night.'

'We've probably got some paracetamol,' he says.

I try to smile. 'That's sweet, but I don't think it's going to quite do the job. I need something of more industrial strength than that. Can you call me a taxi?'

Michael nods.

'This isn't over though,' I say, looking at them both. 'This can't carry on. I know I'm not your parent and I know you're worried about some sort of ramifications from social services or the police or something. But even if there were any, I think they'd be better than what you've got going on here. Do you understand?'

They both nod.

'OK. I need a phone for the taxi. And, while we wait, we need to help your mum. She might be concussed. And we can put a dressing on that scratch,' I reach out and turn Michael's cheek to the side so I can look at the wound. 'Human scratches can very easily become infected, just like animal ones. Do you have any disinfectant?' A silly question, I realise. They just stare at me, blankly. 'OK, don't worry. We'll manage.'

All three of us journey upstairs. On the landing, Evan says he's going to carry on clearing his mum up. He says the bleeding has stopped and he doesn't think her nose is broken. I nod and offer a small smile, grateful for this at least, and Michael and I go into the bathroom.

With nothing else to hand, I order him to stand in the shower and use the flow of the nozzle to direct warm water in a stream across his cheek. 'It stings,' he grunts, but I tell him it will be over soon.

'Do you have plasters or bandages?'

He shakes his head.

'Right, er, do you have anything freshly washed or clean, or something that you could hold to it? Even a clean T-shirt or something.'

He looks slightly offended. 'We have clean clothes, you know. We're not tramps.'

I apologise, even though, judging by the rest of the house, it wouldn't be unreasonable to presume laundry wasn't high on the agenda here. I follow Michael to his bedroom – a lot tidier than the rest of the house – and sit down on the side of his bed. It squeaks slightly, and the corner I'm sitting on goes down a little, as if one of the springs in the mattress has lost its strength. I reach out and hold onto its corner, to stop myself toppling off.

Déjà vu. It's always been a strange feeling. But I've never experienced it like this. Usually, you know something hasn't happened before – it's just a sensation, an edge of familiarity that lingers and makes you think you're experiencing a recurrence. This isn't like that. This is astonishing. The world glides slowly in front of my eyes, rippling slowly, then quicker, shuffling the shapes of the room into something new and yet not new. Michael, me, on this bed, someone pushing me. Shouting at me. And before. In the street. Falling over. Him coming towards me in the hotel. Fish and chips. Southend. Leaving home. Piccadilly. All those people dead. And me and Alec. Crying over the news reports. And a face. A face on the fridge. A name. Facebook. Michael Kelley. Michael Kelley. Michael Kelley.

Jessica.

And I'm back. And I'm looking at him. And I know.

'What's wrong?' he says. He looks at me. I look at him. 'I've remembered. I've remembered everything. And now I know who you are. You're the reason Jessica is dead.'

Chapter Forty-One

THE MOTHER

May. Three months after the attack.

The realisation is cataclysmic. And my reaction is extreme. I start screaming. Shrieking. Flailing. Hitting out at Michael, knocking him back towards his bed, leaving me spinning in the room, not properly registering the pain shooting through my damaged body.

'What do you mean? Hey, get off! What the fuck? What are you doing?' He's looking terrified.

I can't answer his question. I can't even look at him. I just need to leave.

I claw my way out of the room, pushing against the door as if I've lost the proper use of my hands. I can hear Michael calling after me, getting up off the bed, following me. I hurry to get down the stairs and tear the front door open. A wall of rain and wind hits me, bringing me sharply into the present. How could I have forgotten? Forgotten what he did. What he did to my baby.

'Please! Caroline! You're fucking stupid to go out in this.' The sound of him yelling against the roar of the wind follows me as I walk out of the wreck of a front porch and into the street.

'Hold on, I'll come with you!' he yells. I don't wait.

I know this is all my fault. That I was foolish to come here. Foolish to leave Kent and come looking for the boy. But it doesn't dilute the rage I feel towards him. And that's why I need to get away from him. Because if I stay, I don't know what I'll do. I just know that it would be worse than hitting and screaming.

At the bottom of the road, where I had the crash and my life could have ended, I stop to get my breath back up against some tall recycling bins outside a boarded-up off-licence.

'Caroline!' I can hear someone approaching, and I crouch down by the bins as the sound of trainers scraping against the pavement alerts me to Michael's arrival. The wind is still loud, but I try to keep my breathing quiet, in case he senses it above the din. I see, between the green plastic sides of the bins, that the boy, now dressed in his hoodie and tracksuit, is looking left and right, deciding which way I might have gone. Eventually he decides to turn right, the more natural direction of my hotel, towards the seafront. I wait until I see him disappear down another street.

I'm aware that if I'm going back to the hotel at all, I need to aim for the seafront, so I navigate around the more direct route Michael must have taken, keeping to small streets and alleyways, inching around puddles and areas of flooding.

Some roads I can't go down at all due to fallen trees, a hazard to cars and pedestrians alike. I don't know how long it takes me. I could have been walking for years and I wouldn't know. My body is numb. My mind, lit up by the rush of adrenalin that came with the return of my memories, is now threatening to close down and stop. I'm thirsty. I'm hungry. I'm in pain. And catastrophically tired.

When I see the warm, welcoming lights of a Tesco Express at the end of a street I almost cry with joy. When I walk in, I try to stand straighter, look like I'm a completely ordinary person out for an early – very early – trip to buy groceries during one of the worst storms the South-East of England has ever seen. 'Morning,' I croak at the shop assistant unpacking copies of the *Radio Times*. I go straight to the aisle of cosmetics and medication and select a pack of paracetamol and one of ibuprofen and take them to the counter, along with a bottle of water and a ready-made sandwich. 'That will be £3.65, please,' says the middle-aged man behind the counter. I feel in my pockets for my purse and discover nothing there but my phone. I must have left it at the house. Maybe on the makeshift bed where I slept. It's probably joined the gritty, fluff-filled forest of lost items down the sofa by now. And I don't have anything else. No bag. No cash. In a desperate attempt, I try holding out my iPhone to use Apple Pay on the contactless card machine, but the screen stays resolutely dead. That's when I burst into tears. Proper, loud tears.

'I'm sorry,' I say, 'I'm so sorry. I've come out without my purse. I'll have to leave it.' I turn towards the stormy street outside and the rain splashing against the shop-front, the luminous Tesco sign reflected in the water-soaked pavement.

'Are you OK, love?' he says, kindly. Normally I would have rather objected to the 'love', but I don't have the energy today.

'Er… yes,' I sniff, trying to stop the tears from falling.

'Have you been out in that downpour?' He nods to the outside. As we both look, a big cardboard box skates on one of its points across the road, as if pulled by invisible string. It's like the world's been turned upside down.

'Never seen anything like this,' he says. 'Been carrying on for weeks. In some areas they've called the army in, apparently. Because of the floods. We've had trouble getting some of our deliveries in. No celery to speak of for days, now.'

I'm not sure what to say, so I just nod, and then the man turns back to my purchases.

'Are you in pain?' he asks, prodding at the pack of ibuprofen.

I nod again, the tears still spilling down my cheeks. 'I was in a car accident.'

'Christ,' he says. 'Do you need me to call you an ambulance?'

'No, no,' I wave my hand. 'It happened the other week. I've just got some lasting pain.' My hand subconsciously starts rubbing my shoulder and the shop assistant's eyes fill with what looks like pity.

'Oh love, I'm sorry. Here, you take these…' Out of his pocket he brings out a fiver and puts it in the till, then pockets the change. 'Not supposed to do this, but seeing as you're out in this storm all alone.' He hands me the tablets and I continue to cry as I take them.

'Thank you. Thank you so much.'

'Don't mention it,' he says. 'I see your phone's not working. Do you need to call anyone?'

I shake my head. 'No. I'm... I'm heading for the seafront. Someone's picking me up from there.'

He looks even more concerned. 'It really won't be nice down there at the moment. You'll get the weather in all its fury. I can call you a taxi...'

'No, it's fine.' I hold up my hand. 'Really. I'll be fine.'

He nods, still looking worried, and I thank him again and walk out of the shop.

Once outside, I immediately tear open both packs of tablets and take two of each, then one more of ibuprofen, ignoring the recommended dose. I then take large bites of the sandwich, the cheese and ham filling tasting wildly delicious; a symptom of how hungry I must be, even after the takeaway last night. Then, after washing it all down with some water, I set off again, walking downhill towards the sea.

Chapter Forty-Two

THE BOY

I heard her. I heard what she said to Michael. And that's when I worked out what's happened. How she found us. And why she thought it was him.

Now she's gone, and Michael has rushed out to find her. I walk through the house as if in a half-dream, not sure where I'm going or what I'm looking for, a confusion and a sadness and a red-hot anger starting to roar within me. On the outside I don't make a sound, but my hand trembles with rage as I push open the door to the bedroom upstairs. Mum's bedroom. The side of her face red from where the man slapped her. The sheets all tangled. The junk all over the floor. I hate it all. 'It's your fault,' I say out loud, tears starting to run down my face. 'It's all your fault.' Then I leave the room before I start smashing things. Because it's true. If she hadn't got off her face and tumbled down the stairs that day I was supposed to be going to Stratford, I would have left the house on time to go to the train station. If I hadn't helped her upstairs and then taken her to the bathroom so she could be sick, things would have been different. Then, when she came to, she started swearing at me, thinking I was making a fuss, trying to make her 'feel bad for being a shit mum'. I stayed silent, which wound her up even more. So she started saying stuff about Dad. About how I must miss him – miss his visits to my room. She said she was always so jealous that he was more interested in visiting my bed than hers. Then it was my turn to be sick. And then I had to go and lie under the covers in my room and try to stop myself from shaking, screaming, turning the whole house to dust and ruins. Of course, by this point, Jessica must have been waiting on that platform for a long time. At some point, she would have started to hear gunshots. Or perhaps shrieks of panic first. But of course, I didn't know about any of that until later on in the evening, and then what I'd done truly hit home.

Now, all these months later, with everything so fucked up and broken, I go over to my laptop, click onto Michael's Facebook account and look at all our chats. Jessica and me. Everything we've said to each other. On Facebook, at least. All the early stuff happened on Circle. And I can't look at that. Not now. It's too much. I take my laptop over to my bed and scroll to one of the happier conversations we had. One where we imagined our lives together.

JESSICA MACLEOD: I can't say, I don't want to jinx it.

MICHAEL KELLEY: Just imagine.

JESSICA MACLEOD: No, Evan, really. I get

superstitious. But… well, if I did… I'd imagine us living somewhere warm. Away from the grey English weather.

MICHAEL KELLEY: Where?

JESSICA MACLEOD: Somewhere where there are seashells – massive ones – just lying on the sand for anyone to pick up. But people don't pick them up. Because they're beautiful where they are already.

MICHAEL KELLEY: God. I think I'm in love with you.

JESSICA MACLEOD: Haha I'm talking nonsense about seashells.

MICHAEL KELLEY: No you're not talking nonsense. You're saying the best things. Best I've ever had anyone say to me.

JESSICA MACLEOD: So, where would you like to live? If you had the choice.

MICHAEL KELLEY: Anywhere. Anywhere where you are.

JESSICA MACLEOD: ♥

MICHAEL KELLEY: I mean it. Somewhere where nobody would find us. And we'd grow old together. And die together.

JESSICA MACLEOD: Woah. We're getting deep.

MICHAEL KELLEY: I mean it.

JESSICA MACLEOD: I know. I do too.

My tears as I read these messages make my pillow damp. My eyes blurry. But I don't move. I just carry on reading. Until, finally, when the rain outside is at its loudest, I fall asleep.

Chapter Forty-Three

THE MOTHER

May. Three months after the attack.

I reach the pier. I haven't been along it since I was a young girl, here on one of our fleeting visits to England. I seem to remember it burning down at least once, maybe twice, since then. The sign in front of the steps leading up to it tells me that it won't officially open for another four hours. I ignore this, and press ahead, trying the doors that lead to the foyer and the little shops selling postcards. They're locked. I'm suddenly filled with an overwhelming need to be out in the open. To be surrounded by something bigger than myself, bigger than my own awful thoughts. I go round the side of the small building and find some fire exit steps leading round the back. The gate swings open easily – perhaps it's been damaged in the storm – and I follow the steps up until I'm making my way onto the main walkway of the pier itself, which runs alongside the tracks of the little train that shuttles visitors who don't wish to walk from one end to the other.

The rush of being out on a stretch of wood in the middle of the water is so strong, it takes me by surprise. It's like water is hitting me from every angle, the waves below me too low to send much spray upwards, but their noise and the rain make it feel like I'm being immersed by them – in danger of being pulled away by the current to… where? Down the Thames? Out to sea? To a better life?

I don't know how long I stay there, along the pier, having walked about a third of its length and now pressed up against the side, sobbing quietly to myself. *If only my phone were working,* I think as I grip its hard, solid mass in my pocket. *I could phone Alec. Tell him to come and get me. Away from the rain, the wind, the sea, away from that boy who murdered our daughter. Who ripped her from our lives and sent us spiralling off into the worst nightmare a parent could possibly experience.*

I slump down against the pier wall and imagine being in my warm bed, back home in Kent. Alec bringing me a cup of tea. Jessica, rushing in to tell me I haven't signed a form for school, or do I know where her netball kit has got to? It makes me smile.

Then something pulls me out of my little trance. Someone calling my name. At first, I think I'm imagining it. But it gets louder and louder, then eventually I hear footsteps. I feel footsteps, vibrating beneath me. A man is running towards me from the start of the pier. No. Not a man. A boy. Michael Kelley.

'What the fuck?' he shouts when he reaches me. He's still in his hoodie and tracksuit and they're completely soaked against his slim frame. 'Why are you sitting here? You'll... die of cold or something.'

It's only now I realise I'm shivering.

'Come on. We need to leave,' he says, holding out his hand. I look at it – his youthful skin, smooth fingernails, one of them slightly jagged where he's torn it or bitten it. Then I take his hand with my good arm and allow him to help me up.

'How did you find me?' I ask once I've got to my feet.

'I saw you trying the entrance. Thought you'd come back to the street once you realised it was closed, but you disappeared round the back. Figured you'd found a way to get onto the pier.'

I don't say anything. Just stare down at the soaked wooden floor and his waterlogged trainers.

'Why did you start attacking me? Why did you hit me like that and scream like a madwoman? What have I done? What did I do to upset you?'

His baffled expression pulls at something inside me. It makes me want to hug him, comfort him, tell him everything is going to be all right. But it also makes me want to punch him, throttle him, make him suffer for not putting two and two together and realising what's destroying me from the inside out. What he caused to happen.

'You killed my daughter.' I say the words as strongly as I can against the shrieking wind.

He looks completely thrown, his eyebrows disappearing into his wet, sandy-blond fringe that's falling over his forehead.

'What the fuck are you talking about? You told me your daughter died in a terrorist attack.'

'She did.'

'Then why are you saying I killed her?'

'Because you did.' I stare at him straight in the eyes as I say this, but I don't see what I've yearned to see. That fear, that panic, that look of being found out, of everything falling apart. He just looks confused.

'You think I'm some terrorist or something? You think I've got guns and all that shit you need to make bombs and go round killing people? You think I'm part of fucking ISIS and shoot people at train stations? Why would you say that?'

'I'm saying you're the reason why she was there. You're the reason why Jessica was on that platform when those... those men arrived with their guns and started pouring bullets into husbands and wives and daughters and sons and... my little girl.'

His look of complete amazement doesn't leave his face. 'You're mad. I'm sorry, but you're really fucking insane.'

'You were in love with her. Or so you said in your messages to her. You arranged to meet her on Stratford station and you didn't turn up. And that's why she died. She was waiting there for you. For hours. And you just didn't bother to show up.' And with that I hit him. Hard across the face, on the side where his scratch marks from earlier are still raw. It surprises him, I see it in his eyes. He lunges towards me, and for a second I'm not sure whether to steady myself or retaliate, but I abandon thought and just act: I hit him again, jolts of pain electrifying my body as my hand connects again with his face. As he's knocked back again, I push him as hard as I can against his shoulders, sending him scrabbling away, trying to retain balance. But he falls. His legs come out from under him and he starts to collapse, almost in slow motion. And as his head drops down, it hits with a sickening thump against the metal bar of the pier wall. And then there's nothing. Just him, lying very still on the ground in front of me, rain running in little streams across his face, his arms, down his back. He doesn't move.

Whenever I've written a death scene for the screen, I've always described the shock the witness – or in some cases, perpetrator – feels when the terrible moment occurs. I know shock. I know pain. And maybe, for this reason, I feel the curtains closing around my mind. The part of my brain revolting against what I've done, screaming as loud as it can, is being steadily silenced, almost by a self-induced anaesthetic. Moments ago, I would have thought killing Michael Kelley would have brought me peace – an inner calm I didn't think I would know again. But I don't feel calm. There's nothing calm about what I've done. And the stillness I'm now feeling has a strange, unnatural quality, like morphine or a sleeping pill, as if to shield me from the true horror of what I'm seeing.

I don't check his pulse. I don't call an ambulance. I just

feel in his pockets for his phone and pull it out. I think about throwing it over the side, but something stops me, and I pocket it instead. With one last look at the body, slumped and bleeding on the ground before me, I turn away from him and start to walk, slowly and carefully, back along the pier.

Chapter Forty-Four

THE MOTHER

May. Three months after the attack.

The journey back to the hotel passes like a blur. I don't hear the wind, or the rain. I don't notice it stopping. I only realise the force of the storm has abated when I walk up the steps of the hotel and then collapse in the front lobby.

People rush round. Someone shouts to get help. Adamant that I don't need an ambulance, I bat away their concern and struggle to my feet. 'It's my own fault,' I say, 'I went out for a walk before breakfast. Should have eaten something.'

It's too early for the restaurant to be open, and the staff are still clamouring to call paramedics for me, but I'm very firm with them that it isn't necessary. Just a plate of toast sent to my room would be enough, thank you. A lot of worried faces follow me to the lift.

In my room, I sit on my bed, not thinking, not properly

337

comprehending what's just happened. Then the toast arrives and I sit and eat it in one of the armchairs, enjoying its plump, expensive feel compared to the sofas in the house of the previous day. All of that feels like a lifetime ago now.

Then I put my phone on charge and strip off my clothes. Before I get into bed I find my medication from the hospital and swallow more pills than any doctor would advise. At last, I'm ready to get in amongst the covers of a proper big, comfortable bed and go to sleep for an eternity.

I wake at 2pm, quite naturally. Nobody has disturbed me. No hotel staff have called an ambulance for me against my will. No police have come to arrest me. Nothing has changed. I roll over and see my phone is now fully charged, with a buzzing stack of messages from Alec – both texts and missed calls. I ignore them all. I get up, ignoring my pain the best I can, and walk slowly to the shower. Once under its warm rush, I allow myself to cry. Big, gasping sobs, water coming in through my mouth and nose as I do, but I don't care. I just allow the emotion to rush through me, filling every corner of my body. I'm not sure how long I'm in there, but eventually, after I can't cry any longer, I raise my hand to shut off the water.

In the comfort of the hotel dressing gown, I sit on my bed and pick up my phone. Clearing all the notifications on the scuffed, slightly cracked screen, I navigate my way to the website of Skyscanner. In the 'from' column I select 'London (UK)' and in the 'to' column I select 'Perth (AUS)' and click the search icon. Up comes a list of options and I click 'One way'. I select an Emirates airlines flight to Australia. Nineteen hours, including a stop-off at Dubai. I don't think about what I'm doing. I just do it, as if on autopilot. It's the only thing that feels natural. There's nothing here for me now.

I set about making myself look normal and presentable. I wash my hair and dry it. I put on my make-up. Pick out a nice top and black trousers. Then I stand, looking at myself in the mirror. Before I leave, I pop a few more pills, do up my bag, then turn and look round the room. The enormous TV screen glints back at me. *It's all over*, I think to myself. Then I close the door for good.

They order me a car at the desk to take me to the airport.

'There is a very large television in my room,' I say to the woman on the front desk.

'Yes, I know, madam,' she says. Polite, but there's an edge to her voice. Apparently everyone knows about the TV. What a stir I seem to have caused during my visit.

'Please keep it. It is a gift to the hotel.'

She looks like I've just threatened her with a gun. 'Oh, erm, I'm not sure that's possible… we require guests to take all personal—'

'It is a gift,' I repeat. 'And if it's really a problem, please have it shipped to my home address.' I take a sheet of paper from the desk without asking and scribble the address of the house in Kent. 'My husband will pay for courier costs, and any other charges I've incurred while staying here.'

She nods. 'We already have his card on file.'

'Excellent. Well, goodbye and thank you.'

I leave and wait outside for my car on the front porch. The rain has now stopped and the sky shows signs of clearing. Behind the clouds, I can see the first glimmer of sun come out. I've almost forgotten what that looks like.

In the taxi, I look through my bag at my reading material. It should keep me set-up on the flight. It's been a while since I've done something as extensive as nineteen hours. No pressures on one to do anything else, like exercising or laundry or admin. Just hours and hours stretching ahead to be filled. And it makes me desperately sad that it's come at a moment when I can't possibly enjoy it. A time when being a prisoner to my own thoughts for hours feels like torture.

'Are you all right, madam?' The driver is looking at me in his mirror, concerned.

I wipe the tear from my eye and sniff. 'Yes, I'm fine. Don't worry about me. Just… things.'

He nods understandingly, as if he knows about 'things', and doesn't bother me again.

When I get to Heathrow, I go straight to security, thanking the heavens I've always kept my passport in the inside zip pocket of my small travel bag. I don't have any luggage for the hold, just the carry-on.

Before heading for the first-class lounge, I purchase two more books. It's unlikely I'll run out on the flight, but airport book shopping seems like a holiday tradition. In the past I would have eagerly stacked up multiple enjoyably nasty crime novels. I doubt that will ever be possible now. I opt for a Jane Fallon, a Jill Mansell and, as a wild card, a re-issued paperback edition of Nigella Lawson's *How to Cook*.

I spend the ninety-minute wait lost within the pages of the Nigella, finding her writing and calm, considered instructions soothing. I remember my battered old copy of this at home, along with a number of other cook books. I used to enjoy cooking, especially when Jessica was little. She used to sit and help me sift flour or stir sauces. Things my own mother never did with me. I think back to the home I'm travelling towards. I wonder how much has changed. Will it all be the same, or will it have turned into a slick, ultra-modern Americanised landscape? I think back to my life there as a teen. Difficult, uncomfortable, always punishing my parents for this or that, always aware of either their resentment or indifference towards me, depending on the day.

It takes an age to board the plane. First-class passengers are allowed to board first, but even after the economy crowd have settled down we end up waiting an age. An announcement is eventually made – something to do with the luggage doors – and we're told to wait for further instructions.

I fish into my bag, keen to get back to Nigella, and my hand touches against something. Cool, hard glass. It's Jessica's iPhone. It's got very low battery – only sixteen per cent – and I dim the screen and, without thinking too much about what I'm doing, touch the Facebook Messenger icon. I select the messages with the name at the top. Michael Kelley. I scroll back to the beginning. Then I begin to read.

Chapter Forty-Five

THE MOTHER

May. Three months after the attack.

JESSICA MACLEOD: Hi

MICHAEL KELLEY: Hi

JESSICA MACLEOD: Funny to be talking on here. Better than on Circle. Less baggage. More free.

MICHAEL KELLEY: Yeah

JESSICA MACLEOD: Don't go all one-word-answers on me now.

MICHAEL KELLEY: Sorry

JESSICA MACLEOD: That was one word AGAIN!

MICHAEL KELLEY: Soz

JESSICA MACLEOD: Are you trying to wind me up?

MICHAEL KELLEY: Maybe

JESSICA MACLEOD: Cute pic.

MICHAEL KELLEY: Careful. I don't want you getting the hots for my brother.

JESSICA MACLEOD: Don't worry. I won't. You sure he won't see these chats?

MICHAEL KELLEY: I told you – he never uses it.

JESSICA MACLEOD: Why don't you have your own account?

MICHAEL KELLEY: Never got round to it.

JESSICA MACLEOD: Come on, Evan. Tell me.

MICHAEL KELLEY: People at school. They can be dicks.

JESSICA MACLEOD: Like, bullying…?

MICHAEL KELLEY: Something like that. Prefer not to go into it. Kept putting sick stuff on my wall. Kept

sending me messages saying awful things. I thought
I've got enough awful things in my head without others
chipping in.

JESSICA MACLEOD: Oh Evan. I'm sorry.

I stare at the name. Four letters. They go through my
mind, over and over. Sinking in. *Evan. Evan Kelley.* And
then it starts to click. His face. Michael's face. The
confusion. The denial. My blind anger at him. Hitting him.
Stopping him from existing, going about his life as if Jessica
was nothing to him.

But she *was* nothing to him. Because he didn't know she
existed.

I got the wrong boy.

I scream. One long, pain-filled scream.

The woman in the window seat next to me instantly
leaps up and hits her head on the luggage rack above us.
The couple to my right back away, as if I'm about to draw
out a weapon and launch some kind of attack. Within
seconds, members of the cabin crew are swarming round
me. I hear one of them finishing their conversation with a
passenger abruptly, saying, 'Excuse me, we've got a
situation.' That's what I've become. A situation.

The scream is turning into sobs and a young man in
uniform is talking slowly and calmly to me. 'I need to you
breathe deeply. Listen to me, breathe deeply.' I shake my
head, but he carries on talking. 'Can you tell me your name,
madam?'

'Caroline,' I choke out.

'OK, Caroline. Take a moment and then tell me why you're upset. Are you scared of flying?'

A plastic cup of water is produced by one of his colleagues and offered to me. I take it and sip the freezing-cold water like icy razors trickling down my throat.

'No.' I shake my head. 'I mean, yes. That's it. I... I'm not used to doing it alone.' It seems like the most natural reason and I clutch onto it gratefully.

'OK,' he says again, his voice soothing and kind. 'Well, while we're waiting for the preparation for take-off, how about you come up to the front with me. You could even have a chat with the pilot, if you like?'

I instantly feel panic surge in me. 'I don't need to talk to the pilot. Honestly. I'm going to be fine.' I hand him back the empty cup and tuck my hands out of sight so he doesn't see how much they are shaking. 'I'm much better. Really.'

He smiles and nods. 'OK, Caroline. Remember, you can always press the button on the side of your seat and one of us will come to talk to you or get you anything you need.'

I try to look thankful back and nod.

He walks away towards the front of the aircraft and the woman who had been sitting next to me, and extricated herself during my outburst, shuffles back into her seat, eyeing me cautiously. 'You all right now?' she says, although it sounds more as if she's asking, *Are you going to do that again?* rather than asking if I'm OK.

'Yes. I just had a bit of a shock.'

She gives me another wary glance, then settles back into the pages of *Fifty Shades Darker*.

'To all our passengers, this is your pilot speaking. I'm

pleased to tell you the fault has been corrected and we are now ready to begin our journey to the runway. We do apologise for the delay – rest assured we should be on our way shortly.'

This announcement causes mutterings of 'Typical' and 'About bloody time'. I just try and focus on my breathing, trying to keep it long and controlled, and not let my mind go back to Southend Pier and the body of Michael Kelley, lying lifeless on the ground in the rain.

We encounter further troubles in Dubai when they can't get the tunnel that connects the aircraft to the terminal to fit onto the plane. A horde of stressed travellers berate a harassed-looking flight attendant as she explains to them the problem will be fixed as soon as possible. The problem isn't fixed and in the end we have to make our way down a staircase and out into the heat and walk the short distance to the doors of the airport. The temperature, after weeks of chilly rain in England, and the over-zealous air conditioning of the flight, is an assault on the senses. My skin feels as if it's reforming, recalibrating, trying to cope with the sudden change. I try to fish around in my bag for my sunglasses, but someone behind me pushes and tuts, so I give up and use my hand to shield my eyes.

Inside the airport, I go and get a coffee. Over the past hours I've tried to focus on reading, but my mind won't behave. At some points, when I had a short nap, I couldn't help but wonder if maybe it was all just a dream. Maybe today's the day I left Alec in Kent, before the pier, before the crash, before I met Michael Kelley. I told him I was going to Australia on the phone, when he was angry about me leaving without telling him. And now I'm doing just that. Perhaps everything that occurred in the middle was just a nightmare, triggered by grief. It isn't the case. I know that. I just wish it was.

The stopover in Dubai takes four hours, and I spend most of it sitting, staring into space, punctuated by occasional attempts to distract myself by looking in the shops. I browse the paperback fiction, nearly all of it imported from the UK. I can't find anything I want and drift over to the chairs. I look around at the passengers sitting near me. I wonder how they would react if I told them everything that was on my mind right now. How many would sympathise or condemn me if I laid out everything that had happened? About my Jessica. About my strange breakdown, running off to Southend. And my terrible, terrible mistake that has culminated in the death of an innocent, damaged boy. My mind involuntarily flicks back to his body, lying there still and lifeless on the floor of the pier. Was he dead? Could there, perhaps, be a chance he could still be alive? I consider doing a trawl of news sites, trying to discover something definitive, but I know that's beyond me. Even typing the words into Google would jeopardise whatever equilibrium I've managed to maintain since my outburst on the plane. It takes me a while to realise the strange tapping sound that has started to pull me out of my daydream is the noise of my own tears, falling onto the pages of the book in front of me.

Chapter Forty-Six

THE MOTHER

May. Three months after the attack.

'You are fucking kidding me, right?'

My mother's harsh Australian croak of a voice hits me down the phone line like a bullet.

'I thought it would be nice to see you,' I say, holding the phone close to my ear. I'm standing by luggage collection – it's the quietest part of the arrivals area of Perth Airport, with most people now finished collecting their bags and making their happy, though clearly exhausted, way to their hotels.

'Why the fuck are you bothering, Caroline? Really. What's brought this on?'

I feel anger beginning to bubble up inside me. 'Ah, you see, your granddaughter's been murdered by a world-famous terrorist organisation,' I say through clenched teeth. 'Thought maybe that would justify a meet-up. Maybe I was wrong.'

'Don't give me that. That happened months ago and you didn't even want me to come to the funeral.'

'You never met her,' I say, trying to stop myself crying. 'So why would you want to see her coffin? You didn't care enough about her to see her when she was living, so why the hell would you care about her death?'

A small, balding man with a lime-green suitcase is hovering by the luggage conveyor belt and glances over at me. I stare back at him until he can't hold my gaze any more and turns away.

'May I remind you,' my mother says in a slow-talking, are-you-fucking-thick-or-something voice that I know only too well from my childhood, 'that it was you that phoned me today – I don't want you bringing all your baggage to my doorstep. It was you who washed your hands of me, and now you're trying to make out like I'm some kind of wicked witch of the fucking west.'

'I'm at Perth Airport,' I say, ignoring her diatribe. 'Can you come and get me?'

Silence greets this. Then she starts up again: 'You're fucking what? I thought you were phoning from England. You're actually in the country, right now?'

'Yes.'

Some spitting, tutting sound fills my ears, then she says, 'I hope you're not expecting me to put you up?'

'Well, yes, actually I was, but I can get a hotel instead. Actually, you're right, that would probably be best.'

'You won't get any argument from me on that front. Must be nice, being a multimillionaire from making pornographic TV shows.'

This is too much for me. 'They're not pornographic!' I shriek into the phone. The man with the green suitcase has now been joined by a woman, presumably his partner, and they both jump at this. 'What?' I say to them, my arms wide, as if daring them to a fight. They scurry away, the woman turning to get a good look at me before they turn the corner.

I put the phone back to my ear. My mother's still ranting.

'Oh I did watch a couple. I know you think I don't, but no, I thought fair's fair, she's gone and made a go of it. They come on the telly here, on that BBC First channel. Apparently they call graphic depictions of oral sex highbrow *drama* these days.' She says the word 'drama' like it's a new-fangled fad.

'There are no graphic depictions of anything like that. And anyway, I can't talk about this now. I need to sleep. I guess I'll get a taxi to you and then work out a hotel from there.'

My mother doesn't try to argue further. 'Fine. You know the address?'

'Of course I know the bloody address, I lived there for—'

The line goes dead. She's cut me off.

Sighing and wincing as I try to pick up my bag with my bad arm, I start to walk slowly towards the main exit and contemplate whether they'll accept card or insist on me paying with the Australian dollars I haven't had time to get.

Most of the taxis have either a 'CARDS ACCEPTED' sticker or a Visa logo on them, and within minutes I'm in the car, windows down, staring out at the sweeping mass of Perth. The sun's warm, but there's quite a breeze in the air – like a slightly cold summer's day in England, although it's almost midwinter here.

The traffic is light and the journey only takes an hour. Gradually, the streets start to become suburban and familiar to me. Small rows of shops start to trigger memories I thought I'd long forgotten. Memories of drinking milkshakes in a small café called 'Cole's Caff', still there after all this time. Memories of long, drawn-out days of reading books in the town library so as to avoid going home. A second-hand car sales centre, looking more or less identical to how it was before, just with different cars. It used to be staffed by a young guy I'd fancied named Brave. Ridiculous name, I'd thought. Who names their child Brave? He'd have been in his early twenties back then, which means he must be heading towards fifty. What was he doing now, I wondered. Did he have a family?

And what about the kindly old librarian, Mrs Harl, who'd felt sorry for me on those sunny Saturdays when I was tucked inside the library in a dark, quiet corner, away from the heat and the summer fun and, crucially, my parents? She used to bring me ice-cold Diet Cokes from the fridge in their staffroom. What age did she reach before she died? Or Reg Price, the slightly creepy but harmless caretaker who'd lock the big library doors behind me when I had to leave for the day and go back to my uncomfortable home life. He'd been a strange man, frequently to be seen muttering to himself between the bookshelves, probably single-handedly responsible for ensuring the place was often deserted, local mothers with young kids uneasy about being around him. 'There's no harm in him,' Mrs Harl had said, and told me how he'd joined some weird English cult when he was a young man, which had made him go 'just a tad loopy', and he'd never been the same since he'd come back to Perth. I'd nodded at this and decided to always be kind to Reg. He was an outsider, someone who never really fitted into the town he called home. I knew how he felt.

Now, returning after all these years, it seems both incredible and oddly comforting that the place has continued to trundle along without me. Some things changing, some lives coming to an end, but everything largely staying the same.

Before I've managed to properly prepare myself, the Toyota Corolla is winding its way up the driveway to my mother's house. The house I used to call home. And it's changed. The front used to be a grand, impressive sight when you arrived via the long driveway, and part of me as a teenager enjoyed seeing friends' faces as it came into view. We were more than just comfortable. We were wealthy. A family to talk about. Not that my parents socialised much with the neighbourhood. They made it clear when they bought it that they weren't going to be chummy with the two eccentric sisters who lived next door ('There's something distinctly *lesbian* about those two...') or the family of four opposite ('Shifty-eyed, the lot of them'). But both my mother and father were quietly respected – even slightly feared – within our community.

I'd see other mums and dads pointing at them if they bothered to turn up to a parents' evening or school play: 'It's the Byrnes,' they'd whisper and try not to stare. I think it's because they had some strange charisma I'd never quite managed to suss out. And when my father died, my mother was no longer 'Mrs Byrne'. She became 'The Widow'.

Rumours circulated like wildfire about how the accident happened – his fall into the deep cellar, severing both his spine and his neck when he hit the concrete floor below, caused great speculation. I even heard some of my teachers talking about it in the staffroom when they thought everyone had gone home. 'The whole thing was deliberate. Everyone knew their marriage was, well, *weird*. And I think maybe she just snapped and decided to set it all up as an accident. And nobody could prove it wasn't.'

I'd actually enjoyed hearing that. Enjoyed this idea of my mother plotting to kill her bastard husband. Because, if that had been the case, maybe I would have liked her a bit more. At the time, I managed to convince myself that the rumours were false.

But that was then.

'What the hell has happened to the front of the house?' It's the first thing I say to the mother I haven't seen for twenty years as she comes out onto the veranda to meet me.

'Hello to you too,' she says. Some mothers kiss their children and hug them after a long time away. She doesn't.

She folds her arms to make it quite clear there will be no physical contact.

'Hi,' I say, glancing her up and down, taking her in. She's lost weight – quite remarkably so. She'd always been a little plump around her waist and neck. Now she is slim, almost wiry, like some old starving bird. Her long, once-blonde hair – our shared attribute – has gone grey, though in a chic Helen Mirren sort of way rather than looking as if she's gone to seed.

'We had a fire,' she says, raising her eyes to the blackened wood and stone above her. 'It stained most of the front.'

'Jesus,' I say. In spite of everything, there's a twinge of guilt inside me for not knowing. 'Is the place safe to live in?'

She tuts. 'Course it's safe. It will take more than a little chip-pan fire to bring this place to the ground.'

She turns on her heel and walks back inside. I realise that the taxi driver is waiting patiently behind me in the car, avidly watching the odd reunion unfold. I tap my card on his machine, snatch up my bag and follow my mother inside.

'Is that all you've brought with you?' she says, glancing at my luggage. 'Not staying long?'

'I'm here for good.'

She freezes and turns back to me. 'For good?' Although she's speaking quietly – dangerously so – I swear I hear the chandelier above us tinkle slightly from the tension in her voice.

'Yes. I've left Alec. I'm moving back to Australia.'

She stares at me for what feels like a full minute and

then shrugs. 'I'm amazed it lasted as long as it did. What was the final straw?'

I shrug back. 'I don't know. He was too Scottish.'

'Isn't that a racist remark? You always used to have a go at me for my "socially inconsiderate" language. Come on, I'm being serious, Caroline.'

'Are you being serious? Because surely to most people it would be absolutely obvious why our marriage may have imploded. Something to do with me losing a CHILD. A child who was MURDERED.' I shout the most emotive parts of the sentence, but my mother doesn't blink. She just gives me one of her long stares again and then holds up a finger.

'First warning,' she says.

'What?' I spit back.

'You heard,' she comes closer to me now and I can smell her Chanel perfume. Christ, it takes me back.

'If you're staying here, even if it's just for the night, I don't want any hysterics. You were always prone to hysterics when you were a kid and I'd have hoped middle age would have knocked it out of you. If not, then any number of the local hotels are at your disposal. As I said, must be nice being able to splash out on luxuries like that.'

'You're not exactly poor yourself,' I say, gaining back some of the momentum she's tried to kill. 'And while we're at it, why haven't you redecorated since the fire?' I gesture at the walls around me. The wallpaper is brown with smoke marks, some parts of it actually black and cracked. 'This place must be some kind of health hazard.'

'Oh it's not that bad,' she says, rolling her eyes. 'I'll get Xavier to sort it out at some point.'

'Xavier?' I look at her in confusion. Then something occurs to me, 'Mum, have you remarried?'

She lets out a cold, bitter laugh. 'Remarried? I'd rather kill myself. No, Xavier is a sort of live-in assistant. He's been a lifesaver, I have to say. He lives in one of the pool houses, although I let him come inside during the winter months.'

I'm baffled by all this. 'Who the hell is this man? Some kind of servant?'

My mother settles herself down on one of the smoke-damaged lilac sofas. 'I'm not as young as I was, Caroline. It's good to have a strong, strapping lad to lift all the heavy things, do the cleaning, the washing, the ironing, look after the plants and pool.'

'He does all that by himself?'

I see her hands tense. She grips the sofa, the nails digging in. 'It might surprise you to learn that, once upon a time, I did all of that, Caroline. I was the fucking servant to you and your father, and never got a word of thanks.'

'You were not!' Her dishonesty is so audacious, it's breath-taking. 'You make out like you were some put-upon domestic victim. You and Dad were both as vicious as each other. And I did the laundry.'

She's now gone from clutching at the sofa cushions to scratching at them, as if trying to remove a stubborn mark from the fabric.

'Instead of taking a trip down memory lane, why don't you sit down and tell me why you're actually here?'

I take in a breath, sharply and involuntarily. My eyes snap to hers. It's so like my mother. You think she's fooled. You think she's been strung along. But she's been aware of your tricks from your first move.

'I told you. I'm divorcing my husband.'

She shakes her head. 'I don't buy it.'

'Well, it's the truth.'

'That's as may be. But I don't think it's the reason you've come. You don't run away. Unless you have to.'

'I ran away from you.'

She gives me a slow nod. 'Exactly.'

I wait a few seconds. Then, simply because I don't think I have anything else to lose, I say: 'I'm here because I killed someone.'

Her face is motionless. Unreadable. Not even a tremor. This is the woman that gets nauseous at the idea of family bonding or gestures of love, but doesn't blink at murder.

'Is it your husband?' she says at last.

I shake my head.

'Then do go on.'

'I don't think it's worth me getting into it all. The police will be here soon. In fact, I'm astonished they didn't stop me at the airport.'

Still that blank look. 'So why did you bother coming here? Why did you want to see me after all this time?'

I try to match her blank expression, stripping the emotion from my voice as much as I can handle. 'Because I think I now finally understand you. More than I did before. Better than I did before.'

'And why is that?' There's something in her eyes now. Is

it resolve? Or a challenge? Daring me to go further into this new unknown.

'Because we now have something important in common. Something more than most mothers and daughters. We're both murderers.'

Chapter Forty-Seven

THE MOTHER

May. Three months after the attack.

After I've said that sentence, my mother and I stare at each other for a long time. Then she looks away and down at my bag.

'I think,' she says slowly, 'you need to get yourself unpacked. And I'll get Xavier to rustle up some dinner.'

I wait a moment, to see if there's anything else she wants to say. But nothing arrives.

'OK,' I reply eventually. We both stand up and she leads the way out into the living room and towards the stairs. Despite the fire damage, the place is still impressive, though there's more dust than my parents used to tolerate. The place is cavernous, creaking. Why she hasn't just sold it and bought something small and manageable is beyond me. The fact that she and Dad bought it in the first place, when we finally left Saudi, was puzzling at the time. Now its existence seems utterly preposterous.

'I'm afraid I had your old room stripped out and converted into a place for my Sylvanian Family collection.' She says this like it's the most normal thing in the world, and I can't find it within myself to feel hurt. The thought of revisiting my teenage self – posters of pop stars and soap actors I fancied – would have been a bit too intense. 'Xavier sleeps in there, too. Mostly during the winter, although he's yet to move all his stuff from the pool house properly yet. Just don't touch his things. Or mine.'

'How many years has he been working for you?' I ask.

'Since he was sixteen.'

'Christ, I swear that's child labour or something. How old is he now?'

'Eighteen.'

'Surely he should be out enjoying himself or at university getting smashed like most boys his age?'

'He brings girls back sometimes. Has sex with them in there. You see how accepting I've become, Caroline? How tolerant I now am in my old age?'

I let out a sigh, 'What do you want, a sticker or something?'

She ignores this and leads me past the room that used to be mine and towards the guest bedroom. It hasn't changed one bit. Part of me worries the bed hasn't been slept in or made since the 1990s.

'This is where you'll sleep,' she says, stating the obvious. 'I'll ask Xavier to wash the covers tomorrow. They're clean, but might be a bit old.'

'OK,' I say. 'Is he here now?'

Without talking, she walks past me, round the bed and

over to the window. I follow her, and she raises a bony finger to point out to the pool. Inside, the water is rippling, the evening light dancing on its sleek folds. Then, as if on cue, a tanned, athletic-looking teenage boy arrives at the side in a rush and gets out nimbly. He's unclothed, apart from a pair of very small, very tight Tom Daley style swimming trunks. I glance over at my mother, to see if she has visibly registered his near-nudity, but she seems unmoved.

After a few moments, she turns away from the window and goes to exit the room, turning before she leaves completely. 'Have a sleep. Unpack. Come down in two hours. Xavier will have cooked us something by then.'

I nod. 'Do you have any painkillers?'

She eyes me, suspiciously. 'Why?'

'Because I was in a car accident recently.'

I can tell she's not sure whether to take this as a flippant comeback or the truth. Whichever, she decides not to investigate any further. 'I'll have Xavier bring some up.'

As promised, the boy arrives at my bedroom door within ten minutes, now dry and dressed in shorts and a Hollister T-shirt, clutching a pharmacy bag. 'I was told to bring this to you,' he says. 'I'm Xavier, by the way.'

His voice is low, his accent soft, and his eyes focus on me as if he's already slightly bored with my presence.

'I'm Caroline,' I say, holding out a hand.

He shakes it and hands me the paper bag, then says, 'I hear you're here because you've killed someone.'

I can't quite believe the words have come out of his mouth. 'Sorry?'

'Your mother said you're here because you've killed someone. In England. So, are you on the run or something?'

I sit down on the bed and turn away from him. 'Something like that.'

He just sniffs a little and says 'Cool.' Then he leaves the room, closing the door behind him.

I lie back and try to sleep, but I can't seem to drift off. My mind is still buzzing, the strangeness of the situation closing in on me. And all the while, that name, that face, floating before my eyes. *Michael Kelley. Michael Kelley. Michael Kelley.*

I go to my bag and fish out Jessica's phone and unlock it. It only has 8 per cent battery and I'm in the midst of rootling around for my charger when I realise it won't fit in the mains and I don't have an adaptor.

I lower the brightness even further so it's barely even readable and close the curtains. Then, settling back, I return to the conversation I read on the plane and reread it. Then reread it again. On the third time, something strikes me. Circle. The Circle App. There was a reference to it before. In the flirty messages I read between them. Before I'd even met the Kelley boys. And here it was again.

I go back to Jessica's home screen, flick through all her apps, then find it. It's a white square with a black outline of a circle in the middle of it. I click it. A white background with a large grey sphere fills the screen, followed by a login request. I type in her email and then begin guessing passwords. I get locked out after three, but then remember I have access to her email inbox. Within minutes I've reset her password and navigated back to the Circle app. I'm in. And what greets me chills my blood.

> Welcome. Circle is a safe space where survivors of child abuse and neglect can connect, share experiences, and support each other through difficult times. Please see our FAQs section of the app for our full terms of use, as well as dos and don'ts, or visit www.circlesupporthub.com.

My eyes scan over the words again. *Child abuse.*

My hands are shaking when I tap through the welcome message and on to the main home screen. I click on the first page: *Reach Out Stories.*

At the top, a heading unfurls to explain the purpose of the section:

> Reach Out Stories are where members of Circle can introduce themselves and share why they are here and, if they wish, go into detail about their experiences.

I look down at the latest post. It's from someone calling themselves Daniel91. I begin to read.

> Hi, I'm new here (obviously). I'm Daniel, I'm 26, I have a decent job and a girlfriend I love. But I've got to a point in my life where I need to talk about the things that

happened to me when I was ten when my parents sent me off camping with my mate and his dad.

I don't read on. I feel sick. Horrified. And the only reason I'm on there is to find one thing – one thing I'm sure, with devastating inevitability, must be there somewhere. I start scrolling through, madly, trying to go to older posts, not stopping to find a search function or easier route. Then I stop when a name catches my eye. EssexEvan.

I haven't found Jessica. But I've found him.

Hey, I'm Evan. I found out about this app from a leaflet thing in my local library. I go there sometimes to get away from people at school and have been reading stories here on Circle for a month now. I didn't think I'd want to share mine but I think now I'm ready. When I was very small, my dad used to fuck me and my brother. My brother got off a bit lighter compared to me – he put up more of a fight. But for some reason I never could fight back. Then, one day, Dad took me in a van I hadn't seen before and said we were going to meet some friends of his. Friends who wanted to see me. Looking back now, I know who some of them were. They weren't friends of my dad. And some of them were famous. Famous people, paying to do awful things. I didn't know who they were then, but I've worked it out now. Nobody ask me to say their names – that's not why I'm here, so don't push me on it. I just needed to share what happened so it doesn't feel like some sick dream inside my head.

Again, I find I can't read on, but look at some of the comments on his post. Someone called JasmineX2 had commented:

So horrible what people in power get away with. My heart goes out to you.

Another girl called MarissaIre97 said:

I think you should say their names. It would probably help. And then you should go to the police or the press.

And then, from only a few weeks ago, someone named Robert45 commented:

Just seen on the news that a bunch of MPs have been arrested, including one they thought might be the next Prime Minister – Ernest Kellman. Was he one of the guys? Did you end up going to the police? Or was it someone else? Man, this story is going to be BIG.

I remember seeing the news reports that Robert45 had been referring to. I'd barely even thought about them. Didn't think my life would go near anything like that. I should have learned from past experience that's not how it works. Most parents think – hope – it won't be their child killed in a terrorist attack. Until it happens to them. And then they realise anything is possible. Even the very worst things.

I find Jessica's post after a couple of minutes. She's

called herself JessieCAR. Tears start to fill my eyes. It's how she used to write her name on her scrapbooks and drawings when she was a child, even though she knew perfectly well how to spell her name properly, with a little doodle of a purple car underneath. I take a deep breath, then begin to read her post.

My name's Jessica. I'm 16 and have a great life, a great time at school, everything's perfect. Except for a big, terrible secret that I think I'll go mad if I don't share. Which is why I'm here, really. I've never told anyone this, ever. And I don't know if I ever will in real life. But here's the truth: When I was a child, my uncle used to make me do things – sexual things. It happened quite a few times, usually when my parents had him babysitting me when they went out for a meal, or if he looked after me on afternoons when my mum was working, and one time when I went to stay with him and his awful wife when my parents went on a weekend mini-break. I don't really want to go into what he did, and at the time I didn't really realise how bad or serious the whole thing was. I liked spending time with my uncle, and he always used to make it into a 'little game'. I'm now in my teens, and have always struggled to be in his company. I only manage it if I put on a performance, like an actor. I imagine this other girl with my name and how she'd act around her uncle if he'd never done anything wrong. Most of the time it works. But recently, at a family party, he touched my arm – not weirdly, at that moment, but it brought it all back. And one thing has always really upset me, especially now that I'm older. When he used to do what he used to do, he never called me by my real name. He'd just whisper into my ear – something I used to struggle to work out, but the more it happened, the more I became sure. He kept saying my mum's name to me. He kept saying 'Caroline', and telling me he loved me. And that, more than anything, has made it impossible ever to tell her.

Her post ends there. Abruptly. Without any of the positivity with which she started.

I'm done. Finished. And so is the phone. The screen dims. Then goes black.

Chapter Forty-Eight

THE MOTHER

Eleven years to go.

'Caroline. Please. This wasn't a mistake.'

I was standing by the window, my head in my hands. 'Fuck,' I said, taking in a slow, unsteady breath, 'fuck, fuck, fuck.'

Rob let me swear, sitting in silence for a minute, then he came over to me and tried to put a hand on my shoulder.

'Don't. Honestly. I really can't.' I whispered the words, but they still came out as clearly and crisplp as if I'd projected them from a podium. I felt his flinch. His hurt.

'I don't understand. You wanted to. It was you who led me up here.'

'I know,' I said, moving away. Out of reach. I can hardly believe that a few minutes ago I was clawing at the smooth, toned body of my husband's brother, desperate for him, my hands running down his chest, towards his belt, unbuckling it, his lips finding my mouth, his tongue touching mine.

It had only lasted a couple of minutes. If that.

'Maybe we should just sit down. And cuddle. I'd like that, Caroline. I just want to be close to you.'

'Listen, Rob,' I said, turning back round to face him. He knew where this was going. Nobody ever said 'listen' without following it with bad or disappointing news. 'I care for you. I really do. And maybe, if things were different, in another world...'

He lowered his head to the floor, suddenly looking smaller, vulnerable, ashamed. 'In another world, you'd want to be with me,' he said, his voice sounding like he wasn't far from tears. You'd find me attractive. You'd leave Alec for me. You'd love me.'

I couldn't cope with this. I'd have preferred it if he'd stormed out, tried to have a row. But his sudden disintegration was awful to witness.

'You know it's more complicated than that,' I said, doing my best not to let my frustration – my disappointment – show too clearly. 'I do want to be with you. I do find you attractive. But with Jessica and the house... it's not ideal, I know. But I can't stop that. I can't jeopardise that.'

I sat down on the bed and after a few moments, he came over to join me.

We sat there, not saying anything, for almost a full minute. Then he laid his head on my shoulder, his short hair prickling my neck slightly. Then he leant properly into me and I into him, and within a split second we were kissing properly again and leaning back onto the bed, falling into the pillows, and the world was spinning and I was in the centre of it, and it was just me, me and Rob, me and Rob, merging together, becoming one.

There was none of the awkward fumbling one usually gets with first times. After our initial upset, our tear shedding, we were finally ready, emotionally, physically, desperate for each other. He threw off his jeans and shirt and climbed back on top of me, moving rhythmically, our bodies working in sync, silk-like, smooth and perfect, both of us completely caught up in everything we were doing. Although even then I could feel it. Feel the difference. There was an intensity to the sex that was only there for him. Not for me. My thrill was being able – for the first time in so many years – to escape from Alec. Be my own person again. Enjoy a new flavour, a new horizon, a new canvas to paint on. But as I stared into Rob's eyes, there was a focus that was so strong it almost scared me.

We lay together afterwards, our naked bodies entwined, tangled up with the duvet, half of it falling off the bed. Eventually we let it fall, so there was just us, lying there in the afternoon sun. The sound of Jessica watching Disney's *Return to Neverland* downstairs in the lounge. Rob's hands gently stroking my arm, making me feel more loved, more wanted than my husband had in years.

It was only when we heard Jessica downstairs shouting, 'Movie's finished! Ice cream time!' that we sat up. Without saying anything, I got off the bed, pulled on some clothes and walked out onto the landing. 'OK, darling. Give Mummy two minutes, I just need to sort out some things with Uncle Rob for next week. Get all your things together and shoes on, then I'll be down.'

'OK!' she shouted back. Always happy. Always content with whatever explanation she received.

Back in the bedroom, I saw Rob had shifted forwards and was sitting on the edge of the bed, his eyes worried once more.

'Don't say this was a mistake,' he begged, 'I couldn't bear it if you say that again.'

'It wasn't a mistake,' I said, folding my arms, making my decision. 'But we need to be careful.' I saw his eyes widen with interest as I continued. 'I think we could come to an arrangement that works,' I said, speaking slowly, thinking it all through. 'Maybe you could have Jessica like this on Friday evenings, after school. I really enjoy having this afternoon to work on my writing. Just having the house to myself and setting aside some time is a dream. Maybe we could make this a regular thing, seeing as you don't work on Fridays and Alec doesn't get back until late. Jessica likes you, she tells me constantly at home. And then, when I finish… I could come back here and…'

He smiled, and I was relieved. I was worried he was going to ask me to leave Alec, to get a divorce, that he'd decided this was a star-crossed lovers situation. But his grin told me he was more than open to trying out my plan.

'I think it might work out rather well.'

Chapter Forty-Nine

THE MOTHER

May. Three months after the attack.

The hours after I read the truth of what Jessica has been through at the hands of her uncle, Rob MacLeod, pass before me in a blur. It's as if they belonged to those drunken hours when you're a teenager – when you dimly become aware you've staggered home alone when you shouldn't have and there's vomit on your dress and you're not quite sure what time it is or if you're supposed to have school or work in the morning. It's been years since I experienced that. But it all comes back to you, very quickly. And there's vomit. A lot of vomit.

I look at the mess of it on my mother's bathroom floor. I'd run along the corridor into her bedroom – the master bedroom – and ended up in her en suite. I'm rather impressed I had enough in me to throw up so spectacularly, considering the small amount of food I've had in the past twenty-four hours.

If I make any noise during my upset, my mother has either not heard or chosen to ignore me. I get up off the floor and go over to the sink, and splash cold water into my mouth and onto my face. I expect the woman looking back at me to be some grisly, terrifying zombie. A rotting, animated corpse standing where a professional, wealthy, middle-class, middle-aged woman once stood. But it's still me. Maybe looking slightly more tired than usual – although any notions of 'usual' were abandoned in the wake of Jessica's death. I haven't really bothered with any baselines of normality since then.

'Rob MacLeod.' I say the name out loud. Seeing what it does to me. Feeling the pain ripple through my brain as I say it. 'Rob MacLeod. Rob MacLeod.' It's like saying 'Candyman' into the mirror, and part of me hopes some evil spectre will come out through the glass and slaughter me where I stand. But nothing happens. I just stare back at myself, that man's name still reverberating around my mind.

I fucked him, I think. And if I hadn't fucked him, and hadn't wanted to fuck him again and again and again, maybe he wouldn't have been in a position to touch my little girl. Or perhaps, if I hadn't stopped…

There had come a point, after a few months of us spending our Friday afternoons shagging away on his bed like rabbits, when I knew I couldn't carry on. Knew I couldn't continue doing what we were doing. I'd become aware he was getting way too invested – he kept telling me that he loved me. Kept saying we were made to be together. I'd never wanted that. I had felt something for him, but it wasn't proper love. Nothing that could have survived past that honeymoon period of constant sex. Enjoying the slight riskiness of it. Enjoying it being taboo. And the guilt had started to get worse. Even though Alec started to get less and less good at covering his affairs, even when he knew I knew and didn't seem to care. The guilt still weighed me down. Because I knew, if there was one thing that would obliterate the family life I so desperately wanted to achieve, it was him finding out I had slept with the brother he had resented since boyhood. So I'd stopped it. And Rob had cried. Got angry. Withdrawn away from me. And then, to my surprise, offered to continue looking after Jessica on those afternoons. *Just because we can't go on doesn't mean Jessica has to suffer*, he'd said. She'd got used to their routine, he'd told me. They would go to the park or swimming or play in the paddling pool in the garden. He enjoyed spending time with her, he said, and he knew I enjoyed my time writing.

I jumped at the chance. The free childcare. Someone Jessica knew. I was getting more work done since Jessica's birth than ever before, more scripts were being commissioned, I was making a name for myself within the industry. It was an arrangement I didn't want to lose.

I gave my daughter over to a paedophile.

The shock of that sentence reverberates around me. I feel it like it's a bomb blast. I feel as if I'm breaking apart.

There's a rumble in my stomach and I'm worried I'm going to throw up again, but instead of going over to the toilet I race out of the bathroom, back out through my mother's bedroom and along the gallery landing to the room that used to be mine. With a mounting sense of rage, I see she's completely stripped the room of anything to do with me. It's been newly wallpapered, with countertops installed, running all around the room, stopping only for space for the door to open. On them are row upon row of animal figurines – her precious Sylvanian fucking Families. Always, through my childhood, I'd found her toy collection one of her more disturbing eccentricities, and now, looking at them all, I feel repulsed. There are even little houses for them, interspersing the neat ordered lines. Some of them have creatures placed in the weird little bedrooms. Others are empty. There's something deeply unsettling to me about the way the rabbits and cats are all lined up. It looks army-like. Dictatorial. As if I've wandered in on some elite race, ready to take over our chaotic world with their special manufactured brand of logic and order.

In the centre of the room is a camp bed with an old-looking duvet and pillow on top, along with a small jumble of clothes. This is where her pool boy occasionally sleeps, it seems. 'It's all so fucking weird!' I shriek, and kick at the bed, sending everything flying across the carpet, the duvet crumpling as my foot comes down again. I don't stop there. I march across it to the far end of the room towards a row of hedgehogs and bring down my fist, smashing my way through them, breaking up their perfect lines, some of the front row falling onto the floor. Not satisfied with this, I sweep my arm across the countertop, sending animals flying in different directions, the pain in my shoulder stabbing at me, telling me to stop, but I carry on. I spin over to my left and seize one of the little houses and throw it with all my strength so that it hits the wall and shatters in a spectacular, satisfying way, its roof caving in and the sides splitting.

'What the hell?' A low male voice sounds from the doorway. It's the boy. He's standing there, watching the devastation. He gestures to the wreckage around him, but I don't stop.

'Fuck off!' I shriek at him, and grab one of the other houses – one that's inhabited by more little creatures, and fling it at him. He ducks and it hits the side of the door with a crunching sound.

'You're bloody insane,' he mutters weakly, then leaves the room. I hear him running down the stairs and then him talking quickly somewhere on the ground floor. I know what's coming next. With the few moments I have, I throw my arms out madly and gather up a load of the remaining cat figures, lurch over to the window, pull it open, then fling them outside, watching a couple of them splash into the pool below. I snatch up some more and start lobbing them, one by one, into the pool, watching them soar through the cool evening air.

'What the fuck are you doing?' My mother rasps at me from the doorway. Seconds later, I feel her hands clawing at me, pulling me back. The pain in my arm and shoulder catches up with me and I scream. She backs away at the sound, but I keep going. I scream and scream and flail and cry and end up in a small ball on the floor.

My screams become cries. My cries become sobs. My sobs become steady streaming tears and, eventually, deep breathing. And my mother stands there. Throughout all of it. It could be minutes, it could be hours. Until, finally, I manage to make myself look up. Only then does she speak. 'I think you'd better come downstairs. We'll talk this through.' She talks calmly, although there's an edge to her scratchy voice.

'I can't talk it through,' I say, the sob rising again in my voice. 'It's the worst. The very worst thing. And it has fucking ruined me. Ruined everything. Forever.' More tears stream from my eyes and I look away from her to wipe at my face. When I look back at her, I'm shocked to see she's crying too. Without a sound. Without any noticeable sobs or fast breathing. Just a single tear, making its way down her face. Then she slowly lifts up her right hand and holds it out, palm upwards. It's for me. I stare at it for a moment, then back up at her. Then I take it.

Chapter Fifty

THE MOTHER

May. Three months after the attack.

I tell her my story while we sit on the veranda outside. The burnt front of the house towers above us, occasionally sending down a floating flake of ash or charred wood. Under other circumstances, I'd have been afraid of it all falling down upon us. Today, I would welcome such devastation. So long as it killed me.

My mother listens silently while I start at the beginning. What it was like to hear about the Stratford attacks. Knowing my daughter was there. That horror when I couldn't get through to her. Then being told of her death. And spending the next few months living a strange half-life. Somewhere in a hellish in-between. Then how my discovery of Michael Kelley seemed to reignite a sense of purpose in me again. For the first time in months, I had finally been reminded of what it was like to live. I was angry with him, furious with him, I wanted to hurt him. Show him somehow what he'd done. I told her about my crash, my memory loss. And then how, through a set of events that still feel blurred and jagged in my brain, I came to be on Southend Pier with him at five in the morning. And how only one of us walked away alive.

I start crying again when I tell her about what I'd found on Jessica's phone. How my desperate need to find someone to blame had led me to Southend, with tragic consequences. And how, for years, my beautiful little girl had suffered abuse at the hands of her own uncle. A man I was sleeping with behind my husband's back. My mother interrupted me briefly to ask if I'd loved him. I told her the truth: I didn't and never had. I'd just loved the fact he wasn't my husband. I loved the fact that he made me feel safe and wanted rather than tolerated or resented. I loved the sense of escape he brought with him. Something that seems so trivial now, after everything. As I near the last part of my story, I tell her about how desperate I am for closure. For an end. For something to finally put a stop to the hellish rollercoaster the past half-year has been. That's all I wanted. Now I've ruined even that. But I know one thing. That I will not stay silent about what Rob has done. I may have to answer for my crimes, but my God, he will too.

My mother is silent for a number of minutes after I finish speaking. She stares out over the front lawn and the trees that line the winding driveway. It's growing dark now and she shivers slightly, pulling a cardigan from off the back of her chair and wrapping it over her shoulders.

'I've lived through hell,' she says, still not looking at me. 'And it isn't a pretty place.'

I start to mutter how I don't really think any hell she's been through compares to mine, but she silences me with a movement of her hand.

'I think you know what hell I'm referring to, Caroline.'

She looks at me now. And it doesn't take long for me to comprehend what she's referring to.

'You mean... you're talking about... Dad.'

She nods. 'I'm talking about Dad.'

I'm quietly terrified now. I've never thought I'd go down this road with my mother. Always thought it was a sinister rabbit hole best left unexplored. But she seems to want to tell me something and, in spite of myself, I know I need to hear it.

'And I'm talking about the guilt, and the confusion, and the anger at the world and at oneself.'

I hold her gaze. 'When I said we were both murderers, earlier, you didn't object or try to correct me.' I pause, take a breath, then I ask the question. The ultimate question. 'Did you kill him, Mum? Did you kill Dad?'

It's like I'm a little girl again. It's like I've never run away. Like the years of mistakes don't stretch between us.

'Of course I did.' She says it simply but firmly. And she doesn't look away from me.

I let out the breath I've only just realised I've been holding.

'Oh God,' I whisper, and look away. I spend a few moments rubbing my eyes. Then it's my turn to stare off into the darkness. And her turn to stare at me.

'I tell you this, Caroline, so you know that we all have our demons. We all fight the good fight and then realise there was no fucking point to it after all. And then there's something wonderful in standing back and watching it all go up in flames.'

An image swims into my head. Her standing out here, on the lawn, facing the house, and watching the fire rage as it starts to destroy a home built of bad memories.

'I know what you mean about closure,' she says. 'And it's something I've never managed to attain.'

I transfer my gaze to the floor. 'Because you've spent years hiding away.'

She sighs. Not an impatient sigh. Almost wistful. 'Perhaps. But I don't think you're going to have that problem. And I'm envious of it. I think you'll get your day of judgement.'

I turn to look at her, and as I do I sense the flicker of light from the corner of my eye. 'You don't mean... in a religious sense?'

She smiles. A small smile. 'No, not in the religious sense. Something a bit more tangible. That I can be sure about.'

I don't understand what she means. 'Then... why are you so sure?'

'Because,' she says, lifting a hand to point, 'there's a police car making its way up the drive.'

I follow her hand and I see it. The flashing lights. The car coming fully into view. Pulling to a halt in front of us. Then the door opening and the sound of people getting out.

'I think,' my mother says, 'it's time to call it a night.'

Epilogue

The nice police officer – Kathy, the woman who sounds a bit northern – sits down with me. I've worked out her expressions now. She's about to tell me some news.

'I just wanted to tell you, Evan: we've found her. We've found Caroline Byrne.'

I try to speak, but my voice is hoarse. 'Where?' I finally croak out.

'In Australia. At her mother's house. She's going to be brought home for further questioning. It's almost certain she's going to be charged.'

I just nod.

Kathy sits down on one of the sofas in this strange police 'family room' they've brought me to. 'We're going to need to ask you a few more questions, Evan. You haven't really told us much – and we completely understand that, we really do. But for us to do the right thing – for us to properly get to the bottom of what happened to your brother on

Southend Pier – we're going to have to go over some things you might find difficult. OK?'

There's a long silence. The other cop, DS Gracie or something like that, shifts a bit, like he's getting pissed off but knows he shouldn't show it. But Kathy doesn't seem impatient like him. She seems nice.

'How about we have a proper chat now, OK, Evan? It will be recorded. And Maxine, who you met before, will be there, as your appropriate adult. She should really be here now for this little chat, but she's running a bit late and I didn't want to keep you waiting. Is that all OK?'

I just nod.

It takes a while to get everything set up. Then Maxine comes in and greets me with her 'Hello, love', like she did the first time I met her. And then we go into one of their interview rooms.

Kathy says a load of stuff quite quickly for the recording, saying our names and nodding at us as she does, then she starts off her questioning.

'OK, Evan. We're going to start with something we've spoken a little bit about before, but haven't properly. It's about Caroline Byrne and the time she spent in your house.'

I was waiting for this. And I nod, to show I'm OK with her carrying on. I'm OK telling my story, the story of everything that led to this moment. And I'm going to be OK afterwards. It's the first time I've realised that. Because if there's one thing my conversations with Jessica taught me, it's that even when things are as dark as they can be, hope can come along when you least expect it. I've got through terrible things in the past, and I'll get through this.

'Do you have any idea why Caroline Byrne was in contact with your brother, and why she may have been in the house the night your brother died?'

I know she knows already. I know she must have spoken to Caroline's husband. But it's my turn now. My turn to give my side of the story. For me. For Michael. And for Jessica.

'Yes,' I say, my voice catching a bit as I try to speak. 'Me. She was there because of me.'

Acknowledgments

I'd first like to thank all the readers who picked up my three previous books, recommended them to friends and helped bring them to the attention of others by leaving reviews online. I'm enormously grateful.

As always, endless thanks to my parents, sisters Molly and Amy, granny and uncle, and to all my close friends for their support throughout my time as an author, especially during the difficult times of the pandemic and all the uncertainty this period has brought with it.

I would like to thank my wonderful agent Joanna Swainson and everyone at Hardman & Swainson for being such a brilliant team. Huge thanks to Bethan Morgan, Charlotte Ledger, Kimberley Young, Melanie Price, Lucy Bennett, Claire Fenby, Sara Roberts, Emma Petfield and everyone at One More Chapter and HarperCollins. It's brilliant to be at a publisher so enthusiastic and supportive and filled with such kind and generous people. I consider myself incredibly lucky. Many thanks to Phoebe Morgan and the team at Avon for their work during the initial development of this book.

Huge thanks to Bea Carvalho and the whole books team at Waterstones for championing my previous novel, *The Dinner Guest*. It's all been a dream come true and I'll be forever grateful to everyone who helped make that happen. A massive thank you to all my former colleagues in the Waterstones Ecommerce team and to all the booksellers across the world who have been so amazing at pressing my novels into the hands of readers. It's more wonderful than words can say.

ONE MORE CHAPTER

One More Chapter is an
award-winning global
division of HarperCollins.

Sign up to our newsletter to get our
latest eBook deals and stay up to date
with our weekly Book Club!
<u>Subscribe here.</u>

Meet the team at
<u>www.onemorechapter.com</u>

Follow us!
 <u>@OneMoreChapter_</u>
<u>@OneMoreChapter</u>
<u>@onemorechapterhc</u>

Do you write unputdownable fiction?
We love to hear from new voices.
Find out how to submit your novel at
<u>www.onemorechapter.com/submissions</u>